TAMARA

A Play by John Krizanc

Conceived by Richard Rose and John Krizanc

Stoddart

This play may not be performed except by permission of:

Tamara International
151 John Street, Suite 151
Toronto, Ontario
M5V 2T2

Moses Znaimer, Executive Producer

Lawrence N. Dykun and Barrie Wexler, Associate Producers

First published in 1989 by
Stoddart Publishing Co. Limited
34 Lesmill Road
Toronto, Ontario
M3B 2T6

CANADIAN CATALOGUING IN PUBLICATION DATA

Krizanc, John
Tamara

A play.
ISBN 0-7737-5195-5

I. Title

PS8571.R74T35   1989   C812'.54   C88-093857-9
PR9199.3.K755T35   1989

COVER ILLUSTRATION: © Tamara De Lempicka, 1989 VIS-ART Copyright Inc.
COVER DESIGN: Brant Cowie/ArtPlus Ltd.

Menu on page 176 reprinted with permission from Tamara International.

Printed in Canada

This play is dedicated to Richard Rose and Dorian Clark whose enthusiasm and artistry guided it to fruition. I would also like to express my gratitude to the original Toronto cast whose improvisations shaped several scenes.

JOHN KRIZANC

The accuracies I deal in are the accuracies of my impressions. If you want factual accuracies you must go to...but no, don't go to anyone, stay with me.

FORD MADOX FORD

FOREWORD

In the summer of 1980, two schoolmates with vague theatrical interests were discussing the characters in a Chekhov play. John Krizanc, who dabbled in playwriting himself, argued that what interested him most were the servants, the sullen Russian maids and butlers who drop a line here and there and then disappear into the kitchen. They, Krizanc felt, were the only ones to know the underbelly of the social fabric; they were the ones Krizanc wanted to follow. Richard Rose suggested then that perhaps a play could be written, staged in such a way that the audience would be in fact *allowed* to exit with the servants. Krizanc said he might try.

Krizanc was less interested in pursuing a clever dramatic device than in exploring a theme that had always puzzled him. During his life, the theme had come up in many different guises: as a battle between private citizens and the public thing (politics were a common subject at the Krizanc dinner table, his father being an ardent Yugoslav national), as a struggle between the artist and society (which Krizanc saw illustrated in his own everyday attempts to survive, making a living as a bookseller in downtown Toronto), as the clash of civic and official responsibilities (ever present in issues that appeared daily, demanding loyalty to all sorts of causes, Canadian and international). In short, Krizanc's theme had always been the individual versus the state.

The play that sprung from the Chekhov conversation was molded by a number of different circumstances. One was a family anecdote: Krizanc's vehemently liberal father had, as an unemployed student in Italy, briefly put up posters for the Fascist party. Did starving justify his father's moral lapse? Another was a book: the Italian publisher Franco Maria Ricci had brought out in his lavish *Segni dell'Uomo* series a volume reproducing the work of Tamara de Lempicka, a Polish portrait painter who, in the twenties and thirties had became the darling of the European aristocracy. Was the artist justified in portraying those in power or did she have civic responsibilities she should have fulfilled? A third was a film: Bertolucci's *The Conformist,* with its implacable description of bourgeois life under fascism. How did ordinary people live through such extraordinary lack of freedom?

Ricci's book on Tamara de Lempicka included, together with reproductions of Tamara's paintings, extracts from the diaries of Aélis Mazoyer, a woman who had been both the mistress and housekeeper of the great Italian poet Gabriele d'Annunzio. Krizanc read them, went on to read d'Annunzio's work, and eventually d'Annunzio himself became the individual at the core of Krizanc's play. D'Annunzio was an ideal character for Krizanc's purpose. He had been regarded as a war hero by the Italian people after his attempt to preserve for his country the Dalmation port of Fiume in 1919, and he was the bestselling Italian author of his time. His voice would have made a difference in the establishment of the Fascist state and yet, perhaps for the sake of comfort and the supply of cocaine, he allowed Mussolini to keep him locked up for the rest of his life in Il Vittoriale, d'Annunzio's villa on Lake Garda. D'Annunzio, who had both the strength of a great poet and the record of a great soldier, and who chose to remain silent in the face of social evil, represented for Krizanc the extreme example of the artist who first creates an understanding of the world, and then submits to its conventions.

Whoever we are, artist or audience, we move in and out of conventions. First we construct them, laborious Babels to reach some form of superior understanding. Then we undermine them, divide the workers into countless singular languages that banish any illusion of knowledge. First we buttress our inventions by saying, "Once upon a time, this really happened." Then we frame it all by saying, "This is a story that begins 'Once upon a time'." We move in and out of belief and disbelief.

Theatre, the representation of events "as if they happened before your very eyes," begins with the convention of all spectacle: a division of reality. One space is allotted to the audience, the passive viewer, seated to observe; another to the play, the actors, moving to perform. At times throughout history the playwright's skill is perceived to lie in how well he maintains a barrier between those two spaces; at others, his genius is seen in how deftly the barrier is torn down and how completely the spaces allowed to mingle. Racine stands for one, Brecht for the other. D'Annunzio (as a character, not as a playwright) begins with Brecht and ends with Racine.

At all times, however, theatre proclaims the playwright's tyranny. Even when the playwright is replaced by a director, ensemble, *prima donna,* whoever holds the stage holds the strings of the event. Whether brought in or left out of the play itself, the audience must follow the argument of authority: that which the author has determined will be seen by all.

The Fascist state works upon the same principle. Mussolini's nickname, Il Duce, translates as "chief" but also "conductor," "he who conducts," "he who is in charge." Like any ordinary playwright (admittedly on a larger stage), Il Duce determined that which would take place and would be seen, because only that which he chose to show could be witnessed by his public. The *popolo*, the people, had no choice in the matter, and were to find content in obedience and in the surrender of self-determination. From Euripides to Pinter, this is the only requirement demanded by the playwright.

The question Krizanc asked is this: can the public, submitted to the whim of an authoritarian author, be free enough to set against their freedom the stultification brought on by fascism? Can the public, locked up in their seats like d'Annunzio in Il Vittoriale, begin to understand that we do, in fact, have a choice? Krizanc found his answer in Rose's suggested device. He would "free the public," allow them to accompany whatever character and story they chose, servants or masters. The author —Krizanc himself— would become only the provider of material. The builder of situations, he who chooses a point of view, would be the public. As it turned out, each member of the public was allowed to choose his own character and actively follow him or her throughout the house in which *Tamara* was performed. Never before had a theatre-going audience had this kind of freedom. In this sense, *Tamara* became the first democratic play.

Borges pointed out that each writer creates his own precursors. With *Tamara*, Krizanc sets up a series of freedom forerunners: Kafka's infinite novel, *The Castle*, which allows the reader to add his or her own obstacles to the hero's endless quest; the American composer LaMonte Young's *Composition 1960, Number 5*, in which the flight of a butterfly let loose in the auditorium determines the length of time of a section of silence; Ayn Rand's dreary play, *The Night of January 16th*, where the public determines whether the accused is guilty or not; and the most obvious, Julio Cortazar's *Hopscotch* whose interchangeable chapters allow readers to construct their own sequence of events. With the exception of Kafka's novel the others exemplify only the device — not the *need* for the device as an inextricable part of the meaning of the work itself. *The Castle* must remain incomplete because K. must never reach his destination; *Tamara* must allow the audience to choose their stories because the world portrayed by Krizanc is one where choice has been denied.

Unfortunately, because the device is so effective, it becomes almost overpowering, and those who attend a performance of *Tamara* tend not to see the trees for the forest. *Tamara* is not a clever play in which we roam around freely; it is an almost infinite series of plays — one for each possible sequence of scenes — in which we witness characters carefully defined through both actions and language. Language especially. Because in *Tamara* the characters' freedom, curtailed by the omnipresent state, is expressed exclusively through words.

Whoever it is we follow, we find that he or she is a victim of the same set of circumstances. Masters and servants, powerful and meek, the determined housekeeper Aélis or the drunk de Spiga, mad Luisa Baccara or maddening Aldo Finzi, each is what words allow him or her to be. Even Tamara, whose expression lies in shapes and colours, and whose French (or the convention of "English as French" which she speaks with d'Annunzio) is impersonal, Europe's *lingua franca*, finds in words the resolution of her conflicts: "The passion in the artist must be as great as the passion in the subject," she quotes. And then, musing about the artist's responsibility, she says: "For the artist, the whole world is her country and her country is her art. It is a country called freedom." And later still, she says: "Monsieur d'Annunzio believes he is free. He's trapped, not by your guards, but by his own words." Krizanc's characters weave a web of words which paradoxically both traps them in their ideas and offers them a chance for freedom.

Hardly any take that chance. D'Annunzio, prisoner and keeper of his cell, remains at the centre of the maze; Tamara, seeking to paint him and to rise in his society, stands at the entrance; and throughout the play it is Emilia, the maid, who spins the largest number of possible escapes and resolutions. Krizanc has portrayed her as a horribly real Cinderella, condemned to the ashes of the hearth not only by her social standing but by her sex, and triumphantly rising over the condemnation of both. She is, in fact, the Chekhovian servant whom Krizanc wanted to follow; she is a better, wiser heroine than those in whose house she serves.

Because it is a multitude of plays, *Tamara* must be seen a number of times. Nothing replaces the experience of being on stage in the midst of a performance, or on the several stages the play demands. Certainly not reading the book. A play on paper represents only one element of a complex and Protean creature that is another every night and in the eyes of each member of the audience. But reading *Tamara* does afford a luxury that the staging disallows: the reader's concentration on the text, and on the writing of the text. Here, in this book, the reader can make one of two choices: either to become omniscient and read a set of simultaneous scenes, thereby repeating the same time frame from different perspectives; or to choose one character and follow him or her from beginning to end, respecting a linear development that imitates real life — in either case, the reader is made responsible for the outcoming reality. Ultimately *Tamara*, on paper or on stage, becomes the exact antithesis of fascism, because it condemns the audience to the unbearable freedom of a concerned and active witness.

ALBERTO MANGUEL
TORONTO
MARCH 1988

INTRODUCTION

TAMARA takes place on January 10th and 11th, 1927, in Northern Italy near the town of Gardone at Il Vittoriale degli Italiani (The Shrine of Italian Victories), the country home of Gabriele d'Annunzio.

The scenes are played throughout the rooms of a large house. In an ideal setting there is a music room (the Oratorio, in this script), a dining room and a kitchen large enough to accommodate the entire audience standing and sitting. Each of the ten characters has a bedroom (Note: Only three are absolutely necessary for the playing of the scenes), but d'Annunzio also has a study and Finzi has a small room used as an office.

The audience observes the action of the play by following the actors in and out of the various rooms. Scenes run simultaneously with different actors in different rooms often playing as many as eight scenes at one time.

The format and content of this script has evolved over seven years of playing and the evolution will continue. To facilitate the reading of this script and the understanding of the multi-leveled nature of the playing, this version is divided into *twenty-one different sections — A through U— with each section approximately a unit of time in which a number of scenes occur simultaneously.* There are two acts and each covers one day. The scenes are numbered consecutively from the beginning of Act One. However, the numbering of the scenes does not reflect the order in which the scenes occur. The dividing pages for each section are inserted before the set of scenes which occur in that particular space of time. Those scenes, their scene numbers, their locations, and the characters are listed on the page so that the reader can follow the action and the actors he/she chooses.

The playing time of this script is approximately two hours and ten minutes; January 10, Act One, is approximately one hour, three minutes and January 11, Act Two, is approximately one hour, seven minutes. Movement throughout Il Vittoriale is greatly affected by the size of the audience. Therefore, the playing times of each performance will vary accordingly.

The first performance of TAMARA was presented at Strachan House in Trinity-Bellwoods Park, Toronto, Ontario, Canada on May 8, 1981. The original production was created by the Necessary Angel Theatre Company, Toronto, with the following cast:

DANTE Fenzo	Roger A. McKeen
Aldo **FINZI**	Ian Black
Gian Francesco **de SPIGA**	Ramiro Puerta
EMILIA Pavese	Patricia Nember
Gabriele **d'ANNUNZIO**	Frank Canino*
AÉLIS Mazoyer	Shelley Thompson
CARLOTTA Barra	Denise Naples
MARIO Pagnutti	Angelo Pedari
LUISA Baccara	Maggie Huculak
TAMARA de Lempicka	Mary Hawkins

DIRECTION: Richard Rose
ORIGINAL MUSIC: Ramiro Puerta**
ENVIRONMENTAL DESIGN: Dorian L. Clark
COSTUME DESIGN: Linda Muir

* Geza Kovacs replaced Frank Canino on July 26, 1981.
** Original music by Ramiro Puerta is available for use by contacting the composer in care of TAMARA INTERNATIONAL

The first United States performance of TAMARA was presented at Il Vittoriale degli Italiani, 2035 N. Highland Avenue, Hollywood, CA, 90068. The Los Angeles production was produced by Moses Znaimer and Barrie Wexler with the following cast:

DANTE Fenzo	Leland Murray
Aldo **FINZI**	Michael Stefani
Gian Francesco **de SPIGA**	William Schallert
EMILIA Pavese	Sue Giosa
Gabriele **d'ANNUNZIO**	John P. Ryan
AÉLIS Mazoyer	Marilyn Lightstone
CARLOTTA Barra	Wendel Meldrum
MARIO Pagnutti	Robert Thaler
LUISA Baccara	Helen Shaver
TAMARA de Lempicka	Margot Dionne

DIRECTION: Richard Rose
ASSOCIATE DIRECTOR: Phil Killian
CHOREOGRAPHY/FIGHT DIRECTION: Gary Mascaro
ORIGINAL MUSIC: William Schallert
PRODUCTION DESIGN: Robert Checchi
COSTUME DESIGN: Gianfranco Ferré
PRODUCTION STAGE MANAGER: Sam Burgess
STAGE MANAGER: Walter Wood

The present script reflects the third production of Tamara, *which was mounted in November of 1987 at Il Vittoriale, the Park Avenue Armory, in New York City. Moses Znaimer was the executive producer and Larry Dykun and Barrie Wexler were the associate producers. The play opened with the following cast:*

DANTE Fenzo
d'Annunzio's valet, ex-gondolier   Leland Murray

Aldo **FINZI**
Fascist policeman   August Schellenberg

Gian Francesco **de SPIGA**
Inebriated composer, dilettante   Patrick Horgan

EMILIA Pavese
Light-fingered housemaid   Roma Downey

Gabriele **d'ANNUNZIO**
Italia's greatest poet, patriot
and WWI hero   Frederick Rolf

AÉLIS Mazoyer
Head housekeeper and d'Annunzio's
confidante   Marilyn Lightstone

CARLOTTA Barra
Ballerina seeking d'Annunzio's
recommendation to Diaghilev in
Paris   Cynthia Dale

MARIO Pagnutti
d'Annunzio's mysterious new
chauffeur   Jack Wetherall

LUISA Baccara
Former concert pianist and
d'Annunzio's ex-mistress   Lally Cadeau

TAMARA de Lempicka
Aristrocratic French-speaking Polish
exile here to paint d'Annunzio's
portrait   Sara Botsford

DIRECTION: Richard Rose
ASSOCIATE DIRECTOR: Phil Killian
CHOREOGRAPHY/FIGHT DIRECTION: Gary Mascaro
ASSISTANT DIRECTOR: George Rondo
PRODUCTION DESIGN: Robert Checchi
COSTUMES: Gianfranco Ferré
ASSOCIATE COSTUME DESIGNER: Diana Eden
LIGHTING DESIGNER: Brian Bailey
PRODUCTION STAGE MANAGER: Bruce Kagel
CASTING: Johnson-Liff and Zerman
ITALIAN TRANSLATOR: Damiano Pietropalo
FRENCH TRANSLATOR: Gail Armstrong

CONTENTS

ACT ONE

SECTION A

A1	Introduction	20

SECTION B *28*

B2	de Spiga gives a monologue at the piano in the Atrium	29
B3	Luisa gives a monologue in her bedroom	29
B4	Finzi meets Carlotta in the hall outside the Oratorio	30
B5	Finzi monologue	33
B6	d'Annunzio gives a monologue in his room	33
B7	Emilia gives a monologue in the Leda	34
B8	Carlotta and Emilia in the Leda	35
B9	Aélis gives a monologue in the Dining Room	37
B10	Dante and de Spiga talk in the Atrium	38
B11	Luisa goes to d'Annunzio's room	40

SECTION C *42*

C12	Group scene in the Atrium	43
C13	Emilia, Aélis, Carlotta and Luisa wrap presents	50
C14	Carlotta, Dante and Luisa in the Leda	51

SECTION D *54*

D15	d'Annunzio greets Tamara in the Atrium	55
D16	Finzi and Emilia at the stairs	58
D17	Carlotta, de Spiga, Luisa and Aélis in the Oratorio	58
D18	Emilia and Finzi in the kitchen	65
D19	Mario and Dante take Tamara's luggage to the Leda	69

SECTION E *72*

E20	Carlotta and Aélis in Carlotta's room	73
E21	Luisa and de Spiga in the Oratorio	79

E22   d'Annunzio takes Tamara to the Leda   83
E23   Tamara monologue   85
E24   Mario gives a monologue, searching Finzi's
       office   86
E25.   Finzi, Emilia and Dante in the Kitchen, Mario
       joins later   87

SECTION F   *96*

F26   Emilia and Dante head upstairs to the
       Dining Room   97
F27   Group scene in the Dining Room   99
F28   d'Annunzio is joined by Aélis in his room   109
F29   Tamara catches Mario searching her room   112
F30   Mario meets Emilia in the Side Hall   117

SECTION G   *119*

G31   d'Annunzio, Mario and Aélis in the Kitchen   120
G32   Emilia has a monologue on her way to
       Mario's Room   127
G33   Emilia has a monologue on her way to
       the Oratorio   128
G34   Dessert moves to the Oratorio   128
G35   Luisa and Tamara go to the Atrium to
       powder their noses   135

SECTION H   *137*

H36   d'Annunzio, Aélis, Luisa and Tamara join
       the others in the Oratorio.   138
H37   Finzi has a monologue on his way to the
       Dining Room   146
H38   Finzi and Emilia, in the Dining Room   146

SECTION I   *149*

I39   d'Annunzio, Luisa and de Spiga remain
       in the Oratorio   150
I40   Aélis attempts to seduce Carlotta   152
I41   Finzi makes a phone call in his office   156
I42   Finzi and Emilia go from the Dining Room
       to her bedroom   157
I43   Emilia monologue   159
I44   Dante and Mario drink in Mario's Room   160

I45	Brief scene between Emilia and Mario	*172*
I46	Dante in the Kitchen and hall	*173*
I47	d'Annunzio, alone in the Oratorio.	*174*
I48	Aélis enters the Oratorio	*175*

INTERMEZZO

ACT TWO

SECTION J   *178*

J49	Dante and Finzi introduce the second day	*179*
J50	Finzi interrogating audience member	*181*

SECTION K   *182*

K51	Mario and Dante in Mario's room, later joined by Emilia	*183*
K52	de Spiga and Finzi in Finzi's office	*188*
K53	Aélis brings the invoices to d'Annunzio in his room	*191*
K54	Luisa, Tamara and Carlotta are in the Oratorio	*196*

SECTION L   *202*

L55	Mario and Finzi in Mario's room	*203*
L56	Dante and Emilia talk in the Kitchen	*208*
L57	Group scene in the Oratorio	*216*

SECTION M   *221*

M58	Tamara and d'Annunzio in the Dining Room	*222*
M59	Tamara monologue	*223*

SECTION N   *224*

N60	d'Annunzio, alone in the Dining Room	*225*
N61	Group scene in the Oratorio	*225*
N62	Aélis and d'Annunzio in the Dining Room	*231*

SECTION O   *234*

O63	Aélis and d'Annunzio enter the Oratorio, all are present	*235*
O64	Mario, de Spiga, Finzi, Luisa and Tamara prepare to leave for Gordone	*236*

O65	d'Annunzio and Dante, alone briefly in the Oratorio	239
O66	Aélis and Carlotta exit to the automobile	241
O67	Mario sees Tamara giving a note to Emilia	242

SECTION P   *244*

P68	Mario and d'Annunzio are in the Oratorio	245
P69	Finzi and Emilia, in the Atrium	253
P70	Dante cleans d'Annunzio's room	257
P71	Finzi and Dante in the Atrium, "Tumbalalaika"	258
P72	Emilia searches Mario's room	260
P73	Finzi enters Mario's room	261
P74	Finzi makes a phone call in his office	262
P75	Dante enters Mario's room and finds Emilia	263
P76	Mario leaves the Oratorio and encounters Finzi	265

SECTION Q   *267*

Q77	The return of those who left for Gardone	268
Q78	de Spiga and Finzi help Luisa to the Oratorio	270
Q79	Carlotta runs to her bedroom	276
Q80	Dante follows Carlotta to her room	277
Q81	Dante has a monologue	282
Q82	Mario finds Emilia searching his room	282
Q83	Dante finds Mario and Emilia kissing	286
Q84	Tamara finds d'Annunzio in her bed, the Leda	289
Q85	Aélis, Carlotta, Mario and Dante head to the Atrium	293

SECTION R   *296*

R86	Aélis and Dante go to the Oratorio, where Luisa is found	297
R87	de Spiga interupts Tamara and d'Annunzio in the Leda	301
R88	de Spiga and Tamara in the Leda	302
R89	Tamara monologue	305
R90	Dante gives a monologue in the Kitchen	306
R91	Emilia gives a monologue in Mario's room and in her own room	307
R92	Mario has a monologue in d'Annunzio's room	309

R93   d'Annunzio finds Mario in his room   *310*

R94   Dante heads upstairs for a scene with Finzi   *312*

R95   de Spiga monologue   *313*

R96   Mario encounters de Spiga outside
d'Annunzio's door   *314*

SECTION S   *316*

S97   Emilia meets Luisa and Tamara in
the Oratorio   *317*

S98   de Spiga monologue   *318*

S99   Aélis rushes to d'Annunzio's bedroom   *319*

S100   Dante comes to warn Mario   *323*

S101   Finzi phones Roma   *326*

S102   Emilia and Tamara help Luisa upstairs   *326*

S103   Finzi and de Spiga meet in Finzi's office   *328*

S104   de Spiga has a monologue in the Oratorio   *330*

SECTION T   *332*

T105   Luisa alone in her room   *333*

T106   Tamara and Emilia in the Leda   *334*

T107   Finzi encounters Mario and Dante in the
Atrium   *338*

T108   d'Annunzio enters the Leda, throws out Emilia
and attacks Tamara   *341*

SECTION U   *343*

U109   The final scene begins in the Atrium   *344*

ACT ONE

SCENE A1

THE SIDE HALL and THE ATRIUM

DANTE and FINZI introduce the play and give the audience the rules. Piano music can be heard from the Atrium. de SPIGA plays a variety of compositions ranging from his own to Chopin and Debussy.

After members of the audience receive their papers (Carta d'identita — part of the program), they are greeted by DANTE, the valet, in the hall.

DANTE
Buona sera, Signore, Signori! Il Comandante is expecting you but first you will please speak to Capitano Finzi. He will stamp your papers and explain their importance to you. Capisce?

FINZI
(stands behind a small lectern in the hall, dressed in a black Fascist uniform) Papers. *(looks at the passport then hands it back to audience member)* Sign there. You will keep this with you at all times. If you are asked to produce your visa, you will do so and you will be required to know its contents. Read it. Anyone found without their papers will be arrested and deported. I would also ask you to take special note of the date, January 10th, 1927. *(stamps the papers, blows them dry and hands them back to the audience members)* This visa is good for forty-eight hours only.

The audience is then ushered into the Atrium, where Gian Francesco de SPIGA is playing the piano. Champagne is served. As the play is about to begin, EMILIA enters the Atrium where she will dust and begin putting down a carpet of rose petals. DANTE has entered the Atrium and now stands on a chair in order to better see the audience.

DANTE
Bravo! Bravo! Grazie, Signor de Spiga. Buona sera, Signore and Signori.

DANTE repeats his buona sera several times to encourage the audience to call back "buona sera". When they finally do, he continues.

Bene. You are most welcome guests here at Il Vittoriale degli Italiani, the home of Gabriele d'Annunzio. As you can see, it is a most beautiful villa. It was a gift from Mussolini — Il Duce — to Gabriele d'Annunzio, Il Comandante.

d'ANNUNZIO
(suddenly appearing on the steps overlooking the Atrium, dressed in a monk's robes) Dante, is everything ready for Madame de Lempicka's arrival?

DANTE
(crossing his arms and bowing his head) Si, Comandante.

d'ANNUNZIO
Ah, I see Emilia is putting down the carpet of roses. Very good.

EMILIA
Si, Comandante.

When EMILIA finishes putting down the roses, she will exit to the Leda and to PAGE 26.

d'ANNUNZIO
One must never underestimate the importance society women attach to making an entrance; for them, the superfluous is as necessary as...breath. Let us not disappoint. *(exits to his room and to PAGE 33)*

DANTE
Il Comandante has rarely been downstairs in the past weeks. You see he is a very great and very busy man, that is why the task of greeting you has fallen on me, your humble servant, Dante Fenzo. I trust your journey has been a pleasant one. Bene. It is nice to see so many smiling faces. *(sees FINZI suddenly standing on d'ANNUNZIO's chair)* But you must remember, you are now in a Fascist state. Si, Capitano?

FINZI
Si, Dante. *(pause)* If you wish to enjoy your stay here, you must obey our laws.

de SPIGA
Laws are meant to be broken.

FINZI
No, Signore, men are meant to be broken.

AÉLIS comes down the stairs from LUISA's room carrying several unwrapped, boxed presents.

de SPIGA
Aélis, how's Luisa?

AÉLIS
I gave her some more medication.

FINZI
Was that necessary?

AÉLIS
She should be fine by the time Tamara de Lempicka arrives.

de SPIGA
Will Tamara never come?

AÉLIS
Dante, where's Emilia? I asked her to help me.

DANTE
She was just here with the rose petals. Perhaps she's in the kitchen preparing dessert.

de SPIGA
I thought Emilia was dessert.

AÉLIS
Must I do everything?

CARLOTTA
(entering the Atrium from the servants' stairs) Capitano Finzi, would you join me for a walk?

AÉLIS
We'll be having dessert shortly, Carlotta.

FINZI
Another time, Signorina Barra.

AÉLIS
Now, there are many more presents to be wrapped.

CARLOTTA
I should rehearse my dance, Aélis.

CARLOTTA exits to the Oratorio and waits until PAGE 30. AÉLIS exits down the hall and waits until PAGE 26, the hallway.

DANTE
That was Signora Aélis Mazoyer, the head housekeeper here at Il Vittoriale.

FINZI
A foreigner.

MARIO enters from downstairs.

DANTE
Mario, I told you to use the servants' entrance. You're not to come upstairs.

MARIO
Mi scusi, Dante.

FINZI
Mario, I thought you were going to the train station to pick up this Polish woman.

MARIO
I'm leaving, Capitano, I'm leaving.

He exits via the front door and waits until PAGE 55, TAMARA's entrance.

DANTE
That is Mario, the new chauffeur. Not much of a driver...not much of anything.

FINZI
No, he's something all right....I'm sure of it.

DANTE
Now, to begin—

FINZI
Wait! For your own safety, I suggest you listen very carefully to the regulations regarding movement in this house. First: there are ten people who live here. You follow just one of them—

DANTE
Is that an order, Capitano?

FINZI
No, it's a strong suggestion, if you like order. If you are an anarchist you may switch from person to person.

DANTE
You're very kind, Capitano.

FINZI
If you are not following a person, you are breaking the law.

DANTE
Perhaps, you follow Emilia into the dining room and, God forbid, Capitano Finzi enters. Boom! A connection has been made. Now, you may either follow Emilia when she leaves, or switch and follow the Capitano.

FINZI
Anyone found wandering around on their own will be deported.

DANTE
Perhaps you are in the kitchen and noises from the bedroom catch your interest. If you leave on your own and go from the kitchen to the bedroom —

FINZI
You break the law!

DANTE
And this is what will happen. You will miss how the conversation in the kitchen ends, and you will not understand the conversation in the bedroom because you missed how it began. And, you will disturb all the other guests who are obeying the law. Capisce?

FINZI
Third: if one of the people closes a door in your face, do not follow.

DANTE
You will hurt your face, eh, Capitano?... Actually the Capitano is right. For your own safety and the safety of those who live here, please do not open a closed door. Now, I will tell you one more thing...well, actually three. To house his collection of manuscripts and war memorabilia, Il Comandante is adding two more floors and a north wing to the villa; and since they're still under construction, these areas remain off limits. But here, in the living quarters on the first and second floor, you can still see part of the collection which Il Comandante insists you touch only with the eyes. Also, we will be moving very quickly and quietly throughout the villa, so you too must move quickly and quietly.

FINZI
And speak only when spoken to. Capisce?

DANTE
(to audience) Si?

Audience says "Si."

One final word of advice; upon entering a room, those who are in first must move all the way in to the far side of the room. Stay close to the walls, do not get in the way, and do not stand in front of a doorway. *(smiling)* You never know who is going to kick it down.

FINZI
I, too, have some advice, Dante. As a man who once supervised a very large network of informers, I suggest if you are here with friends that you split up, since two pieces of information are more valuable than one.

DANTE
There are no informers here, Capitano.

FINZI
(smiling) You're right, Dante. I call them friends.

FINZI steps off d'ANNUNZIO's chair.

DANTE
(pause) Now to begin. I shall divide you into three groups. Will the lady/gentleman in the green dress *(or whatever he/she is wearing)* raise one hand, per favore? Grazie. Everyone on over *(to his right)* raise one hand, per favore. Ah, grazie. You are Group Number One. Will the lady/gentleman in the beige coat *(or whatever he/she is wearing)* raise two hands, per favore? Grazie. Everyone on over *(to his centre)* raise two hands. You see, Capitano, for me they surrender without a gun. Grazie. You are Group Number Two. Will the lady/gentleman in...ah, well the rest of you are Group Number Three. Now, Group Number One will go with Capitano Finzi. Group Number Two, I will take you upstairs. And Group Number Three — ah, Signore, you will do Dante a favor, si? You will see that none of the guests from Group Number Three leaves the room till Dante returns. Grazie. Group Number Two, Andiamo.

DANTE leads his group upstairs. GROUP THREE remains with de SPIGA, to *PAGE 29, the Atrium.*

FINZI
Group Number One, Andiamo.

GROUP NUMBER ONE goes with FINZI who leads down the hall. He ushers a third of his group into the Dining Room.

You will wait here for Signora Mazoyer. *(if TAMARA's paintings are on display he adds)* You may look at the decadent paintings of this Polish woman while you wait.

AÉLIS enters carrying several wrapped presents.

    AÉLIS
Finzi, you should never have given Baccara that gun.

    FINZI
We were shopping in town and she asked me to buy it. What was I to do? *(steps out into the hall and AÉLIS closes the Dining Room door)*

AÉLIS begins PAGE 37, the Dining Room, as EMILIA suddenly appears in the hall, standing at the door to the Leda.

Ah, Emilia. Will you show these guests to the Leda?

    EMILIA
Si, Capitano Finzi.

FINZI gives half of his remaining group to EMILIA. EMILIA will take them to the Leda and commence her monologue, PAGE 34. FINZI will take the remainder of his group down the hall where he meets CARLOTTA, PAGE 30.

Meanwhile...

de SPIGA, with GROUP NUMBER THREE, begins playing the piano and writing music. In the middle of his writing he begins his monologue, PAGE 29.

Meanwhile...

    DANTE
(with his group upstairs — stops first at LUISA's room; knocks) Signora Baccara? *(hearing no reply, enters with a third of his guests)* Signora Baccara? *(again, no reply; addresses the guest closest to the dressing screen)* Ah, Signorina/Signore, perhaps she is behind the dressing screen?

GUEST will respond "No."
Ah, well, I will leave you here. I'm sure she will return shortly.
He closes the door, leaving the guests alone and waiting for LUISA's monologue, PAGE 29.

(to his remaining GUESTS) You have the privilege of coming with me to the master's quarters. *(leads them to d'ANNUNZIO's room, stops outside and listens)* Shh! Il Comandante is praying. You must enter the master's quarters quietly.

The GUESTS do so, and then d'ANNUNZIO begins his monologue, PAGE 33.

DANTE returns to the Atrium, alone, and quietly asks the guests to move away from the piano and sit. His scene with de SPIGA then begins, PAGE 38.

SECTION B

THE FOLLOWING SCENES HAPPEN SIMULTANEOUSLY:

SCENE B2   de SPIGA gives a monologue at the piano in the Atrium.
Page 29

SCENE B3   LUISA gives a monologue in her bedroom.
Page 29

SCENE B4   FINZI meets CARLOTTA in the hall outside the Oratorio.
Page 30

SCENE B5   FINZI has a monologue in the hall.
Page 33

SCENE B6   d'ANNUNZIO gives a monologue in his room.
Page 33

SCENE B7   EMILIA gives a monologue in the Leda.
Page 34

SCENE B8   CARLOTTA and EMILIA in the Leda.
Page 35

SCENE B9   AÉLIS gives a monologue in the Dining Room.
Page 37

SCENE B10   DANTE and de SPIGA have a scene in the Atrium.
Page 38

SCENE B11   LUISA goes to d'ANNUNZIO's room. **NOTE:** this scene
Page 40   begins within this section but goes briefly into the next.

SCENE B2

THE ATRIUM

de SPIGA

(sitting at his piano, playing "Sono Tre Giorni" — Neapolitan folk song; continued from PAGE 26) Simple melodies. It seems I always come back to them. In my piano concertos, my operas, no matter how I try to be modern, by using atonal chords *(plays a piano chord)* and eccentric rhythms, polytonality, the leitmotif is always the same. A childhood nursery tune or some half-forgotten folksong. It was Luisa Baccara who first gave me the courage to make it simple. She'd take me out to the country and wherever there was a table we'd stop and talk to the villagers. Within minutes she'd have the old men singing honest songs of the field. And as I was furiously transcribing, she'd sit...sit and play cat's-cradle with the children. I wrote a lot in those years. And it was good. Then, everything changed. We stopped going to the country. *(pause)* Luisa met Gabriele d'Annunzio...at my ancestral home, the Palazzo de Spiga on the Grand Canal in Venezia...became his lover...for a time...and I...God, what have I become?

NOTE: When de SPIGA finishes his monologue, he will continue playing and writing music until DANTE enters, PAGE 38.

SCENE B3

LUISA'S ROOM and OUTSIDE D'ANNUNZIO'S ROOM

LUISA

(opening the closet door slightly, sticks her arm out and slowly allows some rose petals to fall to the floor from her hand) ...he loves me not. *(pushes the door fully open)* The place for bullets is through the heart. *(coming out of the closet)* Luisa is getting morbid, Luisa isn't getting anything, anyone. Luisa was getting dressed to meet Madame Tamara de Lempicka. *(sees gun on bed; six bullets lying next to it)* Bullets. *(loading the gun, she puts five bullets in the gun — one for each of the first five names)* Sarah Bernhardt, Emma Visconti, Ida Rubenstein, Isadora Duncan, Eleonora Duse, and Luisa, Luisa Baccara. They all left. Only I stayed. Made the choice between love and art. *(seeing herself in mirror, rising)* Get dressed bang, bang. *(at vanity)* Comb your hair

bang, bang. I must be very calm and pleasant. I'll say, "So pleased to meet you, Madame de Lempicka." Bullets. Bullet for your thoughts. *(picking up the gun)* Bang. Inside every woman *(putting sixth bullet in gun)* you'll find the body of the man who killed her. *(slams chamber shut, then goes to her anteroom, takes a rose out of a vase and heads for d'ANNUNZIO's room; stops outside)* Shh! He's still sleeping. Shh! I'm done with weeping. Shh! No knock knocking. Shh! Stop talking.

LUISA enters d'ANNUNZIO's room, PAGE 40.

SCENE B4

As FINZI comes down the hall to the Oratorio he finds an exasperated CAR-LOTTA picking up the small beads of her broken rosary.

FINZI
Signorina Barra!

CARLOTTA
I've broken my rosary. Watch your step, Capitano.

FINZI
Let me help. *(begins to pick up the beads)*

CARLOTTA
It just suddenly broke.

FINZI
I'll put it back together, don't worry.

CARLOTTA
Nana gave it to me. I don't know how it happened.

FINZI
Maybe you pray too much, Signorina Barra; we've hardly seen you all day.

CARLOTTA
Did you miss me, Capitano? No one else did, not even Aélis.

FINZI
Il Comandante has kept everyone busy preparing for the arrival of this painter.

CARLOTTA
He didn't go to any trouble for me.

FINZI
But he did, Carlotta. May I call you Carlotta?

CARLOTTA
(nodding) I'd like that.

FINZI
Usually guests stay at the Grand Hotel.

CARLOTTA
Unless he plans to seduce them. *(puts a finger to her lips and then crosses herself)* Forgive me...I had a reservation for the hotel but Aélis insisted I stay here. I don't feel right being here. Ever since my arrival I've had the strangest thoughts.

FINZI
That's because there's no discipline here; no one follows a schedule, the servants don't follow orders...so the mind wanders...now, I'm on duty. I have reports to send. *(sees the cross of her rosary under the couch, stoops to pick it up, hands it to her)* Here's your cross. I'll repair it tonight.

CARLOTTA
Grazie. *(holds out her arm so that FINZI will help her up)* I'm glad you're here, Capitano. Without you and Aélis, I wouldn't have anyone to talk with.

FINZI
What about Luisa?

CARLOTTA
I'm not sure she likes me, and...and I know you like her.

FINZI
How did you know?

CARLOTTA
Because you ignore me whenever she enters the room.

FINZI

I've loved Luisa Baccara for a long time. Sometimes I think she loves me. Or loves what I was, and could be again.

CARLOTTA

I still think you're a hero, Capitano.

FINZI

You what? Why would you say that?

CARLOTTA

I read everything about your involvement in the Matteotti crisis...it wasn't right for Il Duce to blame you...after all, this man Matteotti was a Socialist, wasn't he?

FINZI

Si.

CARLOTTA

And aren't they the enemies of fascism?

FINZI

I wish it were that simple.

CARLOTTA

But it is, Capitano. Papà says they should have given you a medal for ridding us of that Socialist menace.

FINZI

And what else does he say?

CARLOTTA

That one day Il Duce will need you back because the country needs decisive men. I just know you'll be first secretary to the Interior again. Just wait.

She kisses him and runs away laughing towards the Leda, PAGE 35. FINZI shakes his head in bewildered amusement.

SCENE B5

THE SIDE HALL

FINZI
Wait. I've been waiting for years....waiting to get back to Roma, waiting for Luisa....I knew when we first met that she understood me. She was still with d'Annunzio, and I was under-secretary to the Interior....never been to a garden party and Luisa took my arm to show me the grounds. I could hear people on the patio talking about us as we walked across the lawn. When I told Luisa they were staring, she said, "Yes, but their eyes are closed." She understood me.

FINZI exits to PAGE 43.

SCENE B6

d'ANNUNZIO'S ROOM

d'ANNUNZIO is kneeling in the centre of the room, leaning on his sword, and he holds one of TAMARA's letters in his hand. He is from PAGE 21, the Balcony.

d'ANNUNZIO
Where is she? Where is the woman who'll save me from this terrible nocturnal orgy of silence; who will show me once again, perhaps for the last time, an unknown aspect of love? *(reading from one of TAMARA's letters)* "I have a train from Firenze to Verona, leaving Verona at 12:45, arriving Gardone at 6:00. I beg you in the name of your clairvoyant love, do not destroy this wonderful state of semi-poisoning, semi-abandonment in which you have immersed me." Semi this, semi that, look what you've done to my little monk. There is nothing semi about him. "I wait, I hope, I want. Tamara." *(puts the letter down)* Any woman who can write a salutation like that understands the essence of desire.

The phone rings, and continues to ring until he answers it.

Tamara! *(rises, places the sword on the fireplace mantle, crosses to the bed, lies down and then picks up the phone, which is next to the bed)* Tamara. *(pause)* If I want to speak to someone in authority, I simply look in the mirror.

(laughing) Yes, yes, it's a quote...mine...Benito, don't steal it; a man's bad jokes are his character. *(pause)* I wouldn't call it "running" a country so much as dragging it. My business, Signor "Conductore," is the whereabouts of a friend of mine.... Of course, it concerns a woman....She's on the 12:45 train from Verona, arriving Gardone at 6:00. Do you know what time it is? *(pause)* Well, it's of national importance to me. Please...I know, I know...well have someone else look into it. Yes. No....*(pause)* No, no, no. I did not....I said I wanted a new editor. Wait, — wait — you promised me a complete edition of my works —never mind my promises — wait — a complete edition — thirty-six volumes. But...yes. But I want the political writings published now. I know they love my poetry...it sold seven million copies, not six. But...*(pause)* of course you have my ear, and when I die I'll have them cut it off and bronze it for you...I'm not...but the people want my voice. I want to speak to them.... What? Fine, another time....Just get me a new editor...someone who can spell. Yes — yes...and Aélis says to send more money....Ciao.

d'ANNUNZIO hangs up phone, rises and begins checking his appearance in the mirror until LUISA enters, PAGE 40.

SCENE B7

EMILIA, the maid, leads her guests into the Leda and closes the door. She begins to straighten the bed.

EMILIA

Me, I clean and serve. And Il Comandante still needs to bring the Polish one. Sometimes he takes me; but not here, in the Leda. No. This softness is only for them. The ladies with the diamond earrings and red lips. This one coming claims to be a painter. Last time it was a sculptor. Il Comandante says I'm the best. Why? Why does he need others? *(holds TAMARA's dress up to herself and swirls about the room)* In a dress like this, in a room like this, I'd know what to do...Mario, the new chauffeur, he knows what to do; last night I went to his room...no. There are things I should not say! "Emilia, your heart is as big as your mouth," Dante keeps saying. It's true. *(gets up and puts the dress back)* Sometimes, well once, I had my bags packed. I'm good...deserve better. Everything I have, I've worked for...not like the Polish one. They'll open the door and Dante will collapse trying to carry all her trunks....And he wants to marry me, "Poveri, siamo poveri." Dante dreams only of Venezia, but never of money. You can't eat dreams. The world takes too much. You have to steal to get back what's yours. *(pockets the earrings)* I'm too poor to marry for love. A man with a fat wallet and a title, then I could go....Il Comandante used to promise he'd help me find a husband. But no men come here anymore, except Gian Francesco de Spiga, and he doesn't count. Il Comandante says all his friends are dead. I think he is afraid to face them....No, I didn't mean to say that...so much work to do.

SCENE B8

CARLOTTA runs into the Leda through the side door, and throws herself on the bed.

CARLOTTA
I kissed him! I kissed him!

EMILIA
Who did you kiss, Signorina?

CARLOTTA
(suddenly noticing EMILIA) What are you doing here?

EMILIA
Preparing the room, Signorina.

CARLOTTA
(noticing TAMARA's dress) Is that another present?

EMILIA
Isn't it beautiful?

CARLOTTA
(holding the dress up to herself and looking in the mirror) Would Capitano Finzi be attracted to someone in a dress like this?

EMILIA
It makes you look like a real woman, Signorina. He'd be attracted to that.

CARLOTTA
A real woman?

EMILIA
Si, Signorina, a grown woman.

CARLOTTA
At home I have only three dresses. Mamma says it's not right to have more. It makes the servants envious.

She drops the dress. EMILIA picks it up.

And now I am envious. Forgive me Father, all my ugly thoughts. *(goes over to the blank canvas stretched on an easel and picks up a piece of charcoal)* This room needs a crucifix. *(makes one on the canvas and goes to exit)*

EMILIA
(trying to wipe the canvas clean) Whenever they ask for forgiveness it means more work for Emilia.

CARLOTTA
(turning in the doorway) I heard that. You wouldn't last a day in my house, not a day, Emilia.

EMILIA
I'm sure I wouldn't, Signorina.

CARLOTTA
In our house the servants never speak, they don't make a sound.

EMILIA
Old Conte Leonni had a servant who was so quiet people said he was invisible. One night the servant strangled the Conte in his bed while the Contessa slept not two feet away.

CARLOTTA
Don't tell me such terrible things.

EMILIA
Il Comandante says that terrible things are the only things worth telling.

CARLOTTA
One day they'll be illegal.

CARLOTTA exits to the Atrium, PAGE 44. EMILIA exits to the Dining Room, where she begins gathering dinner plates until the sound of a gunshot startles her, PAGE 45.

SCENE B9

THE DINING ROOM

After her brief encounter with FINZI in the hall, PAGE 26, AÉLIS enters the Dining Room.

AÉLIS

Ahh! Excuse moi. *(catches her breath and closes the door)* I'm so glad you were able to be with us this evening. I must tell you that there was some question as to whether Roma would allow Il Comandante any more guests but fortunately they relented. *(seeing the dinner plates still on the table)* Emilia! *(pulls upon a cord to summon the servant)* I'm so embarrassed. *(begins to pick up the dinner plates)* I try to run this house but how does Gabri expect me to do my job if he won't reprimand Emilia and Dante for not doing theirs? Every time he locks himself in his room, like some monk in his cell, to plan another great seduction, Emilia stops doing the dishes and Dante...well Dante never needs a special occasion to do nothing. *(puts the plates on a side table and begins to set the table for dessert)* Perhaps it's my fault. I must confess that Carlotta has kept me rather distracted of late. You remember Carlotta? The young ballerina? Of course you do. Does she not have a remarkable freshstrawberries quality about her? Baccara says she's naive, perhaps she's right, but since the Great War I've found that to be a remarkably rare and seductive characteristic. To some extent I think that's what Gabri is hoping to find in this painter, Madame Tamara de Lempicka. Indeed I haven't seen him so obsessed about a woman since he first saw Eleonora Duse on the stage, many years ago. And he hasn't even met Tamara yet. Let me explain. A few months ago on a rare trip to Milano, Gabri happened upon an exhibit of her art, including some very revealing self portraits. Well, since then he has done nothing but talk to me of Tamara, her beauty, her sensuality. Since he was so enamored of her and growing increasingly depressed about his own work, I suggested that he invite her to Il Vittoriale to paint his portrait. And that began an exchange of — Mon Dieu, how do I put it without offending anyone's modesty — highly erotic correspondence. Believe me, when he finally succeeds with her, we will, all of us, at last have cause for laughter. And now you are most welcome to accompany me but I must attend to the last-minute details of Tamara's arrival.

AÉLIS exits to PAGE 43, the Atrium.

SCENE B10

THE ATRIUM

DANTE enters from PAGE 27, the Upstairs, and crosses to audience members. de SPIGA is from PAGE 29, the Atrium; he stops playing.

DANTE
I don't know that opera.

de SPIGA
It doesn't exist yet, Dante. They commissioned me to write an opera about Venezia and even though I lived there half my life, I cannot come up with anything to say. I've found a few melodies based on folk songs, but as for a libretto...nothing.

DANTE
You need a story.

de SPIGA nods yes.

To write about Venezia is to write about love.

de SPIGA
It's been done: Othello.

DANTE
No, I have another story, very sad. Posso?

de SPIGA
I'm listening.

DANTE
This is the story of a man waiting for the woman he loves. *(long pause)*

de SPIGA
And?

DANTE
That's it.

de SPIGA
For three acts?

DANTE
Two. In the third act he kills his valet.

de SPIGA
Why?

DANTE
Because there was no hope.

de SPIGA
He kills his valet because he lost all hope? Why doesn't he kill himself?

DANTE
Oh no, Signore. He thinks too much of himself.

de SPIGA
So he lost hope because the woman didn't love him?

DANTE
She couldn't love him and he couldn't love her because they had both lost hope. Did I mention that in the second act, just when they're about to get together, the Fascists take over?

de SPIGA
No. But people fall in love no matter who is in power.

DANTE
No, Signore. They think only of staying alive...that's how the man kills his valet. He turns him in to the Fascists.

de SPIGA
What does the valet do? Is he a Communist?

DANTE
No, Signore, the valet is a poor Venetian; he just makes his master nervous because he is always smiling.

de SPIGA
That will never make an Italian opera. German, maybe. You depress me, Dante. I had no idea your world was so bleak.

DANTE
It isn't. You see, I'm smiling. But you do not smile, Signore.

de SPIGA
So, I'm the man in your story.

DANTE
For the sake of your valet, I hope not. Permesso.

de SPIGA
(laughing) Si, Dante.

DANTE goes to the front window to check on TAMARA's arrival and de SPIGA continues playing the piano until AÉLIS enters, PAGE 43.

SCENE B11

d'ANNUNZIO'S ROOM

LUISA arrives at d'ANNUNZIO's door from her room, PAGE 30. She points her gun at the door and enters. She stops in the centre of the room. Pointing her gun at d'ANNUNZIO, who is from PAGE 34.

d'ANNUNZIO
(crossing to LUISA) You upset me, Luisa. Did we not agree that our affair—

LUISA
Relationship.

d'ANNUNZIO
...was to be forgotten?

LUISA
I can't—

d'ANNUNZIO
Finished. *(goes to the mirror and checks his appearance)* Over. Not now or again, ever again, never. When Madame de Lempicka arrives, you play the piano, only that. I shall want some soft music around eleven. Perhaps Debussy's "La Cathédrale engloutie."

LUISA

She won't be like the others. I've seen her work; it's new.

d'ANNUNZIO

The young come to me! A day passes and I get older, become legend. *(turning to LUISA)* But you, Luisa, just get forgotten. No one remembers or cares and I'll soon forget you if you don't forget the past.

d'ANNUNZIO hurries out of his room, down the stairs to the Atrium, PAGE 45, leaving LUISA to follow, gun in hand.

LUISA
Inside the body
Of the man who killed me
You'll find a heart
And inside the heart
You'll find a bullet
And my art.

LUISA exits to the stairs and observes the action in the Atrium from above. PAGE 45.

SECTION C

THE FOLLOWING SCENES HAPPEN SIMULTANEOUSLY:

SCENE C12   Group scene in the Atrium.
Page 43

SCENE C13   Brief scene in the Side Hall wherein EMILIA, AÉLIS,
Page 50   CARLOTTA and LUISA pick up the presents for
                TAMARA. They return to the Atrium and then to the Leda
                with the presents.

SCENE C14   CARLOTTA, DANTE and LUISA in the Leda, joined by
Page 51   EMILIA.

SCENE C12

THE ATRIUM

de SPIGA sits playing the piano. DANTE stares out the window. Enter AÉLIS. She is carrying some presents. She is followed by FINZI. de SPIGA and DANTE are from PAGE 40, the Atrium. FINZI is from PAGE 33, the hall. AÉLIS is from PAGE 37, the Dining Room.

AÉLIS
When will the world be quiet?

de SPIGA
There would be no need for Fascists, if there was silence.

FINZI
Aélis, a woman needs a gun. Living in this house, Luisa is at risk. She could be kidnapped by Communists, held for ransom.

de SPIGA
We're already hostages!

FINZI
Signor de Spiga, I was invited to this house at the request of Il Comandante, and take strong exception to your insinuations to the contrary. *(walks over to the window)*

AÉLIS
Francesco, help me with this load. *(puts presents on the piano)* I don't want to hear any more talk of guns, there's too much work to do.

de SPIGA
But I'm a guest.

AÉLIS
After two months you're not a guest, you're a parasite. Now, help me.

de SPIGA
If you'd keep him away from Luisa, I could be gone in a week. It's difficult to plead your love with that black guardian angel hovering about her.

FINZI
(turning around) Don't you think Mario should be back by now?

AÉLIS
Every time Mario goes out, he asks, "Where's Mario, when is he coming back?"...the same question again and again.

DANTE
(turns from window) No sign of them. *(turns back)*

de SPIGA
Any sign of dessert?

AÉLIS
We're waiting for "La Polonaise."

de SPIGA
Aélis, please; let me eat cake!

AÉLIS
Stop it, Francesco.

de SPIGA
Deprived of love, deprived of dessert. Do you want to turn me into a Finzi?

AÉLIS
(laughing) He's not deprived, he's depraved.

FINZI
You may run this house, Aélis, and I may be here as a guest, but you should remember you're French, you are a guest of the Italian government, my government.

Enter CARLOTTA, from PAGE 36, the Leda. She enters leaping and wearing a tutu.

AÉLIS
Carlotta, I asked you not to leap about like that. Something's bound to break.

CARLOTTA
Forgive me, Aélis. I'm so excited, and I feel...whenever I'm happy I need to dance.

FINZI
(quickly to de SPIGA) Francesco, may I have a word?

de SPIGA
No.

FINZI exits to his office where he will open his desk and begin reading a draft of a telegram about MARIO, which he keeps locked in a drawer.

Enter d'ANNUNZIO from PAGE 41, his room.

d'ANNUNZIO
Aélis!

AÉLIS
Oui, Comandante.

d'ANNUNZIO
Is the Leda ready?

AÉLIS
Oui, Comandante.

d'ANNUNZIO
Dante, I'll watch; you help Aélis. You too, Luisa...and Emilia.

CARLOTTA
Can I help, Comandante?

d'ANNUNZIO
Of course. *(sits in his chair)*

CARLOTTA
Grazie, Comandante.

Sound of a gunshot. FINZI runs out of his room, gun in hand. DANTE turns around. EMILIA runs out of the Dining Room. She is from PAGE 36.

EMILIA
(rushing) What was that?

LUISA is on the stairs overlooking the Atrium with a gun in her hand. She fires the gun again. LUISA is from PAGE 41, d'ANNUNZIO's room.

LUISA
It's alive.

FINZI
(coming out of his office with his gun drawn) Luisa, I told you never to do that....Do you want to kill yourself?

LUISA comes down the stairs.

CARLOTTA
Is she...is she sick, Aélis?

de SPIGA
You see, people will kill for dessert! Aélis, don't torture me any longer....I've got a sweet tooth.

AÉLIS
(handing her a duster which has been left on the piano) Emilia, I believe this belongs to you.

d'ANNUNZIO
Luisa, take your gun and this gunslinger *(pointing to FINZI)* out of my Atrium. Out of my sight.

Everyone heads out. EMILIA, CARLOTTA, AÉLIS and LUISA go to the Side Hall, bottom of PAGE 50, for the wrapped presents. FINZI waits for LUISA in the hall, PAGE 50.

DANTE picks up the gifts which AÉLIS had earlier brought in, takes them to the Leda and returns to the Atrium.

de SPIGA
All this trouble for a Polish woman.

d'ANNUNZIO
Do you know what Polish women are like? *(signals to de SPIGA that he would like some cocaine)*

de SPIGA
No. *(pulls out a vial of cocaine and spreads some on d'ANNUNZIO's left hand)*

d'ANNUNZIO
Nor do I, but I intend to find out. A woman like Tamara is rare. She is a lady, yet she speaks not with her mouth, but her sex. She may disappoint....

de SPIGA
Is this Gabriele d'Annunzio I hear? Talking of failure —

d'ANNUNZIO
No, but since I've dreamt so much about her, I might not like her; dreams kill reality. *(snorts cocaine)*

de SPIGA
Society women, they're all sweet sounds and scents.

d'ANNUNZIO
Aélis! Emilia!

Enter AÉLIS, CARLOTTA, LUISA and EMILIA from PAGE 51, the Side Hall.

AÉLIS
Take these. *(giving packages to DANTE)*

DANTE
Are there more? *(takes the presents)* Wouldn't it be nice to be back in Venezia?

d'ANNUNZIO
We're not moving! This is my house, my creation, so stop talking about Venezia, we're not going back. And put on some socks, you're not a gondoliere anymore.

DANTE
Si, Comandante.

DANTE, CARLOTTA, LUISA and EMILIA take presents to the Leda, PAGE 51. EMILIA lingers behind.

d'ANNUNZIO
You've got the flowers...incense?

AÉLIS
Oui, Comandante.

d'ANNUNZIO
Should I get her a necklace?

AÉLIS
You are giving her a beautiful one; it's with the earrings in the Leda.

d'ANNUNZIO
What then? ...something elegant — as she walks in the door.

AÉLIS
I thought this ring.... *(hands him an ivory ring)*

d'ANNUNZIO
(studying it) Aélis, you're marvelous.

de SPIGA
You see, Gabri, you go to all this trouble for these society women, but it's women like Aélis and Emilia who bring you off.

d'ANNUNZIO sees EMILIA following LUISA and CARLOTTA into the Leda with the gifts.

d'ANNUNZIO
Emilia! Don't mention her. She's giving me that corporal's face again. Yes, sir. Yes, sir. And then around the corner without a touch of her.

Emilia exits to the Leda, PAGE 52.

AÉLIS
She's jealous.

d'ANNUNZIO
I don't pay her for jealousy.

de SPIGA
You don't pay anyone.

d'ANNUNZIO
Anyway, there's a difference. Emilia is a whore.

AÉLIS
A maid, Gabri.

de SPIGA
But a specialist. She makes his bed and then lies in it.

d'ANNUNZIO
Tamara is an artist.

AÉLIS
Whore, artist...what's the difference? What am I?

d'ANNUNZIO
Give me your lips, I can't resist a mouth like yours.

de SPIGA
(looking out) She's arrived. She's here and Finzi's outside.

d'ANNUNZIO
Bastard! The first one she'll see is that Fascista! Francesco, don't stand there, take the ladies to the Oratorio. *(takes off his monk's robe to reveal a white military uniform)*

LUISA reenters from the Leda, PAGE 53.

LUISA
(to d'ANNUNZIO) Where's my gun?

EMILIA, CARLOTTA and DANTE enter from the Leda, PAGE 53.

d'ANNUNZIO
(to LUISA) Bang. *(turning to EMILIA)* Emilia, if you don't take that look off your face, I'll lock you in your room. And be nice to Madame de Lempicka. *(throws her his monk's robe)*

EMILIA exits to the Dining Room. She picks up the tray of dirty dishes and begins to exit to the Kitchen. She stops by a pillar to see what TAMARA looks like. To PAGE 55.

Dante, open the door.

d'ANNUNZIO checks his appearance in the mirror and nods for DANTE to open the front doors.

LUISA
(to de SPIGA) Where's my gun?

DANTE opens the front doors to PAGE 55. de SPIGA tries to put his arm around LUISA, but she turns away. He then takes CARLOTTA's arm and, followed by LUISA and AÉLIS, goes to the Oratorio.

de SPIGA
Come Aélis, come Luisa. We'll go to the Oratorio. Luisa will play the piano for us. Won't you?

LUISA
(to AÉLIS) Where's my gun?

AÉLIS
I can't run this house with you flitting about with a gun!

de SPIGA
(to LUISA) Just think of all those keys as eighty-eight little triggers waiting to be pulled.

LUISA laughs.

de SPIGA, LUISA, CARLOTTA and AÉLIS arrive in the Oratorio, PAGE 58.

SCENE C13

EMILIA, AÉLIS, CARLOTTA and LUISA are in the Side Hall to pick up the presents. They are from PAGE 46, the Atrium.

FINZI is waiting for LUISA when she comes into the hall. They are also from PAGE 46.

FINZI
Luisa, give me the gun. You could hurt yourself.

He takes the gun from her, hides it in his office and exits out the front door, closing the doors behind him. He then waits for TAMARA's arrival, PAGE 55. LUISA joins the others in the hall. She picks up a pile of presents from the bench.

AÉLIS
(giving a little bracelet box to CARLOTTA) La petite pour la petite!

CARLOTTA
Grazie....Oh, I never got such things.

EMILIA
She's getting better merchandise than the last one.

AÉLIS
Emilia, keep your tongue in your mouth! *(exiting to the Atrium)*

EMILIA
Signorina Barra, you don't have to carry anything. Why don't you let me take that?

CARLOTTA
Si, I am a guest too. *(puts the bracelet box on top of EMILIA's stack of presents)* I don't have to carry anything.

AÉLIS
I'm watching you, Emilia.

EMILIA
Signora Mazoyer, I never steal.

CARLOTTA
You're right Aélis, servants are not to be trusted. *(takes back bracelet box)*

They all exit back to the Atrium, PAGE 47.

SCENE C14

THE LEDA

CARLOTTA, DANTE and LUISA enter the Leda.

DANTE
Are you all right, Signora Baccara?

LUISA
(quietly) This used to be my room…and now I'm upstairs.

DANTE
Il Comandante wanted you closer to him, Signora—

LUISA
Next, he'll move me up to the new floor.

DANTE
No, Signora, he wouldn't.

LUISA
And then I'll be on the roof with the pigeons. Why can't I fly...?

CARLOTTA
I'm downstairs with the servants, Luisa. The servants.

DANTE
It's a lovely room, Signorina Barra.

CARLOTTA
Did I speak to you?

DANTE
No, Signorina.

CARLOTTA
I feel as if I'm lost in the woods, down there.

LUISA
(*after examining a few boxes of presents*) Everyone, every box...wrapping paper...box...the notes...they're all the same....

LUISA knocks over a pile of presents. DANTE rushes to pick them up. LUISA continues speaking quietly to herself.

Everything that was ours....Why can't he just let me have my memories? ...let them fade....

CARLOTTA
Why did you fire that gun, Luisa?

Enter EMILIA from PAGE 48.

EMILIA
Don't touch them, Dante....I spent all afternoon arranging those presents.

DANTE
Signora Baccara isn't feeling well, Emilia. Perhaps you—

LUISA
I'm fine — *(exits back to the Atrium, PAGE 49)*

CARLOTTA
(following LUISA out) It's this room; it's full of bad thoughts. *(turns the canvas on the easel over again to reveal the cross and exits, PAGE 49)*

DANTE goes to exit and EMILIA follows behind, pausing to steal a bracelet.

DANTE
(turning) I'm watching, Emilia.

DANTE exits to the Atrium, PAGE 49. EMILIA turns the canvas on the easel over again and exits back to the Atrium, PAGE 49.

SECTION D

THE FOLLOWING SCENES HAPPEN SIMULTANEOUSLY:

SCENE D15   d'ANNUNZIO greets TAMARA in the Atrium.
Page 55

SCENE D16   Brief scene between FINZI and EMILIA at the top of the
Page 58   stairs leading to the servants' quarters.

SCENE D17   CARLOTTA, de SPIGA, LUISA and AÉLIS in the Oratorio.
Page 58

NOTE: d'ANNUNZIO and TAMARA after PAGE 57, join the others on
PAGE 60.

SCENE D18   EMILIA and FINZI are in the Kitchen.
Page 65

SCENE D19   MARIO and DANTE take TAMARA's luggage to the Leda.
PAGE 69

SCENE D15

THE ATRIUM and ENTRY HALL

DANTE goes out to the automobile to assist MARIO with TAMARA's luggage. d'ANNUNZIO is visibly upset by the sight of FINZI. d'ANNUNZIO and DANTE are from PAGE 49, the Atrium.

FINZI
(outside) Mario, what took you so long?

MARIO is from PAGE 23, the Atrium

MARIO
Her bags were lost at the station.

Enter TAMARA. Her entrance is blocked by FINZI. FINZI is from PAGE 50, the Side Hall.

FINZI
Your papers, please.

TAMARA
Je ne comprends pas l'italien, Monsieur. [I do not understand Italian, Monsieur.]

d'ANNUNZIO
She doesn't understand a word you're saying....It won't be necessary, Finzi.

FINZI
I decide—

d'ANNUNZIO
Nothing! Is that clear? Nothing. Now, get out.

TAMARA
Monsieur d'Annunzio.

d'ANNUNZIO
Tamara.

As FINZI is leaving the Atrium, he sees EMILIA hiding behind a pillar. He grabs her arm and startles her. They go to PAGE 58.

NOTE: TAMARA and d'ANNUNZIO speak English only when they are alone
— the audience must be clear on this convention.

TAMARA
Pardonnez-moi, mon frère, nous avons été retenus à la gare. [Forgive me, brother, we were delayed at the station.]

d'ANNUNZIO
Je ne suis pas votre frère. Les liens qui nous attachent sont plus forts que le sang. [I am not your brother. The ties which bind us are much stronger than blood.] *(In English)* Dante, Mario, take Madame's bags.

DANTE and MARIO exit to the Leda, PAGE 69.

I hope you'll find the accommodations here adequate. *(slips an ivory ring on her finger)*

TAMARA
Superb!

d'ANNUNZIO
There are so few colours left whose purity have not been corrupted. *(looks very closely at TAMARA)* The craftsmanship is excellent. To mount ivory must be a difficult art.

TAMARA
Why is that man here?

d'ANNUNZIO
Who?

TAMARA
The one in black.

d'ANNUNZIO
Ahhh! Finzi. He was a gift from Il Duce. *(laughs)* Some people give books, perhaps you give paintings. Signore Mussolini gives people. Capitano Finzi is here to keep out unwanted guests.

TAMARA
I thought policemen guarded prisoners.

d'ANNUNZIO
No. No. A writer needs two things: solitude and beauty. And they are one in

you. Come. Let us get the disagreeable task of introductions over with. Then I will show you the "Leda."

TAMARA

(rising) But I can't see anyone, looking like this. I must change.

d'ANNUNZIO

(takes off her coat) But you have already; you've met me. The rest are not important. Could they ever see you? Could common eyes ever perceive such angelic incandescence?

TAMARA laughs.

Come. *(takes TAMARA's arm)*

They exit to the Side Hall where d'ANNUNZIO hangs TAMARA's coat on the coat rack. TAMARA hangs her hat on the same rack and checks her appearance in the mirror.

Come.

TAMARA

When my bags were lost at the station, I thought for a moment it was a sign, that I should not have come.

d'ANNUNZIO

But why?

TAMARA

It was just a moment's hesitation, you understand.

d'ANNUNZIO

Still, you came...was it just for the commission?

TAMARA

Why did you invite me? Why do we do anything — curiosity — the belief that the future lies behind the next door.

d'ANNUNZIO opens the doors to the Oratorio, they enter PAGE 60, in progress.

SCENE D16

THE SERVANTS' STAIRS

This scene begins as soon as FINZI leaves the Atrium, PAGE 55.

    FINZI
(whispering to EMILIA, touching her) Emilia!

    EMILIA
Aldo, you scared me.

    FINZI
I want you!

    EMILIA
Now? You have the money?

    FINZI
I have the money.

    EMILIA
Your office?

    FINZI
Downstairs. I want a peasant girl tonight.

    EMILIA
Let me serve dessert. Then I'll serve you. *(grabs a tray of dishes, goes downstairs to the Kitchen, PAGE 65)*

SCENE D17

THE ORATORIO

CARLOTTA, de SPIGA and LUISA enter from PAGE 50, the Atrium, followed by AÉLIS. LUISA goes to the piano and begins to play Chopin's Waltz Op. 70, #2, quietly. CARLOTTA starts to dance.

de SPIGA

Have I ever told you about my friend Agideo's coffin piano?

CARLOTTA

Oh, Signor de Spiga, you're trying to tease us.

AÉLIS

(to LUISA) You all right?

LUISA nods yes. AÉLIS massages her shoulders for a moment then focuses her attention on CARLOTTA.

de SPIGA

I live in a town called Asolo which is not so much a town as a mountain of fools. No comments, Aélis. I live there because the people keep me entertained. True. Agideo, for example. He makes a living as a dung collector. He used to prosper until the bottom dropped out of the market.

CARLOTTA

But Signor de Spiga, things are wonderful. The Monsignor told me only last week that my generation will do in twenty years what was done in a thousand. Life is exciting! And God shines on the new Italia.

LUISA

Apparently not on Asolo.

AÉLIS

Always so negative, Luisa.

de SPIGA

Do you want to hear my story?

AÉLIS

Do we have a choice?

de SPIGA

No. Agideo is a lover of music. *(stands on d'ANNUNZIO's tomb)* Now most Italians love opera, but Agideo, his secret passion is the piano. Of course, he couldn't afford to buy one, so he decided to build one *(pause)* out of a coffin. It's true, I swear! I told him a piano had eighty-eight keys —

CARLOTTA

(laughing) He built it in a coffin?

de SPIGA

Yes! He said he only had room for three octaves but Pagnucco, the local pasta dealer, was going to sell him his mother-in-law's coffin, and she was five octaves wide!

CARLOTTA

Did you play it?

de SPIGA

Amazing acoustics. Baccara, you'd love it.

LUISA

I've been living in a coffin for three years. Aélis, don't let him bury me. I want to be burned. Fire.

de SPIGA

Oh, this Italian obsession with melodrama.

AÉLIS

(going to LUISA) She'll be here a few days, that's all.

LUISA

And then the next one comes...it starts again.

CARLOTTA

(exercising as she talks) The Church doesn't approve of burning, Luisa, except for heretics.

de SPIGA

We could leave right now, Luisa. The automobile is just outside. Mario could drive us anywhere you want.

AÉLIS

I'm warning you, Francesco. If you upset Gabri there'll be no coming back. Now let's talk of other things. *(pause)* For instance, have you noticed what beautiful eyes Carlotta has?

de SPIGA

On that, dear Aélis, we see eye to eye, though observing you I've noticed other...aspects of her seem to hold a greater fascination.

LUISA begins playing a Chopin waltz again. She stops abruptly when d'AN-NUNZIO and TAMARA enter from PAGE 57, the Atrium.

d'ANNUNZIO
(with TAMARA on his arm) Ladies and Gentlemen, may I present Madame Tamara de Lempicka: artist and art.

de SPIGA
How beautiful!

d'ANNUNZIO
En français, Francesco. [In French, Francesco.]

de SPIGA
Beauty is its own language.

d'ANNUNZIO
Puis-je vous présenter Gian Francesco de Spiga, compositeur. [May I present Gian Francesco de Spiga, composer.]

de SPIGA
Enchanté.

TAMARA
Bon soir. J'aimerais vous entendre jouer votre musique. [Hello. I would love to hear you play your work.]

de SPIGA
Gabriele ne me permet pas de jouer ma musique; plutôt ce sont ses chiens qui ne le permettent pas, mais après le dessert je vous jouerai du Chopin. [Gabriele won't allow me to play my own work, or rather, the dogs won't allow it, but after dessert I'll play some Chopin for you.]

TAMARA
Je préfère Debussy. [I prefer Debussy.]

d'ANNUNZIO
Non, Tamara. Cet honneur reviendra à notre chère Luisa Baccara. [No, Tamara, that honour will fall to our dear Luisa.]

TAMARA
Luisa Baccara—

de SPIGA
First, dessert!

No response.

LUISA
(to d'ANNUNZIO) She's more beautiful than I imagined.

d'ANNUNZIO nods his agreement.

TAMARA
J'ai tellement entendu parler de vous, Madame Baccara. Je vous admire beaucoup. Je vous ai vue jouer une fois à Zurich. [I've heard a lot about you, Madame Baccara. I am an admirer of yours. I saw you play once in Zurich.]

LUISA
What did...she say?

AÉLIS
She saw you play in Zurich.

LUISA
Tell her I've abandoned touring. *(to TAMARA)* Fini, fini.

AÉLIS
Elle dit qu'elle ne fait plus de tournées, et cela la choque qu'il y ait quelqu'un qui s'en souvienne. [She says she no longer tours, and is surprised anyone remembers.]

d'ANNUNZIO seems upset by this.

d'ANNUNZIO
Et voici Carlotta...

AÉLIS
Barra.

d'ANNUNZIO
Elle espère aller à Paris et danser pour Diaghilev. [She hopes to go to Paris and dance for Diaghilev.]

TAMARA
(takes her hand) Bonsoir, ma petite. [Hello, little one.]

CARLOTTA
When the devil caresses you, he wants your soul.

TAMARA
Êtes-vous une jeune Pavlova? [Are you a young Pavlova?]

CARLOTTA looks to AÉLIS for a translation.

AÉLIS
Are you a young Pavlova?

CARLOTTA
(curtly) No, Maria Taglione. I am Italiana. *(exits crying, to her room, PAGE 73)*

AÉLIS
Carlotta!

TAMARA
Ah! Vous les Italiens, vous avez une telle passion.

d'ANNUNZIO
Aélis, save me. There are too many artists in this room.

AÉLIS
Tous les artistes ont une telle passion! [All artists are passionate!]

d'ANNUNZIO
She reminds me of you when you were young, Luisa. Always storming out of rooms.

LUISA
It was you who taught me that bad manners were a sign of talent.

d'ANNUNZIO
(to TAMARA) Je vous présente Aélis. C'est ma femme de charge. Si vous avez besoin de quelque chose, vous pouvez le demander à elle. [This is Aélis, my housekeeper. If you need anything at all, ask her.]

AÉLIS
A votre service, Madame. [At your service.]

TAMARA
Quel nom étrange, Aélis. [An odd name, Aélis.]

AÉLIS
En vérité je m'appelle Emilie, mais Le Comandant préfère Aélis, alors, c'est

Aélis. [My real name is Emilie. But Il Comandante calls me Aélis, so Aélis it is.]

TAMARA
Je l'aime bien. [I like it.]

AÉLIS
Merci, Madame. Will you excuse me, Comandante, I should like to see what's the matter with Carlotta. *(goes to exit, turns to TAMARA)* Nous prenons le dessert en quelques minutes. Voulez-vous nous joindre? [We're having dessert in a few minutes. Will you join us?]

TAMARA
Avec plaisir. [Yes, with pleasure.]

AÉLIS exits to CARLOTTA's room, PAGE 73.

de SPIGA
Another sweet tooth!

d'ANNUNZIO
I will show Madame de Lempicka her room, and then we will join you for dessert. *(goes to exit)* Perhaps.

de SPIGA
(taking LUISA by the arm and going to the piano) Luisa, come to the piano and we'll discuss the virtues of the minor seventh.

d'ANNUNZIO
(exiting the Oratorio with TAMARA on his arm) You should not discuss what you do not have, my friend.

de SPIGA
The minor seventh?

d'ANNUNZIO
Virtue.

d'ANNUNZIO exits smiling, with TAMARA, to PAGE 83, The Atrium /Leda.

de SPIGA
(to himself) The things we don't have are the only things worth discussing.

LUISA
(sits at the piano) Poor girl. *(begins playing Debussy's "La Plus Que Lente")*

LUISA and de SPIGA continue talking, PAGE 79, the Oratorio.

SCENE D18

THE KITCHEN

EMILIA enters the Kitchen carrying dishes from the Dining Room. FINZI fol-lows. They are from PAGE 58, the Stairs.

FINZI
So...she is very beautiful.

EMILIA says nothing. She begins washing the dishes.

Her skin is soft and white as flour.

EMILIA
I didn't see her.

FINZI
She's much more attractive than you. And she carries herself—

EMILIA
If I had nothing better to do, I could fix myself up better than her. I work.

FINZI
Mario looks like he's in love with her already. They seemed to be having quite a conversation in the automobile.

EMILIA
Mario likes a woman, a real woman. He's not—

FINZI
Not what? What isn't Mario?

EMILIA

Only children play with dolls. *(goes to FINZI)* Carlotta told me she kissed you.

FINZI

An innocent kiss, nothing more. I'm not like your Mario. He'd chase anything in skirts.

EMILIA

He wouldn't!

FINZI

It interests me, Emilia, that I have been in this house over two years and I've never heard you mention your cousin Mario — yet you know him so well, you even know his taste in women.

EMILIA

The men in my family are all the same. My father picked my mother, and his brother's wife is just like my mother. It's easy to see what kind of women they like.

FINZI

And you? Do you like your men to be like Mario?

EMILIA

I don't have time for men.

FINZI

Unless they pay.

EMILIA

(goes back to the dishes) The Polish one, you think she's different? Did you see the dresses, the jewellery — all those things we carried to her room? She gets paid. Too much....

FINZI

You didn't charge Dante.

EMILIA

Nine years ago, what you could get for free then costs a lot today. Besides, I paid. *(quietly)*

FINZI

Ah, yes. Your daughter, Caterina.

EMILIA

You talk to me, ask questions; it's your job. I answer. You pay me money, I let you into my bed. We're not friends, capisce? No talk about Caterina.

FINZI

I went to your room last night.

EMILIA

Did you? I saw you going into Baccara's room. Did you need both of us?

FINZI

You were in Mario's room.

EMILIA

Sometimes we talk. I've hardly seen him since before the war. There's lots to talk about.

FINZI

Does he ask questions about Il Comandante?

EMILIA

Who wouldn't?

FINZI

Does he ever ask political questions? "What does Il Comandante think about Il Duce?" Things like that?

EMILIA

He's young, he thinks of girls.

FINZI

You know what I find interesting, Emilia, is how Josko, the old chauffeur, left for Christmas and without warning, failed to return.

EMILIA

He missed Fiume.

FINZI

No, I checked with the police there; he never arrived. In fact, I sent telegrams out all over Italy and no one has seen him.

EMILIA

His mother lives in Fiume.

FINZI

I know where his mother lives. What fascinates me is how your long-lost cousin showed up at the door — as a qualified chauffeur, no less.

EMILIA

It's the "zimbracca."

FINZI

(allowing her lie) Ah...si. That's what Il Comandante calls it when someone reads minds, the "zimbracca?"

EMILIA

Si, Mario was at the Grand Hotel with the Principessa d'Avignon and decided to see me. She was going to Capri and Mario hates the heat; so he took the job. Now enough about it. Basta.

FINZI

The next time you two have a late-night chat, I want you to tell him I'm watching him.

EMILIA

You tell him yourself.

FINZI

I know I don't have to repeat myself. Do I?

EMILIA

No.

FINZI

Bene.

DANTE enters and the three of them continue, PAGE 87.

SCENE D19

THE LEDA

MARIO and DANTE take TAMARA's luggage to the Leda. They are from PAGE 56, the Atrium. They put the luggage down by the table of gifts. MARIO begins "checking the room out" — looking out windows, behind the dressing screen, etc. DANTE does not notice as he closes the door.

DANTE
I don't know why these society women bring so many clothes. You watch, Mario. Il Comandante will have her in here in five minutes, undressed in ten, and she will stay that way until you drive her back to the station. Il Comandante says, "A woman like her wears her nudity like a uniform." And it's true. I wear a uniform and it suits me. Well, maybe not as good as my gondoliere's outfit, but I like it. I'm at home in it. But you, Mario...you don't look right.

MARIO
Where do these stairs go?

DANTE
To Il Comandante's quarters. *(adjusts MARIO's cap)* Josko, the old chauffeur, used to wear his cap like this. No. It just doesn't suit you. You look too good.

MARIO
Grazie. *(begins to unpack TAMARA's bags)*

DANTE
Employers don't like it if you look so good. *(noticing what MARIO is doing)* Mario! Chauffeurs don't unpack a lady's clothes. Leave that for Emilia.

MARIO
Mi scusi.

DANTE
You'll learn...in time.

MARIO
Do all of Il Comandante's women stay here?

DANTE
(goes to the dressing screen where a gown is hanging; takes it to the settee and

lays it out) All of the society ones, the whores stay at the Grand Hotel and, of course, there's Aélis and Emilia. A busy man.

MARIO
Emilia?

DANTE
Don't be so shocked, Mario. She may be your cousin but she still is the woman I love. Get used to the pain.

MARIO
But how can she?

DANTE
Food, a roof, where have you been Mario? Servants don't just serve, they service. Capisce?

MARIO
If you love her, why do you stay? Why don't you take her away?

DANTE
You think I don't want to? Listen, Mario, you're her cousin, maybe you could talk to her?

MARIO
Si, Dante.

DANTE
She doesn't listen to me. It's like we're in a cave, there's light in one direction but Emilia won't follow; she's convinced there's a treasure, that if we go deeper, she'll find it. Gowns, pearls; it's all fairy tales. What saddens me about you Catholics is that you'll commit any sin to find salvation.

MARIO
I don't go to church.

DANTE
(going to the bed; picks up one end of the mattress and removes a flask of vodka; has vodka bottles and flasks hidden all over the villa) No? When I asked Emilia why you were always sneaking off to Gardone, she said you went to mass.

MARIO
(laughing) The bordello. Dante, what about this whore...the one d'Annunzio uses? Defelice. Where could I find her?

DANTE
(puts flask back) Listen, Mario, three things: one, you couldn't afford her and two, she doesn't like men who ask questions, and three —

MARIO
Dante, I meant—

DANTE
There's work to do, Mario....*(goes to exit)* How about a drink after I serve dessert?

MARIO
Done.

DANTE exits to the Kitchen and PAGE 87. MARIO exits to FINZI's office, PAGE 86.

SECTION E

THE FOLLOWING SCENES HAPPEN SIMULTANEOUSLY:

SCENE E20   CARLOTTA and AÉLIS in CARLOTTA's room.
Page 73

SCENE E21   LUISA and de SPIGA in the Oratorio.
Page 79

SCENE E22   d'ANNUNZIO takes TAMARA to the Leda.
Page 83

SCENE E23   TAMARA monologue.
Page 85

SCENE E24   MARIO gives a brief monologue while searching FINZI's
Page 86   office.

SCENE E25   FINZI, EMILIA and DANTE in the Kitchen. MARIO enters
Page 87   halfway through the scene.

SCENE E20

CARLOTTA'S ROOM

CARLOTTA is in her room, lying on her bed, crying. Enter AÉLIS. They have come from PAGES 63 and 64, the Oratorio.

AÉLIS
Carlotta, how could you embarrass me like....*(seeing CARLOTTA, goes over to her)* Oh...Carlotta, I don't understand what's gotten into you.

CARLOTTA
I've been here six days, and he still hasn't seen me dance.

AÉLIS
Soon. I promise.

CARLOTTA
(jumps up and begins exercising) Everyone says "soon." I don't have time. I'm getting old, Aélis. Il Duce says we must build, now. I have to start my career.

AÉLIS
Carlotta, you're seventeen years old!

CARLOTTA
My sister became a nun when she was sixteen.

AÉLIS
You're so sweet. Let me close the door. *(closes door)* So sweet.

CARLOTTA
Why does he pay so much attention to her?

AÉLIS
She only just arrived. He's being polite.

CARLOTTA
All those presents. He was waiting at the door, Aélis. He didn't do that for me. She gets a room upstairs and I'm forgotten with the servants in the basement.

AÉLIS
(looking around) Have you seen your present?

CARLOTTA
Where?

AÉLIS takes a dress from behind the dressing screen.

AÉLIS
I bought it this morning when we went out shopping.

CARLOTTA
For me! You...Aélis! Thank you.

CARLOTTA hugs her. AÉLIS prolongs it.

You're so nice to me, Aélis. Everyone else....

AÉLIS
They like you.

CARLOTTA
Not like you. Can I put it on? I'll look better than that Polish woman! I'm so
excited. *(begins to undress)*

AÉLIS
May I help you? Your thighs are so beautiful. *(touches CARLOTTA's thighs)*
How do you manage to keep such powerful thighs?

CARLOTTA
Exercise.

AÉLIS
Il Comandante loves firmness.

CARLOTTA
Do you think he will give me a recommendation?

AÉLIS
That all depends. *(sitting down in a chair)* Show me your exercises, Carlotta.
I'll sit right over here.

CARLOTTA
(doing pliés in camisole and underwear at the end of the bed) I do eighty every morning.

AÉLIS
Eighty!

CARLOTTA
Sometimes I think as soon as I stop exercising or dancing, I'm not beautiful. If I stop, I feel as ugly as a stick.

AÉLIS
Do you have a boyfriend?

CARLOTTA
No. Mother says I'm not to have romantic thoughts until it is time.

AÉLIS
And when will that be?

CARLOTTA
When I marry.

AÉLIS
That might be too late.

CARLOTTA
It's not for me to question these things.

AÉLIS
But if you had someone who loved you, who'd take care of you, buy you presents, take you places, then perhaps you wouldn't feel...what did you say? ... "as ugly as a stick" when you stop dancing.

CARLOTTA
Have you ever felt it, Aélis? Felt love?

AÉLIS
Just once...oh...you....

CARLOTTA
Sometimes I think I...well, just recently actually, here at Il Vittoriale I thought I felt it....I mean, I felt the way this woman I read about in a book called *The*

Dawn of Love felt, when she saw her lover for the first time. Papà said I shouldn't have read it...you see it was left on the train and I didn't know what it was about...but when I got off the train in Padoua I had a hundred questions and...*(pause)* life became more complicated after that. *(goes behind the screen to put on her dress.)*

AÉLIS

I was just your age when first I fell in love. At least I thought it was love and then one day I was asked by the Comte de la Bretonne to be a companion to his niece Isabelle.

CARLOTTA

(turns around for AÉLIS to do up her zipper) So you had to leave the man you loved?

AÉLIS

Oui, but after arriving in Britanny I never thought of him.

CARLOTTA

You didn't write him?

AÉLIS

Isabelle took all my time. Day and night.

CARLOTTA

Was she sick? *(sits beside AÉLIS)*

AÉLIS

No. Actually she was as young and healthy as you are....

CARLOTTA

Did she dance?

AÉLIS

Not even a waltz. Horses were her life. Her thighs were as firm as yours from hours in the saddle...on her beautiful black-and-white mare. Do you know what she wanted to be, Carlotta? A cowboy. She wanted to sell the chateau, move to America. Perhaps if she had, she might still be alive.

CARLOTTA

She died?

AÉLIS

On her twentieth birthday her uncle gave her a huge red stallion....I begged her not to ride it...it threw her...broke her neck.

CARLOTTA

What did you do?

AÉLIS

...went to England for a time, I was devastated, and then returned to France, where I met Il Comandante.

CARLOTTA

So you gave up the man you loved to become a servant, to serve others.

AÉLIS

What?

CARLOTTA

Father Lotti says those who serve others, serve God first.

AÉLIS

That's not exactly what I meant.

CARLOTTA

What did you mean then?

AÉLIS

Oh, Carlotta. Now enough remembrance. Let's get upstairs to dessert.

CARLOTTA

Will the Polish woman be there?

AÉLIS

Yes.

CARLOTTA

I don't want to go.

AÉLIS

Carlotta, please. Do it for me.

CARLOTTA

You didn't say you like my dress.

AÉLIS
It's...incroyable.

CARLOTTA
Is that good?

AÉLIS
The best.

CARLOTTA
Am I ready?

AÉLIS
(touching up CARLOTTA's hair) Voilà. Vous êtes parfaite. [There. You're perfect.]

The scene continues as they walk upstairs to the Dining Room.

I can't understand why you took such an instant dislike to Madame de Lempicka.

CARLOTTA
I don't like foreigners. I can't understand what she says and everybody clusters around her and forgets me. Even Capitano Finzi went out to greet her.

AÉLIS
I'm a foreigner, Carlotta.

CARLOTTA
But you speak Italian and you care about me. You listen. We're friends.

AÉLIS
Yes...we're friends. *(pause)*

As they are about to enter the Dining Room, AÉLIS stops CARLOTTA.

I should tell Il Comandante dessert is served.

CARLOTTA
Aélis, don't leave me.

AÉLIS
The saints are with you, Carlotta. Go in. I'll be right back.

CARLOTTA enters and AÉLIS exits to d'ANNUNZIO's room, CARLOTTA to
PAGE 101, AÉLIS to PAGE 109.

SCENE E21

THE ORATORIO

LUISA is in the Oratorio with de SPIGA. She is playing Debussy's "La Plus
Que Lente" while he is taking advantage of her. They are from PAGE 65.

LUISA
Francesco, we're here to play the piano.

de SPIGA
If music be the food of love...

LUISA
Francesco!

de SPIGA
...play on.

LUISA
Francesco, stop! *(stops playing)*

de SPIGA
Just think of what they're doing! You forgot the refrain.

LUISA
There is no refrain.

de SPIGA
Why won't you leave d'Annunzio? My house is big. I can give you all you
want. Asolo is such a beautiful place. How can you love him? He doesn't love
you. Stop waiting, Luisa. Those days are past. He doesn't want a permanent
relationship.

LUISA
He does.

de SPIGA
With death. Why don't you give him your gun? At least he'll have a use for it.

LUISA
How morbid.

de SPIGA
This house has become a mausoleum.

LUISA
Il Vittoriale is a museum for the Italian people.

de SPIGA jumps on d'ANNUNZIO's tomb and gives a mock Fascist salute.

de SPIGA
d'Annunzio! d'Annunzio!

LUISA
(crossing upstage of tomb and picking up a dagger sitting on a pedestal)
Aren't you his friend?

de SPIGA
Of the man, yes. Of the artist, yes, but not of the collector. Gabriele plays the role of the Egyptian pharaoh a bit too much for my tastes. When he dies he wants to take all of us with him. On that day I intend to be in Asolo. Luisa, look at him. Since his days as the ruler of Fiume, he's aged thirty years in the last seven. Where will you go? What will happen when he dies?

LUISA
Will the name d'Annunzio ever die?

de SPIGA
(going to LUISA) Who remembers Luisa Baccara? A debut with Toscanini no less, and you give it up to service this, yes, this old man!

LUISA
You think I don't know the cost? Francesco, you're so sweet, but you don't understand women. Some of us think. *(pause)* Some dream. Some hope, wait. But all of us want, and will get, revenge. *(dropping the dagger back on the pedestal, returns to the piano)*

de SPIGA
(going to LUISA) Such a Venetian. Who would have thought that under such

alabaster breasts there could hide such a black heart? Revenge is so bourgeois, Luisa. Now, murder — "la crime passionelle" — I might write the opera.

LUISA
(hitting a note on the piano) It's out of tune. *(walking away)*

de SPIGA
(going to LUISA) It's you who are out of tune, Luisa. Out of step, out of touch, out of his sight, out of his mind. Luisa, come to Asolo. For nine weeks, I've worshipped at your feet; I've got a concerto due next month which isn't written. You're alive, Luisa. You can leave!

LUISA
(crossing away) I can't...I'm afraid.

de SPIGA
Why? It's not Gabri, he's too old to frighten you. Who?

LUISA
It's me, just me.

de SPIGA
No, Finzi. Last night he went to your room.

LUISA puts her hands over her ears.

I saw him. I listened. *(grabs LUISA)* Don't cover your ears. I didn't cover mine! Is that how you like it? Hard? Do you want me to be tough? *(pause)*

LUISA
This house has something of mine and I want...to...I want to get it back.

de SPIGA
There's nothing here! Everything this house takes, it kills. I understand you.

LUISA
No.

de SPIGA
I try to understand you. But I can't understand how you fornicate with Finzi.

LUISA
I won't be insulted. *(crossing away once again)*

de SPIGA

That you live under this roof and breathe this septic air is insult enough, for
you and me. Please, come with me, away from Gabri and that black-shirt bastard, Finzi —

LUISA

Don't say it out loud.

de SPIGA

(going to LUISA) There are two concerns in my life, music and you.

LUISA

There's no music in prison.

de SPIGA

For saying he's—

LUISA

Yes. Every day, men disappear for less than that. Have you been to Venezia?
Or Milano? They're everywhere. Maybe not yet in the precious hills of Asolo,
but soon. Soon, Francesco.

de SPIGA

You don't take Finzi seriously? Boys in costume —

LUISA

Five years. They've run Italia for five years.

de SPIGA

Like five-year-olds.

LUISA

Don't. Some people can make jokes. Gabriele d'Annunzio —

de SPIGA

Amen. *(crosses himself)*

LUISA

Yes, he can get away with it. As long as his jokes are private. He knows when
to stop. But you, Francesco, you shouldn't start.

de SPIGA

A hint of concern! She cares for me! I care for you. Why do you always say his name like that — "Gabriele d'Annunzio," "Il Comandante" — I don't understand why you worship him. It is worship. This place is like a shrine. Why, if you love Gabri, do you sleep with Finzi?

LUISA
(confessing) Because Gabri wants me to! He wants to know what Finzi is up to.

de SPIGA
I don't care what d'Annunzio wants. All I care about is what you want, Luisa. What is it? What can I give you, what can I offer?

LUISA
(begins to exit the Oratorio) Let's have dessert.

de SPIGA
(pause) Let's.

They exit to the Dining Room and PAGE 99.

SCENE E22

THE LEDA

TAMARA and d'ANNUNZIO come from PAGE 64, the Oratorio. TAMARA enters the Dining Room, d'ANNUNZIO follows.

d'ANNUNZIO
I should warn you, many others have tried to paint my portrait; but it seems mine is not a life which can be expressed in two dimensions. It still intrigues me to try to see what an artist sees in me.

TAMARA
How will I paint you? Is that what you're asking?

d'ANNUNZIO nods yes.

Will I paint you as the poet, as the brilliant man who rekindled the conscience of a nation, or the warrior whose actions helped bring the war to a close, or the creator of the Free State of Fiume, the man who almost won back for Italia the territory she was promised for entering the war? No, those achievements don't interest me. *(she walks out into the hallway)*

d'ANNUNZIO
Then what—

TAMARA
I want the great seducer. Yes, I know all about you. And I think all the portraits I've seen of you fail to capture your essence.

d'ANNUNZIO
That's because…what was the phrase you used in one of your letters?

TAMARA
The passion in the artist must be as great as the passion in the subject. How do you feel about posing in the nude? I want to paint you in an unguarded moment—you do have…unguarded moments?

d'ANNUNZIO
Let me show you the Leda. *(kisses her)*

He flings open the doors to the Leda and motions for Tamara to enter.

Lie down. Lie down beside me. *(coaxes her down beside him)* I know your journey was long, but not so long as my yearning.

They kiss and roll around, etc.

TAMARA
Wait I.…*(laughing)* Monsieur d'Annunzio, you may have put me in this bordello, but I should remind you, you are paying me to paint your portrait. What follows after that, if anything, is not something I want to dispense with like some small formality. I am an artist, not a whore.

d'ANNUNZIO
I am well aware of the distinction between an artist and a whore. A whore has better manners.

TAMARA
I know I'm too defensive. It's just not what I imagined…a woman wants a lover to draw her out, to write poems to her to make her feel special…not to act like her husband. I'm sorry.

d'ANNUNZIO
No. I bought you a few presents. *(goes to the settee)* Would you indulge me by wearing this...and this necklace in to dessert? It will go well with...where are they? There was a box of earrings. *(no reply)* Perfume, a bracelet, there are hats...do you like hats?

TAMARA
No. No. I couldn't. You're very kind but....

d'ANNUNZIO
Let me see you in it— *(goes to her and begins caressing her breasts)*

TAMARA
Monsieur d'Annunzio, what are you doing? *(slaps him)*

He exits to PAGE 109, his room.

SCENE E23

TAMARA, IN THE LEDA

TAMARA
I insulted...after all those letters...not in the house five minutes and I insulted him. *(begins changing for dessert)* But is it just a matter of — my name is Gabriele d'Annunzio, let's make love?

Everything seemed so different in Paris. I'd write to him, reveal my most intimate thoughts and it was as natural as writing in my diary. His replies would arrive by special courier, at the oddest hours, and it was as if he knew my mood exactly. For the first time in years I didn't feel alone with my thoughts; finally there was someone else to help me fight the emptiness of abstraction.

But then I arrive, and he abruptly leads me to this room — this bordello. Where is his sensitivity? Has he misread me completely? Perhaps it's my fault. He wanted me to come last week and I wrote and said, "I'm prevented by the laws of nature." What did I imagine he'd be expecting...discussing such things with a...yes, he's a stranger.

What must he think of me? The house is full of serious artists, Luisa Bacarra
— she probably thinks I'm just his night's diversion. Ah, this brain! Analyzing, analyzing, always speculating...just paint his portrait. You'll never get
down to work if you're always reliving the past and dreaming about the future.
You're here, it's what you wanted; an opportunity to work. Paint the damn picture. If there is to be anything between us I'll find it through the work....This
house is full of images and possibilities.

*TAMARA lapses into silence and goes behind the screen to put on her gown
just as MARIO enters. He begins searching her luggage, PAGE 112.*

SCENE E24

FINZI'S OFFICE

MARIO'S BEDROOM

*MARIO is from PAGE 71, the Leda. He enters, turns on the desk lamp and
begins searching FINZI's office. He goes to the desk and searches the drawer.
In it MARIO finds a draft of a telegram. It is written in Italian but spoken
rapidly in English*

MARIO
January 9, 1927.

To General Foscarinni, Ministry of State:
Request for information on the whereabouts of Serbian National Josko
Petranelli, a chauffeur, formerly in the service of Gabriele d'Annunzio. Stop.
Disappeared December 30. Stop. Local inquiries being made. Stop. Mother
believed to be living in Fiume. Stop. Also all or any information on a Mario
Pagnutti, cousin to Emilia Pavese, a maid here at Il Vittoriale, see file number
PO 07371. Stop.

If they find Josko's body...if...if...it's always if! You get an order, you act and
then you wait, *(at safe)* and hope. I've been here a week *(at desk)* and ac-
complished nothing. They said two days: in, out, yes or no. Everything planned. *(at stuffed chair)* I've no weapon. Finzi knows or will know. And now the
woman who painted my mother's portrait suddenly arrives. Why? Is it just
coincidence? Or....*(pause)* I need a gun.

I've got to talk to d'ANNUNZIO, now. *(exits abruptly to d'ANNUNZIO's room)* Il Comandante?

No one is there.

He's probably downstairs with Tamara...and if she opens her bags and finds the orders from my contact Defelice...if...if.... *(he finds a gun in d'ANNUN- ZIO's desk and, after hiding it in his belt, exits to his bedroom)*

(talking as he descends the stairs to the Servants' Quarters) Dark halls and passages. When I was young I used to go exploring all the old rooms. Father couldn't imagine owning a house in which he had seen every room. Masters abandon them to children and the servants. Wherever I explored, all corridors led to the kitchen. If you were hungry— or afraid, there was always a maid to comfort you. Last night Emilia came to my room. There was no talking; the silence was bringing us closer. I tried to hold back. But I surrendered. For a moment, there were no fears. No lies. No politics. It was like being set free.

Entering his bedroom, he hides the gun behind his bed. He removes his hat, leaves it on the bed and exits to the Kitchen, PAGE 91.

SCENE E25

THE KITCHEN

FINZI is talking to EMILIA as DANTE enters from the Leda, PAGE 71.

DANTE
I'm trying to decide what kind of man would give a woman a gun.

FINZI
A wise man.

DANTE
No, the wise men brought gold, frankincense...what else, Emilia?

EMILIA
Dante, I don't —

DANTE
Myrrh. That was it — myrrh.

EMILIA
(at sink) If you two are going to start, go out to the kennels. I've got work to do.

DANTE
Do you give guns to all the women in your life? Your mother, for example?

FINZI goes to grab DANTE, but misses him.

The feet of a gondoliere! Quick. Agile. You have to be on your toes in the fog, a steamboat could ram you. Did you get a gun, too, Emilia?

EMILIA
You've been drinking. Always. You start talking about Cain and Abel and —

DANTE
Don't steal my words. I saw you....*(goes to her and hugs her, putting his hand in the pocket of her apron while singing)*

Emilia, Emilia, the flower of my heart,
Emilia, Emilia, never shall we part.

EMILIA
Go away.

DANTE
Ahhh! What's this? *(takes a box from her apron which, when opened, contains a set of earrings)*

EMILIA
Dante, give them back!

DANTE
I'm surrounded by gangsters and thieves. Emilia, you promised you'd stop.

EMILIA
Dante, give them back! She doesn't need them. I've worked for them. Give them back.

FINZI
(crossing towards DANTE) Dante, give them to me.

DANTE

They belong to Madame de Lempicka. Now Il Comandante, he has good taste.
Didn't always, but after five years of living in Venezia, he has the good sense
to give a woman diamonds instead of guns.

FINZI

(to EMILIA) You must understand, Emilia, there are two types of Jews: the
practical and the romantic.

DANTE

And now the Fascist! No, Aldo, don't say you're a Jew. I am a Jew. I'm poor
and getting old. I've seen change and maybe I've changed but there are some
things I still cling to. You don't have to worry, because, yes, I'm afraid of you.
I am afraid of the way you strut about the kitchen when no one else is around,
because I know that you, too, are scared.
You attach yourself to the strong. I used to scrape the barnacles off my boat.
They're small, but they can slow you down. The way you slowed down Il
Duce. Aldo Finzi, first secretary to the Interior, and a Jew. They scraped you
off. We'll never be like them.

FINZI

My dismissal was a temporary measure, you'll soon see me back in Roma.
Barnacles! One day you'll wish you attached yourself to me!

DANTE

The price is too high.

EMILIA

So much talk. Dante, help me with the cake.

DANTE brings the knife to her. She cuts the cake.

FINZI

What's taking Mario so long?

DANTE

(to EMILIA) Are you going to stop taking things?

EMILIA

I take what I need.

DANTE

(to EMILIA) If you'd marry me you wouldn't have to keep stealing —

EMILIA
Marry you. I'd have to rob to fill three mouths.

DANTE
I could take care of you and Caterina.

EMILIA
No, you couldn't. Get it out of your mind. I take care of her myself. Me.

DANTE
There was a job in Venezia for a maid and a valet, husband and wife. Mamma clipped it out. The pay's better and we'd get an apartment above the boathouse.

EMILIA
I told you, no.

FINZI
Have you noticed how Mario talks? His accent is Milanese, yet he says he's Roman.

DANTE
I'll put these back. This is the last time I cover for you, Emilia. If Aélis catches you, you're finished.

FINZI
Not if your Comandante fails with the Polish one. If he does, he'll want Aélis; Aélis will say she has a headache and your beloved Emilia will be called in to service Il Comandante.

DANTE
You bastard!

DANTE attempts to hit him, but FINZI is ready and punches him quickly.

EMILIA
(rushing to DANTE) Every day you two start this. *(to DANTE)* Are you all right?

DANTE nods yes.

Let me see. There's no bleeding.

DANTE
I'll never bleed. Not like they made my father bleed. I will not.

Enter MARIO from PAGE 87, FINZI's office, and his bedroom.

MARIO
Dante...?

FINZI
Ah, Mario, I was just asking about you.

MARIO
The fan belt was loose. I had to tighten it. Dante, what happened?

EMILIA
He slipped. Don't worry about it.

MARIO
No, he was punched.

FINZI
The signs of violence are not unfamiliar to you.

DANTE
It's nothing, Mario. I'm fine.

FINZI
I punched him. It is important we understand each other, Mario. I am not an evil man, but I will not shirk from violence when it is the only course. *(turns his back on MARIO)*

MARIO
I was in the war; I understand your kind.

MARIO grabs a knife off the counter as if to attack FINZI but then says casually.

Dante, have some cake. *(cuts the cake)*

EMILIA
Mario, it's not for us.

FINZI
(turning to MARIO) I'm glad we understand each other. When two people know where they stand, one of them is more likely to succeed.

MARIO
Just a small piece.

EMILIA
Don't touch. It's Il Comandante's favourite —

FINZI
With that Polish one upstairs, he won't be eating cake.

EMILIA
I'm sick of hearing about her.

DANTE
She's very beautiful. Her skin is —

EMILIA
Stop it. Soft skin, soft hands, if I —

MARIO
(holding EMILIA's hands) Emilia, rough hands come from honest work.

EMILIA
Your hands are soft.

MARIO
(awkwardly) Grazie.

EMILIA
She does nothing. Why does he want her?

MARIO
Because she doesn't want him.

DANTE
You know those society women, they are always walking around with their noses up in the air. You know why?

EMILIA
No.

DANTE
To keep their brains from running out on to their tits.

Even FINZI laughs.

EMILIA
Basta. Are you going to help me serve, Dante?

FINZI exits to the hallway outside the Kitchen and waits for MARIO.

Mario, will you help me with the wine?

As EMILIA and DANTE exit with the cake and serving platters, they pass by FINZI who remarks sarcastically.

FINZI
He likes you, Emilia.

EMILIA
We're cousins.

EMILIA and DANTE exit to PAGE 97, a travelling scene which begins in the hall and ends in the Dining Room. FINZI detains MARIO for a talk.

FINZI
Mario, a moment.

MARIO
Yes.

FINZI
I find myself in some difficulty.

MARIO
Il Capitano has done something wrong?

FINZI
Not I. Luisa is in charge of employment here. I'm very fond of Luisa; I would not like to see her position compromised. You see, Mario, Luisa neglected to make the mandatory inquiries before signing your employment certificate.

MARIO
What are you talking about, Capitano?

FINZI
I'm having your references checked right now.

MARIO
I'm Emilia's cousin.

FINZI
Catholic?

MARIO
Si.

FINZI
I thought Catholics disapproved of incest. Let's be clear. I listened at your door last night. You two weren't saying your prayers....

MARIO
Capitano, we're lovers.

FINZI
You've gone to a lot of trouble if it's only a simple matter of "chiavare."

MARIO
A man needs a woman.

FINZI
Apparently your needs are greater than most.

MARIO
I'm in love.

FINZI
I can understand your little deceit as a man, but Roma will not understand.

MARIO
Roma?

FINZI
It looks very bad, Mario. They might think you had other motives for being here. It wouldn't be the first time a Communist had tried to get in to see Il Comandante.

MARIO
Automobiles are all I know about.

FINZI
Our last chauffeur, Josko, was very mechanical. It's odd how he disappeared. You were very fortunate to be in the right place....

MARIO
I'm young; women are soft for me.

FINZI
Did you obtain your last job by sleeping with a maid?

MARIO
No. My capitano in the war, he was a Visconti, was a friend of the Principessa d'Avignon.

FINZI
This Visconti, he was from —

MARIO
Milano.

A bell rings in the Kitchen.

I'm needed upstairs, Capitano.

FINZI
I'll take this. *(takes the wine tray from MARIO)* Il Comandante does not like the new servants upstairs. I suggest you stay in your quarters...and we'll continue our talk later.

FINZI exits to the Dining Room, PAGE 102. MARIO pretends to go to his room but then runs upstairs to TAMARA's room, PAGE 112.

SECTION F

THE FOLLOWING SCENES HAPPEN SIMULTANEOUSLY:

SCENE F26   EMILIA and DANTE head upstairs to the Dining Room.
Page 97

SCENE F27   Group scene in the Dining Room with DANTE, EMILIA, de
Page 99   SPIGA, LUISA, CARLOTTA, MARIO, FINZI and
                 TAMARA.

SCENE F28   d'ANNUNZIO is joined by AÉLIS in his room.
Page 109

SCENE F29   TAMARA catches MARIO searching her room.
Page 112

SCENE F30   MARIO meets EMILIA in the Side Hall.
PAGE 117

SCENE F26

EMILIA and DANTE head upstairs to the Dining Room. They talk on the way and the scene ends in the Dining Room.

DANTE
Why did Finzi say that?

EMILIA
What?

DANTE
"Mario likes you": what was that about?

EMILIA
Dante, he's my cousin. Finzi just wants to upset you.

DANTE
Why's he questioning Mario?

EMILIA
(exasperated) It's his job.

DANTE
Emilia, if there's anything you're not telling me....Did he lie about his references?

EMILIA
No.

DANTE
They check every detail.

EMILIA
He's family. That's all I know about him and that's good enough for me.

DANTE
I'm just trying to protect you.

EMILIA
You worry too much. *(gives him a kiss)*

DANTE

I'll keep Finzi away from Mario but you tell your cousin he's not to come upstairs unless he's called. There's only one valet here...and if he thinks he can take my job....

EMILIA

Dante, he loves his automobile, he doesn't want to work in the house.

DANTE

His place is downstairs or out in the garage.

EMILIA

I asked him to help me tonight. I'm sorry. I'll get the wine. *(goes to exit)*

DANTE

Ring the bell, he'll come.

EMILIA pulls a cord which rings in the Kitchen hall.

EMILIA

We need another maid.

DANTE

I swear Il Comandante keeps adding rooms just to see how much the Fascists will pay for his silence. The third floor is empty and the fourth...who'll go up there when it's finished? I'm not going to climb those stairs. In the last five years Il Comandante has doubled the size of the house but still refuses to hire more servants.

The scene continues as de SPIGA and LUISA enter the Dining Room, PAGE 99.

SCENE F27

THE DINING ROOM

EMILIA and DANTE are setting the table from PAGE 98 as de SPIGA and LUISA enter from the Oratorio, PAGE 83.

LUISA
What are you complaining about now, Dante?

DANTE
Signora Baccara, I was just saying the house has gotten too big.

de SPIGA
Perhaps we've gotten smaller.

EMILIA
Il Comandante keeps adding on rooms —

de SPIGA
The way some people gain weight.

EMILIA
When we first came there were just ten rooms, now there're thirty.

de SPIGA
Luisa, do you remember that first weekend?

LUISA
It was...there were just the four of us!

de SPIGA
That's right.

EMILIA
Il Comandante was waiting in Venezia and Signore de Spiga brought us down to open the house.

DANTE
There was no master that weekend.

LUISA
I remember playing the piano and dancing.

de SPIGA
We danced for the first time in years. And Dante got so drunk —

EMILIA
He didn't, Signore.

de SPIGA
Well, I did.

DANTE
A trip to the country and no bombs, of course I got drunk.

EMILIA
(to LUISA) You let me wear that dress, with...it shined!

LUISA
The red one, with the sequins?

EMILIA
Si, Signora.

LUISA
(to EMILIA) And we went to town and they thought you were the Principessa de Monte Neveso.

EMILIA
Si!

de SPIGA
Was that the time you saw the ghost, Luisa?

LUISA
I tell you I saw Franz Lizst. I did. The piano used to belong to him and he came back that weekend.

de SPIGA
Well, I've certainly never heard a better "Pelerinage."

DANTE
For a year, in 1921...I was happy. The war was over; Fiume was behind us; we

thought we'd finally find peace...and then in 1922, my papà was killed, Il Comandante—

de SPIGA
(*noticing a change in LUISA*) Don't go on, Dante. We could still be happy....

LUISA
1922, I hated that year.

de SPIGA
The four of us could escape to my house.

No response.

EMILIA
Everything changed after Il Comandante fell off the balcony.

DANTE
Someone pushed him!

LUISA
I was playing the piano!

de SPIGA
We know. No one's accusing you.

LUISA
My favourite year was the one before I was born.

de SPIGA
Emilia, your dessert will have to be especially sweet tonight to coax Luisa out of this prenatal depression.

EMILIA
This what, Signore?

de SPIGA
Nothing. Some wine, Dante.

DANTE
It's coming, Signore.

Enter CARLOTTA from outside the Dining Room, PAGE 79.

LUISA
Carlotta, it was impolite of you to walk out on Madame de Lempicka.

CARLOTTA
My papà taught me that if we think someone or something is wrong we must let them know. *(sits down)*

LUISA
My father said the same thing. He used to think that only he was right. He died before I could tell him he was wrong.

de SPIGA
Well, I'm glad to see someone is attending to the moral education of our ballerinas.

He sees FINZI enter from PAGE 95, the Kitchen hall, via his office, to the Dining Room.

There's a black cloud on the horizon.

LUISA
Aldo, you shouldn't be here.

FINZI
Since Mario's new I thought it best for him to remain downstairs, so I brought the wine. I've hardly seen you all day, Luisa.

FINZI hands it to EMILIA. DANTE takes it and pours a glass for de SPIGA and LUISA.

de SPIGA
You may go now, Finzi.

CARLOTTA
Please don't go, Capitano.

de SPIGA
I'm sure the Capitano has better things to do than eat cake.

FINZI
Better the cake than the crumbs. Isn't that true, Luisa?

No response.

CARLOTTA
Here, Capitano. Sit beside me.

FINZI
I'd be delighted to, Signorina Barra. *(sits down)*

de SPIGA
Luisa, I'm losing my appetite.

No response.

FINZI
Dante, some wine.

DANTE pours him a glass, after receiving a nod from LUISA.

DANTE
Should I serve now, Signora Baccara? *(setting a place for FINZI)*

LUISA
Wait. Il Comandante will be here in a minute.

EMILIA
(trying to leave) I could get him?

LUISA
No.

de SPIGA
I'm sure Gabri is having dessert in the Leda.

CARLOTTA
Aélis went to see him.

de SPIGA
Then he has two reasons not to join us. *(looking at FINZI)* And I have one to join him.

FINZI
Would you like some wine, Signorina Barra?

CARLOTTA
I don't usually...but why not?

FINZI
Dante.

DANTE pours wine for CARLOTTA.

de SPIGA
He'll corrupt you, Carlotta.

LUISA
Francesco.

CARLOTTA
If you think kindness to another is corruption, Signore, then I shall corrupt him
as well.

de SPIGA
You'll put a lot of women out of work if you start mistaking sex for kindness,
Carlotta.

FINZI
(standing up violently) Apologize!

CARLOTTA
(grabbing FINZI's hand) Please, Capitano. I'm not offended by Signor de
Spiga. I feel sad for people who cannot see the virtue in others because they
have none themselves; but I do not take offense.

de SPIGA
I stand corrected, Carlotta, and I am a humbler and better man for it. Do sit
down, Finzi, you're starting to take root.

FINZI sits down slowly.

EMILIA exits to the Side Hall where she meets MARIO, PAGE 117.

CARLOTTA
Papà says that wit is the last refuge of the weak.

de SPIGA
It's just that we're the only ones who get the jokes, Carlotta.

CARLOTTA
Men like Aldo make you jealous; that is why you say these things.

de SPIGA
What do you think, Luisa, am I jealous of Finzi? Should I be?

LUISA
Serve us now, Dante.

EMILIA returns

DANTE
(quietly to EMILIA) You'd better get de Spiga his cognac.

DANTE begins to serve dessert. Ladies first, then de SPIGA and FINZI.

FINZI
You look lovely tonight, Carlotta.

CARLOTTA
Grazie, Aldo.

FINZI
Is that a new dress?

CARLOTTA
Do you like it?

FINZI
It's very becoming.

CARLOTTA
Aélis gave it to me.

de SPIGA
That was very corrupting of her...excuse me, I meant kind.

TAMARA enters the Dining Room from the Leda, PAGE 116.

TAMARA
Bonsoir. [Good evening.]

de SPIGA stands as she enters and indicates where she should sit. DANTE rushes to her to assist with the chair.

de SPIGA
Bonsoir, Madame. Voulez-vous...[Would you like...] *(indicating her chair)*

LUISA
She's very beautiful.

de SPIGA
Elle dit que vous êtes très belle. [She says you are very beautiful.]

TAMARA
(indicating her dress) Un cadeau de Monsieur d'Annunzio. [A present from Monsieur d'Annunzio.]

de SPIGA
She said —

LUISA
I understood that. Serve her now, Dante.

TAMARA
Est-ce que Monsieur d'Annunzio est toujours si impatient de faire l'amour? [Is Mr. d'Annunzio always so anxious to make love?]

de SPIGA
Oui. Toujours. [Yes. Always.]

TAMARA
Une femme a besoin de connaître un homme avant de penser à ces choses-là. [A woman needs to know a man before she can think of such things.]

LUISA
What did she say?

TAMARA
(eating the cake with her hands) Même alors, je ne sais pas si je le ferais. Il se peut. [And even then I don't know if I would. Perhaps.]

CARLOTTA
Dante, she needs a fork.

DANTE brings it.

de SPIGA
Vous devez suivre votre coeur dans ces affaires-là, madame. [You must follow your heart in these matters, madame.]

CARLOTTA
Doesn't she know any Italian?

de SPIGA
None.

LUISA
What was she saying about Gabri?

de SPIGA
She said that she cannot decide whether or not...how can I put this delicately...whether or not to accept Gabri's advances.

LUISA begins to cry softly.

CARLOTTA
These foreigners have no morals. *(crosses herself)*

de SPIGA
Time will teach you, Carlotta, that in matters of love, nothing is black or white.

Enter AÉLIS from d'ANNUNZIO's Room, PAGE 112.

AÉLIS
Is everyone enjoying dessert?

There is no response. She hands a tray with a poem on it to TAMARA.

C'est pour vous, Madame de Lempicka. Monsieur d'Annunzio descendra dans un instant. [This is for you, Madame de Lempicka. Mr. d'Annunzio will be down shortly.] I'll be right back, Carlotta. *(seeing FINZI in d'ANNUNZIO's chair and muttering under her breath)* Finzi, get out of this room.

AÉLIS exits to the Kitchen, PAGE 121.

LUISA
(watching TAMARA read the poem) I'm not hungry. *(pushes her plate away)*

de SPIGA
Anyone else for seconds? No? Well, it's a shame to let that go to waste. *(reaches across the table and takes LUISA's dessert)*

FINZI
Have you noticed how Signor de Spiga always takes seconds? It was second place you took at the music festival in Genova last month, wasn't it?

de SPIGA
It is difficult to win first prize when the orchestra can only play the national anthem.

LUISA
I'm going to the Oratorio.

de SPIGA
Are you all right, Luisa?

She does not respond.

FINZI
(standing) Will you play for me? *(turning to de SPIGA)* You didn't have to translate that.... You really are a malicious bastard, Francesco.

LUISA exits without answering. She is followed by CARLOTTA, FINZI and TAMARA, PAGE 128.

DANTE
(to de SPIGA) Café, Signore?

de SPIGA
No. Cognac in the Oratorio.

de SPIGA joins the others in the Oratorio, PAGE 128.

DANTE
(to EMILIA, who has returned from PAGE 118) Where's the cognac?

EMILIA
Mario said he'd bring it. Men. Do I have to do everything?

DANTE
I'll see where he is...after all, it's still my job, not his.

DANTE exits to PAGE 160. EMILIA follows behind DANTE, but pauses at the base of the servants' stairs for a brief monologue, PAGE 127.

SCENE F28

d'ANNUNZIO'S ROOM

After leaving TAMARA, PAGE 85, the Leda, d'ANNUNZIO enters his room. He sits at his desk and tries to write. He writes with a quill.

d'ANNUNZIO
...how can she expect me to write poetry if she refuses...me. Does she think me some German masochist....I am Latin!...Success is my inspiration. I've never failed with a woman. But if we learn from our failures...then what do I really know? Nothing. *(pause; gets up and goes to the mirror)* These teeth have grown rotten feeding on the sweets of success. Teeth which used to bite into and hypnotize and inspire the crowds can't even...can't even....Silence! Is there nothing left to inspire me? No woman, no eyes, lips, breasts? No cause that still wants words and not canons to sing its praises? Or are there...just...no words...my lovers and conspirators, gone.

Enter AÉLIS from PAGE 79, outside the Dining Room.

AÉLIS
Dessert is served, Comandante.

d'ANNUNZIO
I hate sweets!

AÉLIS
But it's your favourite dessert. *(pause)* Well, what should I tell "La Polonaise?" It's embarrassing.

d'ANNUNZIO
You push me, Aélis. Tell her what you please. No. No, wait. Tell her Il Comandante does not wish to see her. Nothing else.

AÉLIS
I could, perhaps, say—

d'ANNUNZIO

No! Say just that. She only understands bluntness.

AÉLIS

Things are not going well?

d'ANNUNZIO

It's a cold breeze that blows from the north.

AÉLIS

So you will be writing all evening? Carlotta wanted to dance for you.

d'ANNUNZIO

They all want to dance. It's a matter of who will lead. In the nineties, a woman wore three corsets. Now, a layer of lace. Why is it more difficult to remove lace?

AÉLIS

She is very fragile.

d'ANNUNZIO

Don't let that delicacy fool you; it's just gold leaf on stone. She is of the new breed. Women who look like women, but have the souls of men. No, it started at Gomorrah, with Lot's wife. She turned to stone.

AÉLIS

I thought it was salt.

d'ANNUNZIO

Salt, then. Yes, salt, to rub into the loins of men.

AÉLIS

Comandante, work on your poetry. In the meanwhile, if you need someone, I'll call your favourite, Defelice.

d'ANNUNZIO

Tamara...this poem...will I never finish anything? Aélis, I couldn't even come up with a simple stanza...not a word.

AÉLIS

Of course you couldn't...you haven't eaten all day....Gabri, don't push yourself like this. Come, let's eat.

d'ANNUNZIO
(crossing towards bed) Women demand poets to write them poems. They expect it...and I have nothing to offer.

AÉLIS
This room is full of poems. *(goes to the bookcase, opens it and takes out a loose manuscript)* There are poems to heroes, poems to buildings, not many, let's see...water...ah, women: actresses, ballerinas....I should show these to Carlotta.

d'ANNUNZIO
I know what I've written.

AÉLIS
Ah! This one is good. This one is very good. You wrote it for Romaine Brooks, another painter.

d'ANNUNZIO
(suddenly interested) Is it dated?

AÉLIS
No. And it's in French.

d'ANNUNZIO
(hesitating) I can't do it.

AÉLIS
She won't know, it's unpublished. And, when you succeed with Tamara, you will have her to write about.

d'ANNUNZIO
(kisses AÉLIS) Take it to her...we'll rendezvous in the kitchen.

AÉLIS
But Gabri, what about dessert?

d'ANNUNZIO
Aélis, don't mention sweets, I'm about to make you the best frittata you'll ever have. I feel my inspiration returning.

He heads out of his room, followed by AÉLIS.

AÉLIS
(now out on the stairs) But Gabri!

d'ANNUNZIO
Shh! They'll hear. Where are they, in the dining room?

AÉLIS
Yes, but Gabri, you know how much Emilia hates it when you don't let her cook. I'll get her—

d'ANNUNZIO
Who runs this house?

AÉLIS
You, Comandante.

d'ANNUNZIO
And I say I'm certainly allowed to break a few eggs. Now, you go into the dining room and give Tamara the poem. Get going. Allons; marchez, mon petit soldat.

d'ANNUNZIO exits singing opera to PAGE 120, the Kitchen. AÉLIS exits to PAGE 107, the Dining Room.

SCENE F29

THE LEDA

Enter MARIO from PAGE 95.

TAMARA coming out from behind a screen.

TAMARA
(after a pause) You haven't seen my necklace by any chance?

MARIO
(recovering from the surprise) Permesso, Signora. *(bows and goes to exit)*

TAMARA
Don't go, Marchese Visconti. And please, stop pretending you don't understand me.

MARIO
Madame is mistaken.

TAMARA
I was in Zurich —

MARIO
I've never been.

TAMARA
Four years ago.

MARIO
We've never met.

TAMARA
No. But your mother keeps your picture by her night table.

MARIO
Mothers do.

TAMARA
I've painted many faces from memory. You're Emma Visconti's son.

MARIO
This is one face I suggest you forget.

TAMARA
A handsome face, which also has character; it is difficult to forget.

MARIO
So, you painted my mother's portrait?

TAMARA
Yes, and she left for Marienbad without paying.

MARIO
Did she speak of me?

TAMARA
She told me about her son....(*suddenly excited she races to her luggage and starts searching it*) That's why my bags were lost at the station. You didn't put it in my bags too?

MARIO
What?

TAMARA
Explosives! She told me your friends smuggled explosives in her luggage. *(finds a letter)* What's this?

MARIO takes the letter and reads it to himself. It reads: "Ship, the *Helen* — leaves Genoa January 12, 1800 hours bound for Marseilles. If he does not come, eliminate him."

As MARIO speaks, he lights the note on fire and drops it into a waste paper basket.

MARIO
It's unfortunate she told you that story. And I must also apologize for using you as a courier.

TAMARA
What did the note say?

MARIO
Here's your necklace. *(picks it up off the vanity)* Another gift from d'Annunzio?

TAMARA
Yes.

MARIO
Allow me. *(goes to put it on her)* Turn around.

TAMARA
Are you trying to frighten me?

MARIO
Why would I?

TAMARA
You use your own mother and now me, an innocent stranger—

MARIO
No one is innocent in Italia. The clasp is stuck.

TAMARA
After the Russian Revolution there were no innocents left.

MARIO
There. *(does up the necklace)*

TAMARA
Only murderers.

MARIO
You survived.

TAMARA
And I have nothing because of your comrades. No home. No money. Half my family dead! *(slaps him)*

MARIO
(grabs her hand) You're alive.

TAMARA
I escaped!

MARIO
To go on?

TAMARA
Yes!

MARIO
And find freedom in France?

TAMARA
Yes.

MARIO
(walking away from her) Then understand: I work for freedom here, in my home, my country: Italia. And I will do whatever I must to win that freedom, for everyone. However unpleasant the task. Understood?

TAMARA
Yes...yes.

MARIO
Any mention of my name, or this message, will only implicate yourself and another, even more...innocent party.

TAMARA
I don't want to know about politics! Just let me paint his portrait and go. Please. I need this commission.

MARIO
(pause) How much does Mother owe you for her portrait?

TAMARA
Are you trying to buy my silence?

MARIO
No. Even I still believe discretion is one of the few virtues aristocrats possess. I'm simply offering to pay a debt. How much?

TAMARA
In lira...perhaps 50,000.

MARIO
There will be 100,000 in your suitcase when you depart.

TAMARA
And when will that be?

MARIO
Whenever you wish. Now shouldn't you be in the dining room eating dessert?

TAMARA
No one gets hurt? You're just a servant and I'm a guest, correct?

MARIO
Si, Signora.

TAMARA
(walks to the door, turning and smiling) Then, clean up my room.

TAMARA exits to the Dining Room, PAGE 105.

MARIO exits out the other door to the hall where he meets EMILIA, PAGE 117.

SCENE F30

THE SIDE HALL

Enter EMILIA from PAGE 104, the Dining Room.

EMILIA
(running to MARIO) Mario! Hold me. It's too much.

MARIO
(holding her in his arms) Don't talk.

EMILIA
Finzi keeps asking....

MARIO
Shh! Calm. He can't do a thing.

EMILIA
What if he finds out why you're here?

MARIO
Why am I?

EMILIA
I...I don't know.

MARIO
To hold you in my arms. To kiss your lips, your eyes. Just tell him the truth —
we met in Gardone, I gave you a lift in the Principessa's automobile, you told
me about the job, and we became lovers. The truth.

EMILIA
But it isn't, you —

MARIO
(his hug becomes a bearhug) It is...only that...believe it Emilia and we'll all
stay free. Kiss?

She kisses him.

You should get back. Dante's alone with the savages.

EMILIA
(laughs) Can I come to you later?

MARIO
You better.

EMILIA
I should get de Spiga his cognac.

MARIO
Go back, I'll bring it in a minute.

EMILIA
(exiting back to the Dining Room , PAGE 105) There better be some left.

MARIO exits to the Kitchen and PAGE 120 begins.

SECTION G

THE FOLLOWING SCENES HAPPEN SIMULTANEOUSLY:

SCENE G31   d'ANNUNZIO discovers MARIO in the Kitchen. MARIO is
PAGE 120   dismissed and d'ANNUNZIO cooks AÉLIS a fritatta.

SCENE G32   EMILIA has a brief monologue, travelling to MARIO's
PAGE 127   room.

SCENE G33   EMILIA has a brief monologue on her way back to the
PAGE 128   Oratorio.

SCENE G34   de SPIGA, TAMARA, CARLOTTA, FINZI and LUISA in
PAGE 128   the Oratorio. EMILIA enters later with cognac.

SCENE G35   LUISA and TAMARA go to the Atrium.
PAGE 135

NOTE: *I44 PAGE 160, MARIO's room/and back to the Kitchen, begins following MARIO's dismissal from the Kitchen, PAGE 122. This scene continues through until Intermezzo. (end of Act One).*

SCENE G31

THE KITCHEN

MARIO enters the Kitchen from PAGE 118, the Side Hall, and pours himself a cognac.

MARIO
1891....It was such a bad year that the only thing the French could do with it was to sell it to the Italians. *(hears someone singing out in the hall)*

d'ANNUNZIO
(entering) I expect my servants to bow when I enter a room.

MARIO
Mi scusi, Comandante! *(bows)*

d'ANNUNZIO
(crossing rapidly to MARIO) Hands under the arms!

MARIO obeys.

Drop the glass.

The glass shatters.

Good. *(pinching him on the cheek in a friendly manner)* You're the new chauffeur?

MARIO
Si, Comandante.

d'ANNUNZIO
Mario, isn't it?

MARIO
Si, Comandante.

d'ANNUNZIO
So...tell me how a chauffeur knows so much about cognac?

MARIO

I...in the war, there was this Capitano Visconti...I was his orderly. His mother used to send him cognac to help him dim the sound of the guns.

d'ANNUNZIO

This Visconti, was his mother's name Emma?

MARIO

Si. Comandante, I was hoping to speak to you about an important matter.

d'ANNUNZIO

Clean up this mess.

Enter AÉLIS from the Dining Room, PAGE 107.

AÉLIS

Mario, what are you doing here?

MARIO

(sweeps up the glass.) I came down to get the cognac.

AÉLIS

And there...you have it.

MARIO

Permesso.

d'ANNUNZIO

Get me some zucchini, Aélis. Wait. I'm about to undertake one of the great works of my career: a frittata con zucchini. *(at the stove)* Did you know, Aélis, that Mario here knows Emma Visconti's son? Remember Emma, with the most nimble fingers in Europe?

AÉLIS

I remember what Emma cost you, a month in Baden-Baden. We're still paying for her gambling debts.

d'ANNUNZIO

The woman likes casinos.

AÉLIS

You may go now, Mario.

MARIO goes to exit.

d'ANNUNZIO
Wait. What was this important matter you mentioned?

MARIO
It was…just about the automobile, Comandante. It can wait. Permesso. *(bows)*

MARIO turns to pick up the glasses and exits to his room, PAGE 160.

d'ANNUNZIO
Fascinating young man.

AÉLIS
Why is everyone interested in Mario? Emilia fawns over him; Finzi seems positively infatuated with him.

d'ANNUNZIO
Cut the zucchini! *(stirring the eggs)* Are they sleeping together?

AÉLIS
Who?

d'ANNUNZIO
Mario and Emilia!

AÉLIS
Don't be ridiculous.

d'ANNUNZIO
Keep an eye on his room.

AÉLIS
What do you mean?

d'ANNUNZIO
Since he came, Emilia has had a headache. Have you noticed? Every night. A headache. If they're sleeping together, fire him. Salt? Is there salt?

AÉLIS
Gabri, even I can appreciate his virility; but they are cousins.

d'ANNUNZIO

He wants something. What, I'm not sure. Watch how he looks at you. The eyes. Always the eyes, in love or death. Wait and see.

AÉLIS

If he's a thief, I should —

d'ANNUNZIO

No, Aélis. Just wait.

AÉLIS

Wait. You always say wait. How can I do my job? I try to pay bills, you say wait. I can't schedule anything because you always put everything off. It's been over a week now and you still haven't seen Carlotta dance.

d'ANNUNZIO

Tamara has kept me waiting...for how many months, how many letters? A man can only wait for so long, seduction is a precise art.

AÉLIS

Like cooking. Maybe you should cook for her.

d'ANNUNZIO

Show my soft side, is that your idea? No, a woman like that wants to be beaten. She has her husband to keep her world soft.

AÉLIS

Will you go to her again this evening? *(pause)* I think she liked the poem.

d'ANNUNZIO

We'll join them in the Oratorio. I'll have Luisa play some soft Debussy, then while everyone listens, I'll lead Tamara to the altar and speak of music and Paris in the old days; working with Debussy before the war, all the stories the young like to dream about.

AÉLIS

No. All that makes you sound old, like you're finished. She's modern. Talk to her like an equal. No, try it. Talk about her letters, how they move you.

d'ANNUNZIO

Reading her letters is like watching a woman undress.

AÉLIS
That's it. Say that.

d'ANNUNZIO
Reading her letters is like watching a woman undress.

AÉLIS
Oh, no Gabri, that was terrible. You have to make it more direct, forte, masculine, manly.

d'ANNUNZIO
Reading your letters is like watching a woman undress.

AÉLIS
Too much. Relax. It should be erotic and mysterious.

d'ANNUNZIO
Reading your letters is like watching a woman undress.

AÉLIS
Yes, Gabri, that will work. A little wine, Gabri? Some mineral water?

d'ANNUNZIO
Water. I want my mind crystal clear when I go to Tamara.

AÉLIS pours, they clink glasses.

AÉLIS
Bonne chance, mon ami! [Good luck my friend!]

d'ANNUNZIO
A toi aussi. [And for you too.]

They begin eating the frittata. d'ANNUNZIO spits it out.

AÉLIS
Careful, Gabri. You don't want to burn your tongue.

d'ANNUNZIO
Well, was I inspired?

AÉLIS
Mmm...encore un petit soupçon de sel. [A little hint more salt.]

d'ANNUNZIO
Nonsense; it's perfect. Just because you've been having better luck than I in seducing women of late, Aélis, it doesn't make you an expert in all the appetites. Hah! You'll never understand what a man endures waiting for a woman.

AÉLIS
Do you think it's easier for a woman?

d'ANNUNZIO
I have this horrible feeling that no matter how I respond to any of your questions, they all lead back to Carlotta. Even you can't seriously believe she'll surrender.

AÉLIS
She liked the dress I bought her; gave me a very tender embrace.

d'ANNUNZIO

Doing better than I am.

AÉLIS
Gabri, we'll both succeed. Tamara just needs to be pushed a bit. She wants you. Am I not right?

No reply.

Bien donc, Gabri. She didn't come here just to paint your portrait. She knew what you wanted.

d'ANNUNZIO
It's what she wants that is at issue. And Carlotta, I suppose she didn't come just for a recommendation, but to —

AÉLIS
If you would watch her dance, I might get what I want. Please.

d'ANNUNZIO
Soon.

AÉLIS
You always say soon. When is soon?

d'ANNUNZIO
Tomorrow. On one condition.

AÉLIS
Which is?

d'ANNUNZIO
If you succeed with her, I want to watch.

AÉLIS storms out of the Kitchen and into the hall, pursued by d'ANNUNZIO.

What? What's wrong?

AÉLIS
You know very well.

d'ANNUNZIO
Enlighten me!

AÉLIS
Your heart's as dark as this hallway.

d'ANNUNZIO
For saying...but you didn't mind when I watched you with Defelice.

AÉLIS
It was a show. Something cheap and ugly. We did it for you, and that whore
was paid.

*She walks away; d'ANNUNZIO manages to stop her halfway up the servants'
staircase.*

d'ANNUNZIO
Aélis, I'm sorry....I rely on you not to be offended. You're the only woman I
can be direct with. I —

AÉLIS
Gabri, I...perhaps I overreacted but you have to allow me some private life.

d'ANNUNZIO
By all means. If it's privacy you want why not take Carlotta on a trip? I'll
pay...wherever you want.

AÉLIS
And you won't be hiding in the hotel closet?

They arrive outside the Oratorio.

d'ANNUNZIO
I promise. But don't plug the keyhole.

They laugh.

Now, how do I look?

AÉLIS
(adjusting his tie) There.

They enter the Oratorio, PAGE 138.

SCENE G32

THE BASE OF THE SERVANTS' STAIRS

EMILIA is travelling from the Dining Room, PAGE 109, to MARIO's room.

EMILIA
(walking from the Dining Room she stops at the bottom of the stairs) How can Mario be so calm? Look at me, I'm shaking. It wasn't supposed to be like this. Defelice said he'd be in the house three days and it's been a week, and now he's in my bed. It has to stop. I'll just tell him to quit and if he doesn't I'll threaten to tell Finzi everything and plead for mercy. *(continues to walk)* Maybe if I gave the money back he'd leave...but I've spent it all on Caterina's convent school....Emilia, this time you've really done it. This time there isn't going to be a happy ending.

EMILIA enters MARIO's room, PAGE 161.

SCENE G33

THE SERVANTS' HALL

EMILIA
(heading up the stairs with the cognac) Why couldn't I just say get out. Leave.
Just say it....I wanted to....Dante was there. Excuses. Always, poor Dante's
fault....I almost did, but then Mario looked at me with those wounded eyes,
those terrible, beautiful eyes...and he just "makes the bread fall right out of my
hand"...what could I....Oh, Emilia, your heart will be the death of you. *(takes a
swig of cognac and then enters the Oratorio, PAGE 131)*

SCENE G34

THE ORATORIO

*de SPIGA, TAMARA, CARLOTTA, FINZI and LUISA enter the Oratorio from
PAGE 108, the Dining Room.*

FINZI and CARLOTTA, as they walk:

FINZI
Signorina Barra, please allow me to compliment you on the way you respond-
ed to Signor de Spiga's cruel remarks.

CARLOTTA
People always think me young, Aldo, but actually I'm more mature than I ap-
pear.

FINZI
You're a unique young woman.

CARLOTTA
Grazie.

FINZI
Excuse me a moment. *(goes toward de SPIGA)*

de SPIGA and TAMARA as they walk:

de SPIGA
(turning to TAMARA) Veuillez nous accompagner, Madame? Peut-être nous pouvons persuader Luisa à jouer. [Will you join us, Madame? Perhaps we could convince Luisa to play.]

TAMARA
Cela me frustre tellement de ne pas pouvoir communiquer avec Luisa. Il y a toute une histoire dans ses mains. Ça me ferait tant de plaisir de les peindre. [I feel so frustrated being unable to speak with Luisa — she has such history in her hands. I'd love to paint them.]

de SPIGA
(to LUISA) Tamara was just saying she'd love to paint your hands.

LUISA
Tell her they're tied to Gabri's.

de SPIGA
Luisa, please, let's have a quiet evening.

The two conversations join.

FINZI
Francesco, I need to speak to you.

de SPIGA
(to LUISA) Finzi shouldn't be here.

LUISA
Il Comandante won't be down. Let him stay.

CARLOTTA
Luisa, you must play. I want to dance! *(begins to dance)*

LUISA
No, I don't want to.

FINZI
Si. Luisa, play for me.

de SPIGA
I'm sure Madame de Lempicka wants to hear you play again.

LUISA plays one chord of Debussy's "Submerged Cathedral" then plays Johann Strauss' "Emperor's Waltz."

CARLOTTA
(going to FINZI) Capitano Finzi, will you dance with me?

FINZI
No, I —

CARLOTTA
Please!

FINZI
All right, I'll try.

FINZI and CARLOTTA dance.

de SPIGA
Aldo, you're not marching.

CARLOTTA
He's very good.

de SPIGA
Aldo has great rhythm, but bad timing.

LUISA
Shhhh.

TAMARA places herself in front of de SPIGA and offers her hand to dance.

de SPIGA
Very well, I'll dance; not for duty, but beauty.

They begin to dance but he stops.

Est-ce que je vous serre un peu trop? Tout est serré en Italie, n'est-ce pas? [I'm sorry, am I too close? In Italia everyone is too close.]

TAMARA nods yes.

Here we are "tutto in famiglia." [All in the family.]

FINZI
Can't you dance, Francesco?

They all dance.

de SPIGA
The family is not always happy. We have our unruly sons. They dress in black
to mourn the death of their reason.

LUISA
(stops playing) Francesco, play us some of that music Americana.

de SPIGA
If it's jazz you want, I'll need some gin.

LUISA
There's only cognac this evening.

de SPIGA
Well, I'll pretend it's gin if you pretend this is jazz.

*de SPIGA goes to the piano and plays "Be My Baby Bumble Bee" (Marshall
and Murphy). TAMARA dances vigorously to the music. She laughs as she
dances.*

CARLOTTA
Is she sick, Luisa?

LUISA
It's the "Ridicolo." All of Paris is doing it.

FINZI
It is most unusual.

CARLOTTA
It is unnatural.

*LUISA begins to dance with TAMARA. EMILIA enters from PAGE 128, her
monologue, carrying the cognac on a tray.*

EMILIA
(to FINZI) What are they doing?

FINZI
(crossing to EMILIA and taking a drink) Everything and nothing. *(turning to CARLOTTA)* You're watching the last steps of the dead rulers, Carlotta. Soon fascism will bring forth a new order.

EMILIA
You frighten me, Capitano.

CARLOTTA
Only the guilty are afraid, Emilia; it's in the scriptures.

de SPIGA
(seeing EMILIA, he stops) Ah, nourishment.

LUISA and TAMARA stop; LUISA seems exhausted.

LUISA
I haven't been to Paris in years. Come, Madame de Lempicka, let's powder ourselves.

TAMARA turns to de SPIGA. She does not understand Italian.

TAMARA
(to de SPIGA) Monsieur?

de SPIGA
Elle a dit que nous ne sommes pas tous "pasta." [She says we're not all "pasta."]

TAMARA laughs.

Veuillez la suivre au boudoir. [Please follow her to the boudoir.]

TAMARA
D'accord. [All right.]

LUISA
Francesco, Carlotta is in your care.

LUISA and TAMARA exit to PAGE 135, the Atrium.

de SPIGA
(clutches CARLOTTA) No harm shall come to her!

CARLOTTA
You are silly, Signore de Spiga.

de SPIGA
In Italia we are always mistaking the wise men for fools and the fools for wise men.

CARLOTTA
(to FINZI) You have a difficult job, Capitano Finzi.

FINZI
He doesn't mean what he says. These aristocrats just hate to follow. One drinks cognac after years of fermentation. Our government—

de SPIGA
Regime.

FINZI
Our government is young, but it will grow and ripen. In time, Signor de Spiga will find the taste of fascism quite palatable.

de SPIGA
In case you ladies missed what your friend said, I will explain. What was it? Ah! Cognac....*(drinking)* Cognac takes years to age, and so does fascism. That is why fascism is presently hard to swallow. Not unlike castor oil. Have some cognac, Carlotta.

CARLOTTA
A glass of wine, that's more than enough for me.

de SPIGA
Nonsense, you're a dancer. A descendant of the bacchantes, worshippers of the vine!

CARLOTTA
I know nothing of any "bunch-of-cunties" though I think what you say is bad. You may insult me, Signore, but I will not let you insult my family name. My father is a banker; his father was before.

de SPIGA
I did not mean —

CARLOTTA
...as was my great, and great-great grandfather. In my town, all know the Barra

family worship our Lord, Jesus Christ. *(crosses herself)* My father led the committee to buy pews for the Church of St. Catherine.

de SPIGA
A simple jest, sweet Carlotta, that is all. Let's say amen to it, shall we?

CARLOTTA
I forgive you, Signor de Spiga.

FINZI
For you know not what you do.

de SPIGA
If ladies were not present!

CARLOTTA
I think you are a man who has doubts; this is why you drink.

EMILIA
My father says the best way to find the hole is to pour liquid in the bag.

de SPIGA
Which means?

EMILIA
I'm not sure, Signore.

de SPIGA
The only reason to drink is no reason. To paraphrase Sant'Anselmo, "I drink because it's absurd."

CARLOTTA
I think you are afraid. This is why you drink.

de SPIGA
I have nothing to fear.

EMILIA
Then it's either a woman or a secret.

de SPIGA
Since you offer, I'll take the woman.

CARLOTTA and EMILIA laugh.

de SPIGA
Have a drink, Emilia.

EMILIA
I'm on duty, Signore.

de SPIGA
So is Finzi. *(hands her a drink)*

EMILIA
I have never tasted....*(drinks)* It is strong.

LUISA, TAMARA, AÉLIS and d'ANNUNZIO enter the Oratorio simultaneously as EMILIA drinks, PAGE 138.

SCENE G35

THE ATRIUM

LUISA and TAMARA leave the Oratorio and go to a large mirror in the Dining Room.

TAMARA
Le voyage m'a tellement fatiguée. J'espère avoir assez d'énergie pour commencer le portrait de Monsieur d'Annunzio demain. [The journey has left me so tired. I hope I have enough energy to start on Mr. d'Annunzio's portrait tomorrow.]

LUISA
I don't understand.

TAMARA
Le portrait, vous comprenez? Portrait. [Portrait. Understand?] Je déteste cette barrière entre nous. Je parle quatre langues mais pas l'italien. [I hate these boundaries between us. I know four languages but not Italian.] *(sees a mirror*

hanging on the wall, goes to it, takes out her lipstick and draws a cartoon of d'ANNUNZIO on the mirror) Portrait.

LUISA
Si, si.

LUISA notices a chain around TAMARA's neck which she pulls on to reveal a locket worn under TAMARA's dress.

TAMARA
Ça vous plaît? Monsieur d'Annunzio vient de me le donner. Il veut que je le porte avec cette robe. Je l'aime bien. Il choisit des cadeaux très originaux! [Do you like it? It was just given to me by monsieur d'Annunzio. He wanted me to wear it with this dress. I like it. He picks out very personal gifts.]

LUISA takes out her locket which she wears around her neck. It is identical to the one TAMARA is wearing. After pausing for a moment, TAMARA goes to exit back to the Oratorio. As she does so, she sees LUISA kissing the lipstick cartoon of d'ANNUNZIO. LUISA and TAMARA return to the Oratorio, PAGE 138 .

SECTION H

THE FOLLOWING SCENES HAPPEN SIMULTANEOUSLY:

SCENE H36   d'ANNUNZIO, AÉLIS, LUISA and TAMARA join the
PAGE 138   others in the Oratorio.

SCENE H37   FINZI has a brief monologue on his way to the Dining
PAGE 146   Room.

SCENE H38   FINZI and EMILIA are in the Dining Room.
PAGE 146

DANTE and MARIO continue SCENE I44, PAGE 160.

SCENE H36

THE ORATORIO

d'ANNUNZIO and AÉLIS enter the Oratorio from the Kitchen. LUISA and TAMARA enter from the Atrium to find de SPIGA feeding cognac to EMILIA. d'ANNUNZIO and AÉLIS are from PAGE 127. LUISA and TAMARA are from PAGE 136. TAMARA crosses to the altar while the following dialogue is taking place in the centre of the room.

    LUISA and AÉLIS
(together) Emilia!

    LUISA
A lady doesn't drink spirits.

    EMILIA
(to LUISA) Just a taste...I....

    d'ANNUNZIO
(laughs) Drink up...there's a hard night ahead of you....

    EMILIA
Grazie, Comandante.

    FINZI
(standing at military attention) If you'll excuse me....

    CARLOTTA
Please don't go, Capitano.

    FINZI
Until tomorrow.

    d'ANNUNZIO
Excused!

    CARLOTTA
Buona notte, Capitano.

FINZI exits to PAGE 146, the Dining Room.

d'ANNUNZIO
(crossing to EMILIA and patting her behind) I may need you tonight, my little corporal.

d'ANNUNZIO crosses to TAMARA. LUISA and de SPIGA talk by the piano, PAGE 139. In the centre of the room, CARLOTTA, AÉLIS and EMILIA talk, PAGE 141. At the far end of the room, d'ANNUNZIO talks to TAMARA at the altar, PAGE 143. All this happens simultaneously.

de SPIGA
What I can't understand is how a dancing nun like Carlotta can have a crush on Finzi.

LUISA
She doesn't.

de SPIGA
Didn't you hear her at dessert? ...defending him with all the zeal of a martyr...not that I mind...they deserve each other.

LUISA
When I was her age I used to dream of men in uniforms.

de SPIGA
And now?

LUISA
Now...they give me nightmares.

de SPIGA
I suppose we all have to wrestle with our demons.

LUISA laughs. de SPIGA observes d'ANNUNZIO speaking with TAMARA.

How is Gabri doing with Tamara? Is the seduction proceeding on schedule?

LUISA
Perhaps she only wants to paint him.

de SPIGA
How can you say that after what she said at dessert?

LUISA
I only heard what you said she said. *(pause)* You've seen her work?

de SPIGA
No.

LUISA
Nude women in front of buildings.

de SPIGA
Aélis must like it.

LUISA
Tamara's very good. Very good.

de SPIGA
Jealous?

LUISA
Not of her.

de SPIGA
After all these years, how can you have any feelings for him?

LUISA
Will he succeed?

de SPIGA
With that look on his face, and his imperious tongue, certainly. But let's stop talking about them. *(pause)* I need a drink.

LUISA
So do I.

de SPIGA
You don't drink.

LUISA
Everyone has something they're locked to. Chained to. *(pause)* Francesco, when you drink do you still feel? Can you see, or does it all blur?

de SPIGA
He'll never go away, Luisa. It's you who'll have to leave.

LUISA
How do you say "say no," in French?

de SPIGA
Dites non.

LUISA
Dites non.

de SPIGA
Don't pronounce the "s."

LUISA
(properly) Dites non.

de SPIGA
Yes.

Their conversation is interrupted by d'ANNUNZIO, PAGE 144.

CARLOTTA, AÉLIS and EMILIA:

AÉLIS
Did you miss me, Carlotta?

CARLOTTA
Yes, but Capitano Finzi was good company. Aélis, now that Il Comandante is here, could I dance? I must dance if I'm to get my recommendation.

AÉLIS
He has much to discuss with Madame de Lempicka.

EMILIA giggles.

But I have his promise that he will see you dance tomorrow.

EMILIA
Besides, there are other ways.

AÉLIS
(gets EMILIA to stop by slapping her tummy) You've gained weight, Emilia. Not pregnant?

CARLOTTA
(laughing) Aélis, how could she be? She's not married.

AÉLIS
Carlotta has a very good exercise for the thighs.

CARLOTTA
Would you like me to show you?

EMILIA
I don't need to exercise, I work for a living. Permesso?

AÉLIS
Va t'en. [Go away.]

EMILIA exits to PAGE 146, the Dining Room.

CARLOTTA
Did we insult her?

AÉLIS
It's just a game she plays.

CARLOTTA
I think this house is full of games.

AÉLIS
Why's that?

CARLOTTA
Signor de Spiga insulted me.

AÉLIS
What did he say?

CARLOTTA
He called me a "bunch-of-cunties." He said it was funny. It was not funny, Aélis.

AÉLIS
(laughing) It's the way you say it. I'm sorry, Carlotta. You're so sweet...but you mustn't take offense....de Spiga insults everyone.

CARLOTTA
Especially Capitano Finzi.

AÉLIS
They hate each other.

CARLOTTA
I think Signore de Spiga just pretends to hate Aldo. It is another game, Aélis.

AÉLIS
Enough talk of games. Let's talk about serious things. Let's talk about us. Would you like me to exercise with you tomorrow?

CARLOTTA
I start very early.

AÉLIS
Your body inspires me. Is there hope for mine? *(sits in a chair by the small table)*

CARLOTTA
My mother has two secrets for staying young: exercise and prayer.

AÉLIS
Your mother again. She sounds very wise.

CARLOTTA
Yes, and beautiful. I'll be up early if you want to join me, but my exercises will be especially hard tomorrow as I must prepare for my dance.

CARLOTTA begins dancing quietly as AÉLIS sits and watches until d'AN-NUNZIO interrupts, PAGE 144.

d'ANNUNZIO and TAMARA:

d'ANNUNZIO
Reading your letters is like watching a woman undress.

TAMARA turns away.

Are you still upset with me?

TAMARA has her eyes on LUISA, she does not respond.

Since silence is pure consent, you have made a declaration. When I left you earlier, I wished for a moment you had not come. The seeds of desire are planted deep within a man. Their roots web the body, from the mind to the loins, intersecting the veins of reason, blocking the flow of what we call everyday life. They create a parallel body, a body whose breath is this yearning we share, a body that can only free itself by union with another. But why do I speak? I know these thoughts are yours.

TAMARA
(turning to d'ANNUNZIO) I was thinking about Luisa. You are lovers, aren't you?

d'ANNUNZIO
It was a long time ago.

TAMARA
She still loves you.

d'ANNUNZIO
And what would you have me do — put her out onto the street? Do you think her sadness does not tear my soul? Our love died and I cannot revive it. Nor can I abandon a friend. At least here she has a home, a piano. And I have her music to accompany my solitude.

Pause. d'ANNUNZIO addresses LUISA. This stops the conversation between AÉLIS and CARLOTTA, and LUISA and de SPIGA.

We've forgotten Debussy.

de SPIGA
What would you like to hear?

d'ANNUNZIO
No, Luisa, you play. Francesco has a tendency to dress him up as if he were an Italian pimp.

LUISA plays approximately six measures of "Toccatta" from Debussy's "Pour Le Piano." She plays fast and loud.

Luisa!

LUISA stops.

(pleading) It's too late for that.

LUISA
And for us?

LUISA begins to play a quiet piece, Debussy's "Submerged Cathedral," very slowly...everyone is attentive. de SPIGA remains at the piano nursing his cognac and watching LUISA. CARLOTTA dances quietly as AÉLIS sits and watches her.

d'ANNUNZIO

(sitting on the end of the tomb, he begins talking to himself) His music always haunts me...like a voice heard on the opposite side of a lake. We became very close in Paris....I remember when they gave me the news of his death...my squadron was just heading out for an air-raid over Pola...and for the first time in my life I didn't care if I lived or died. I remember taking the plane down to a thousand feet, the anti-aircraft guns bursting all around my head and thinking, now is the time to die. To die in action, that's the only honorable death, and I was certainly ready for it; for what good was a world without Debussy....I should have crashed that plane....Death did not come....I wait and sit but still...it does not come...you hear only...the voices of friends...far off...off across the water.

TAMARA goes to d'ANNUNZIO and kneels on the floor. He gently lowers his head down and begins kissing her. de SPIGA, seeing what is happening, goes to LUISA and whispers in her ear.

de SPIGA

The seduction is proceeding.

de SPIGA sits at the piano and takes over the playing of the piece so that it proceeds uninterrupted, while LUISA goes over to TAMARA and d'ANNUN-ZIO. She begins playing with the locket she wears around her neck, as if it were a noose. CARLOTTA has also noticed what is happening. She reacts silently, but in horror. AÉLIS notices this and goes to comfort CARLOTTA, who has walked out into the hallway. AÉLIS arrives in the hall and PAGE 152 begins.

TAMARA

(looking up and seeing LUISA, then speaking to d'ANNUNZIO) Une autre fois. Bonne nuit. Bonne nuit, Luisa. [Another time. Good night. Good night, Luisa.] *(exits to her room and INTERMEZZO)*

To follow her into the second day, see DANTE's introduction to Act Two, PAGE 179.

d'ANNUNZIO

(laughing) Fiasco! Fiasco! Fiasco! *(sits up)* That's the last time I take advice from Aélis.

LUISA

Tamara is not like the others.

d'ANNUNZIO
No, she's a blockhead! She makes me babble until my tongue speaks nothing but empty bubbles.

LUISA
Like a cartoon, poeta?

d'ANNUNZIO
Like a fart in the bathtub. She'll drive me crazy.

LUISA crosses slowly around and to the far end of the tomb where a dagger sits on a pedestal. She picks it up and crosses to the tomb where d'ANNUNZIO is sitting on the funeral bier. de SPIGA segues from "Submerged Cathedral" to "La Plus Que Lente." He will continue playing to d'ANNUNZIO and LUISA, PAGE 150.

SCENE H37

FINZI leaves the Oratorio, PAGE 138, and heads to the Dining Room.

FINZI
Excused! Excused he says as if I was some schoolboy, some dog that pissed on his carpet. Well, I'll have him licking that same carpet, soon enough. *(pauses as he arrives in the Dining Room)* Mario. He's the key. If he isn't who he says he is...if d'Annunzio knows...if....*(picks up the cake knife and smiles as he thinks of the consequences of his logic)*

SCENE H38

THE DINING ROOM.

FINZI hears EMILIA coming and hides. Enter EMILIA from PAGE 142, the Oratorio. She begins picking up the dirty dishes. FINZI begins crossing toward her, hiding the knife behind his back.

FINZI
I need you tonight.

EMILIA
Now? You have the money?

FINZI
No more money, Emilia.

EMILIA
No more Emilia. *(continues cleaning the table.)*

FINZI
(grabs her by her hair) You lied. Mario is not your cousin!

EMILIA
You're hurting.

FINZI pulls the knife from behind his back and puts it to EMILIA's throat.

FINZI
Who is he?

EMILIA
(in pain) I don't know.

FINZI
Why did you lie? How much did they pay you?

EMILIA
Ten thousand lire.

FINZI
Ten thousand lire! A name — does he have a name?

EMILIA
I don't know!

FINZI
How did they make contact?

EMILIA
Defelice.

FINZI
d'Annunzio's whore. Who does she work for?

EMILIA
I don't know.

FINZI
What do they want from d'Annunzio?

EMILIA
Aldo, please, they didn't tell me anything. I swear!

FINZI
(satisfied by her reply, he lets her go) Go get ready.

EMILIA goes slowly to her room, PAGE 157. FINZI heads to his office and makes a quick phonecall, PAGE 156.

SECTION I

THE FOLLOWING SCENES HAPPEN SIMULTANEOUSLY:

SCENE I39   d'ANNUNZIO, LUISA and de SPIGA continue in the
PAGE 150   Oratorio.

SCENE I40   AÉLIS talks to CARLOTTA in the Oratorio and then the
PAGE 152   Side Hall.

SCENE I41   FINZI makes a phonecall in his office.
PAGE 156

SCENE I42   FINZI and EMILIA continue from the Dining Room into
PAGE 157   EMILIA's bedroom.

SCENE I43   EMILIA has a monologue.
PAGE 159

SCENE I44   DANTE and MARIO continue.
PAGE 160

SCENE I45   Brief scene in the Kitchen hall between EMILIA and
PAGE 172   MARIO.

SCENE I46   DANTE in the Kitchen and hall.
PAGE 173

SCENE I47   d'ANNUNZIO alone in the Oratorio.
PAGE 174

SCENE I48   AÉLIS enters the Oratorio and joins
PAGE 175   d'ANNUNZIO.

SECTION 139

THE ORATORIO

LUISA, d'ANNUNZIO and de SPIGA are from PAGE 146, the Oratorio. de SPIGA plays Debussy's "La Plus Que Lente" while LUISA and d'ANNUNZIO talk.

d'ANNUNZIO
(lying back on the tomb) You were talking to her.

LUISA
(turning back and approaching him) We went to powder ourselves.

LUISA has picked up the dagger from a pedestal and crosses slowly to d'AN-NUNZIO.

d'ANNUNZIO
Did she say something to you?

LUISA
I didn't know what she was saying, it was French.

d'ANNUNZIO
Nothing about us? Did you try to —

LUISA
Nothing.

d'ANNUNZIO
What do you think of her?

LUISA
(stepping up on the tomb) It's tasteless. Talk to Aélis about her, but don't have the gall to talk to me!

d'ANNUNZIO
The Barracuda angry? It brings back memories. We had our best nights after a day of fighting.

They embrace and kiss.

LUISA
(breaking away) I just play the piano, remember.

d'ANNUNZIO
Luisa, come to Gabri, come.

LUISA
I used to crawl but I'm learning to walk, and one day when I stop falling down, I'll run.

d'ANNUNZIO
Luisa, don't leave me in this condition.

LUISA
Why not? You've kept me in it for three years.

d'ANNUNZIO
A man needs —

LUISA
I know what you need, but who knows what Luisa wants. Go take Emilia. She does floors.

d'ANNUNZIO
There are some women who say no to love, but I have not yet met a woman who says no to money.

LUISA
I can remember a time when they used to pay you...when you were the one who received the gifts. *(placing the dagger on d'ANNUNZIO's chest)* Good night...Poeta.

d'ANNUNZIO
Do you remember when you first gave me this dagger?

LUISA
(on the way out) San Sebastian's Day, 1920. I still believed in saints then.

LUISA exits, leaving her audience with d'ANNUNZIO. She goes to her IN-TERMEZZO. See DANTE's speech, PAGE 179, to follow LUISA into the second day. d'ANNUNZIO and de SPIGA continue on PAGE 174. de SPIGA ends his music with a crescendo as LUISA exits.

SCENE I40

THE SIDE HALL

CARLOTTA is out in the hall when AÉLIS joins her from the Oratorio, PAGE 145.

AÉLIS
(quietly) Carlotta, don't leave —

CARLOTTA
They were kissing, Aélis.

AÉLIS
But that shouldn't offend you. When people are attracted to each other —

CARLOTTA
That's what frightened me, Aélis.

AÉLIS
A kiss shouldn't frighten; if you said that it made you feel flush, if it made your skin tingle....

CARLOTTA
That's the terrible thing of it...it did Aélis....I try to stay strong and...it's this house....you know after dinner I, well...a thought came to me...an unhealthy one, and to fight it I started to say the rosary. Father Lotti says that nothing is stronger than a whole rosary...but here....Before I'd finished one "Hail Mary" the string on my rosary broke....every day I have these thoughts, feel strange sensations and...I think perhaps I should leave now.

AÉLIS
Carlotta, you stay right where you are. I'm not having you sleep in torment. We're going to sit right down and talk this through. Sit.

CARLOTTA sits down on a couch beside AÉLIS.

Carlotta, you're as knotted as a rope. Let me massage you. It will help you sleep. Tomorrow's an important day.

CARLOTTA
Prayers are all I need.

AÉLIS
Nonsense. Your body's full of tension.

CARLOTTA

Aélis, I try to relax but this is the first time I've been away without a chaperone, everything here is different...everything is the opposite of the way I've been brought up.

AÉLIS

Lie down. On your stomach, that's it.

CARLOTTA complies. AÉLIS begins massaging her.

You shouldn't worry yourself because things are different here. You should see your stay here as an adventure.

CARLOTTA

I'm frightened.

AÉLIS

But why? Because things are different? Because we eat whatever and whenever we want? Or say what's on our mind?

CARLOTTA

It's not you...or this house. It's me...when I saw Il Comandante kissing her I wanted to hold someone and to —

AÉLIS

Kiss them?

CARLOTTA

I should go to sleep.

AÉLIS

Who did you want to kiss, Carlotta?

CARLOTTA

(turning over to face AÉLIS) Why can't it be that we can be Christian and say yes to our feelings. Doesn't God want us to feel pleasure?

AÉLIS

If you kissed this person how would you feel; not afterward but while you were doing it?...

CARLOTTA

People always feel happy when they're sinning, Aélis, it's afterwards....

AÉLIS
There doesn't have to be an afterwards; you can keep on feeling happy.

CARLOTTA
I couldn't—

AÉLIS
Kiss me.

CARLOTTA
What?

AÉLIS
I said kiss me.

CARLOTTA
I—

AÉLIS
(kisses CARLOTTA deeply) There.

CARLOTTA
What a funny kiss.

AÉLIS
Now was that a sin?

CARLOTTA
(awkwardly) We're friends.

AÉLIS
So you didn't feel guilty?

CARLOTTA
Why should I? It was just a sign of friendship.

AÉLIS
Then it's all right for friends?

CARLOTTA
Aélis, I know you want to help me but I don't think you understand about certain things.

AÉLIS
I think I do.

CARLOTTA
There's a difference between friendship and what I'm feeling.

AÉLIS
Passion, is that the word?

CARLOTTA
I never thought I...all those years in the convent school...everyone telling me I was such a saint....It was....I think maybe God is punishing me for being....I've been arrogant, Aélis. Arrogant to think I had no base thoughts.

AÉLIS
(taking CARLOTTA in her arms) You're only human, Carlotta. There's nothing unnatural about what you're feeling.

Enter de SPIGA from PAGE 174, the Oratorio. He is retiring for the evening.

de SPIGA
Quaint. How very quaint. I thought virgins were out of season.

AÉLIS
Good night, Francesco. *(to CARLOTTA)* Don't listen to him, he's drunk!

CARLOTTA
I'll pray for you tonight, Signore.

de SPIGA
And I'll drink to you, Sant' Carlotta. *(toasts CARLOTTA, and laughs; exits to INTERMEZZO)*

To follow him into the second day, see DANTE's introduction to Act Two, PAGE 179.

CARLOTTA
I must go to bed. Are you going to exercise with me?

AÉLIS
Yes. What should I wear?

CARLOTTA
Nothing. Sometimes the body has to breathe.

AÉLIS
Eight o'clock?

CARLOTTA
Six. Then no one will be up. Buona notte, Aélis. And...and...oh, I'm so grateful to you. *(kisses AÉLIS and exits to her room to her INTERMEZZO)*

To follow her into the second day, see DANTE's introduction to Act Two, PAGE 179.

AÉLIS
(to herself) Now was that a friendly kiss or a passionate one? *(turns to the audience)* All this talk of exercise has left me hungry. Come. Let's eat.

She leads the audience into the Dining Room where they are greeted by maids serving food. Their INTERMEZZO has begun. After picking up a strawberry to eat on the way, AÉLIS discreetly exits to the Oratorio and to PAGE 175.

SCENE I41

FINZI'S OFFICE

FINZI enters his office and picks up the phone. He is entering from PAGE 148.

FINZI
Garda Barracks, please...Corporale Tittoni. *(pause)* Tittoni, Capitano Finzi....I need three squads at Il Vittoriale immediately. Three....What? No. I can't say. Tell them it's an exercise. Just have them outside and dug in by twelve hundred hours. Si, si, outside the gate and out of sight. No one enters. No one, without my authorization. And Tittoni, get onto that policeman Capitano Mutti and have him detain the whore Defelice. She may be involved in a conspiracy....What do you mean disappeared?...Find her, I need her....I've no time for your jokes, Corporale Tittoni. Find her. Buona notte. *(hangs up)*

He exits to EMILIA's bedroom, PAGE 157.

SCENE I42

EMILIA'S BEDROOM.

EMILIA has just come from the Dining Room, PAGE 148. She enters the room, goes to the radio, turns it on. The prelude to "La Traviata" is playing and continues throughout ACT ONE. She then turns the overhead lights off. Leaning against a wall, she unbuttons her blouse and waits for FINZI. FINZI enters.

FINZI
(going to EMILIA) You betrayed me.

EMILIA
No, Aldo. No.

FINZI
(quietly) Knives. Guns. Fists. Do you think I enjoy this? *(crossing away from EMILIA)* Look at my boots. I didn't have shoes until I was in the army.

EMILIA
(going to FINZI) I'm poor too, Aldo!

FINZI
But you don't understand. I was eighteen when I finally decided that nobody was going to call me a "kike" and keep standing. If they were going to kick with leather on their feet, I was going to kick harder. I used to kick at the door until every toe was bloody, then bandage my feet with rags and keep kicking and kicking until I broke down the door. When the party took me on and said hit, hit harder, I hit. Me. Aldo Finzi. It was the only way out, Emilia. That's the way it will always be for the poor.

EMILIA
You use your body, I use mine. Poor us.

FINZI
When we took the socialist Matteotti out for a drive, they said shake him. So I shook him, and the bastard died on me. They said I was too rough for Roma; they teach you to act and then change the rules. Now I file reports. I do a good job, nothing escapes me. Generale Foscarinni says a promotion is imminent but you don't want that to happen.

EMILIA
Aldo, I do!

FINZI
By bringing Mario here! You want to get me in trouble! After everything I —

EMILIA
Aldo, I needed the money for the payments to keep Caterina in the convent school.

FINZI
Bringing her up to be a lady. You don't want her to know what she is, the daughter of a gondoliere and a whore.

EMILIA removes FINZI's gunbelt and he lies back on the bed. EMILIA gets on top of him.

What am I, Emilia?

EMILIA
What do you mean?

FINZI
A Fascist? A Jew? No, I am poor. I know what I am, and I'm proud to say it. I'm poor....When I was first secretary to the Interior, I was still poor — the way Mussolini is still poor.

EMILIA unbuttons his jacket.

I expected you to be loyal to me. *(undoes her bra)*

EMILIA
Aldo, I am.

FINZI
No, you want to be rich, to have your own maids, to —

EMILIA
Si, I want to be a lady like that Madame de Lempicka. Is that so wrong? You want me to end up like Dante's mother — starving while her husband was leading the gondolieri on strike.

FINZI
Dante's father led the strike?

EMILIA
Did he have a choice? The steamboats would have put every gondoliere out of business if they didn't do something.

FINZI
Dante? Where's Dante?

EMILIA
He...I think he's with Mario.

FINZI
(shoving EMILIA off of him and beginning to get dressed) Dante's with Mario!

EMILIA
No, No! Shhh! Let's relax. You're getting worked up about politics....You men and your games.

FINZI
It's Dante! Dante, too. It's all of you!

FINZI exits to the Kitchen, PAGE 171. EMILIA follows but FINZI chases her back to her room.

Get back in your room and stay there!

EMILIA goes back to her room, PAGE 159.

SCENE I43

EMILIA'S ROOM.

EMILIA
Dear Lord, I beg you to protect Dante and Mario from Finzi — I know I've not been to church as often as I should and...but why do I say these things?— you know my heart. Lord, forgive me for the sin I am about to commit. Please understand I do it for love and please forgive me all my lies and give me the strength to survive. I just want to survive.

She exits to the hall where she encounters MARIO, PAGE 172.

SCENE 144

MARIO'S ROOM.

MARIO enters his room carrying a decanter of cognac. He sits down. He has come from PAGE 122, the Kitchen.

MARIO
Questions. Everyone questions. Emilia will talk if Finzi keeps question-ing....And me...why do I go on? What can we hope to achieve with d'Annun-zio? Learn to make a better omelette? Is that the revolution I'm fighting for? *(pours more cognac)* Father used to get so angry because I thought I knew all the answers....What are they now?

Enter DANTE from PAGE 109, the Dining Room.

DANTE
Time for a little drink, Mario? You said you were in the war?

MARIO
Why?

DANTE
(spoken quickly) In a few moments Emilia will realize the cognac is missing. If she goes to Luisa or Aélis we will have them explode upon us like an Austrian 70 mm. Boom! The end of Mario. If, and this alternative you should pray for, if Emilia comes directly here, it won't be too bad for you, Emilia being a dud grenade compared to others. But all women are witches.

MARIO
Salute! *(drinks)*

DANTE
(sniffs the cognac) Do you drink this?

MARIO
It's not very good.

DANTE
Do you want a real drink? I'll get you some of my own strictly private stock.

EMILIA comes to the door from PAGE 127, the hallway.

EMILIA
There you are. Are you trying to get me fired?

DANTE
Emilia, he was just dusting off the decanter.

MARIO
I'm sorry. The last thing I want to do is get you into trouble, cousin Emilia.

EMILIA
(after a pause) I have to go.

EMILIA takes the cognac and exits to the hallway, PAGE 128.

DANTE
There, you see — a slight thud, a little wiggle, and away she goes. Now, turn around and I will get you a real drink.

He exits to the hall where he retrieves another of his many hidden vodka bottles. He returns through a side door to the bedroom and surprises MARIO.

Presto. I give you a word of advice, mysterious Mario. Don't trust anyone poorer or richer than yourself.

MARIO
Why?

DANTE
Don't be alarmed, my friend. I give only advice. You see, you are a chauffeur and I am a gondoliere. This makes us equal, si?

MARIO
Si.

DANTE
Not quite. But we will talk of that later. Have a drink.

MARIO
Where are the glasses?

DANTE
No glasses. We are going to have a toast to my patrono.

MARIO
Il Comandante!

DANTE
He doesn't even pay my wages.

MARIO
Who, then?

DANTE
The Soviet foreign minister.

MARIO
Chicherin?

DANTE
So you know him? *(opens the bottle)*

MARIO
I read about his visit here in the paper.

DANTE
I, too, read the papers. A toast to Minister Chicherin.

They toast.

MARIO
Vodka! Bene! Who are you?

DANTE
It is you who are the mystery. I'm not a Communist, if that's what you mean.
This vodka was given to me for saving his life.

MARIO
Where? In Russia?

They sit on the trunk.

DANTE
Here. Drink. Three, four years ago, he came to dinner. After dinner, Il Comandante takes the Russian into the Oratorio. On the altar, there's a large sword
given to him by the Italians of New York for liberating Fiume. You've seen it?

MARIO
I know it.

DANTE
This, remember, is all true. Il Comandante picks up the sword. He unsheaths it. A big sword, no? The foreign minister, he doesn't know what to do. Il Comandante says nothing for...maybe...five minutes. Then he says: "My dear friend," you know how he talks. "My dear friend, for reasons which I did not wish to tell you beforehand, I have resolved to cut off your head." True. Really. The minister, he's scared. That's when I came in. Il Comandante was furious. He looked at me, mad, very upset, then he turns to the Russian and says, like an Englishman, "A pity I am not in form tonight. I am afraid I'll have to postpone the matter to another day." That's how I saved Chicherin's life. Drink. It was all a joke, of course, but the Minister, he did not think it was funny. Five months ago I received the vodka. Communists are slow to say thank you, no?

MARIO
The Fascists never say thank you.

DANTE
This is true, but some things we should not say.

MARIO
I know nothing of politics. I just drive the automobile.

DANTE
Automobiles? They are for old men and old ladies. They are wheelchairs. A bambino this big *(indicates size)* could drive an automobile.

MARIO
His feet wouldn't touch the pedals.

DANTE
It takes no skill to drive. Thank God Venezia does not have them. Venezia has the gondola!

MARIO
I've never been.

DANTE
To go once is never to leave. We will compare: automobiles and gondolas. I'm driving your automobile. It takes no skill to drive this stupid thing. Now, when I'm inside this automobile of yours, can I hear the birds singing in the trees?

MARIO
Si.

Spoken simultaneously.

DANTE
No.

Can I smell the beautiful country air?

MARIO
Si.

Spoken simultaneously.

DANTE
No.

Can I talk to someone coming in the opposite direction?

MARIO
Si.

Spoken simultaneously.

DANTE
No.

Mario, we're not agreeing. Look, we're heading for Venezia. Narrow road, automobile coming head on. Do I yell "premi," [right] "stali," [left] what?

MARIO
Premi. [Right.]

MARIO and DANTE exit to the Kitchen. MARIO takes the vodka with him.

DANTE
I say nothing, he says nothing, and the world's a worse place for it. Here we are. I park the automobile, and we get on the train for Venezia. *(takes his hat off of a hook on the wall and puts it on)*

MARIO
What are you doing now?

DANTE
I'm going to show you Venezia by gondola. Ah! The causeway. Three
thousand metres long, forty-eight secret explosive chambers for quick demoli-
tion. I counted the arches once, two hundred and twenty-two of them. Are you
listening, Mario? It was built in 1846 by the Austrians. We Venetians never
thought of it. My father, he hated it, but some progress is good. Now, the
tourists come. We're here. Stazione Venezia — Santa Lucia. Like everything
in Venezia, the station was built on the ruins of a church. This one house is the
remains of Santa Lucia. She was done to death, for refusing to marry.

MARIO
Like Emilia

DANTE
Sant' Emilia.

MARIO
Of the single bed.

DANTE
Years ago we had a double bed! True. It's all in the guidebook. To be a gondoliere, you must know the guidebook.

MARIO
Dante, this is a nice game. But I can't see Venezia.

DANTE
Drink. When they drain the canals, you don't see where they dig, you smell it.
(climbs up the long table) But it's still very beautiful. Venezia. La mia
Venezia. [My Venice.]

MARIO
Il Comandante wears too much perfume.

DANTE
Not too much for Venezia. The Grand Canal.

MARIO sits on the table.

Three kilometres long, average depth 2.5 metres, three at the Rialto. Don't
look that way. The steamboats dock there. Almost ruined us when they first
started. Società Vaporetti Omnibus di Venezia; run by Frenchmen. It was hard.
My father led the strike, the Roman Catholics prayed to the Holy Mother. She

was kind. We were not entirely wiped out. My gondola! Not like your automobile. Look at her! Nine metres long, 1.5 at the beam. See how she leans, not drunk like us. They're built like that, to take the one-oared rower.

MARIO
Dante, enough. *(gets off the table)* How can I talk to Il Comandante?

DANTE
You will not. After a year, he might say hello. Three years, you're a second cousin. Ten years, famiglia.

MARIO
When is he alone?

DANTE
When he's in your automobile.

MARIO
I've been here a week and he still hasn't gone out.

DANTE
(picking up a broom and getting up on the table) Mario, you got a problem? See Aélis or Signora Baccara.

MARIO
I have to see Il Comandante.

DANTE
Come, I'll take you to him. Get on board.

Mario jumps on the table.

MARIO
Now? If I went to his study...?

DANTE
He would strike you down.

MARIO
Has he—

DANTE
Tried to hit me? Like a father hits a child, that's all. We're off. See my feet?

Like in ballet. The oar has to be at the waist level, then you twist the body in the opposite direction. Listen. We're on the canal. That's the Scalzi Church on your right. Baroque, I think.

MARIO
How long have you been with Il Comandante? *(sits down on the table)*

DANTE
Caporetto, when was that?

MARIO
October, 1917.

DANTE & MARIO
Caporetto! *(toast)*

MARIO
So you met him at Caporetto?

DANTE
No. My regiment withdrew to Venezia. We were stationed at Palazzo de Spiga. Signor de Spiga, being one of the most Italian of Italians, was hiding his little ass in Roma.

MARIO
No one can hide there now.

DANTE
That's true. This is funny. Maybe it's not so funny, but it's true. de Spiga had a gondoliere. Un nome inglese. [An English name.] Andrew was his name.

MARIO
Si.

DANTE
It's hard to say, because I am a gondoliere also. He was...how do you say...omosessuale.

MARIO
A "frocio." [fag.]

MARIO is drunk.

DANTE
Si. He had a friend. Young boy. They used to do these things together. The young boy's father was in the "amici."

MARIO
Mafioso?

DANTE
Si. They don't like these things. Found him impaled on a "bricole" in the lagoon. Completamente nudo. [Completely nude.] I was the only gondoliere in the regiment, so I got the job. Grazie, Andrew.

MARIO
"I should not see the sandy hourglass run
But I should think of shallows and flats
And see my wealthy Andrew doc'd in sand."

DANTE
(laughing) Shakespeare.

MARIO
You know it?

DANTE
I hate it. *Merchant of Venice.* See the steeple? San Fosca. My family lives next door. This, no, don't look, it is ugly, Palazzo Barbarigo. The Austrians bombed it for us, but it still stands. Too bad. *Merchant of Venice*, a bad play. Before the war, 1907-1908, I met this American, a poet, not good like Il Comandante, but I liked his funny Italian, so we talked sometimes. His name was Ezra Pound. He was broke, said he wanted to be a gondoliere. I showed him a few strokes. Smell the fish?

MARIO
That's the pescheria.

DANTE
And this is the Erberia, the best vegetable market in Italia.

MARIO
That's not true. Genova has a very good one, and so does Milano.

DANTE
So, I lie. This one's easy to steal from.

MARIO
That's important.

DANTE
When you're hungry, and I'm always hungry. The oldest church in Venezia, San Giacomo di Rialto. Fifth century.

MARIO
Ezra Pound?

DANTE
He said he liked the *Merchant of Venice* because the Jew got what he deserved. Here it is, the deepest point in the canal, three metres. This is the Rialto Bridge. Don't look up. The shops are terrible, and the kids spit on you. Bad. Built in 1588.

MARIO
What did you say?

DANTE
Built in 1588.

MARIO
To Pound?

DANTE
I said: "I am a Jew, and I deserve an apology."

MARIO
Or a pound of flesh. Did you get it?

DANTE
I threw him into the canal before he could open his mouth.

MARIO laughs.

Palazzo Papadopoli, built by Gian Giacomo dei Grigi. Renaissance. Sixteenth century.

MARIO
You know a lot.

DANTE
Not like a chauffeur. Palazzo Grimani, now the court of appeal.

MARIO
How do you appeal to a Fascist?

DANTE
On your knees.

MARIO
And beg.

DANTE
(handing MARIO the broom and taking the bottle from him) Here, row. Behold, Palazzo Ducale. *(points opposite)* My great-grandfather worked there, in the kitchen. The Contessa was host to Byron, Shelley, Keats, many others. Brilliant men with pure ideas.

MARIO
Fascism is for people afraid to commit suicide. It is a disease for liberals who can't quite pick up the gun. It takes away liberties, one at a time. A sort of death. Death in moderation.

DANTE
Mario, you're rocking the gondola. Palazzo Balbi, the most beautiful in Venezia. Built by Vittoria in 1582. Napoleon watched the regatta from the balcony. The present government wants to build a shortcut to the station, using the Ca Foscari, here, and adding on a new canal. I dislike shortcuts.

MARIO
Everything is —

DANTE
Keep it down, Mario. This is the Palazzo Giustiniani, where Wagner wrote the third act of *Tristan*. You know, the wail of the shepherd's pipe? It was inspired by the gondoliere's call. "Premi." [Right.] "Stali." [Left.] And here it is, Palazzo de Spiga. The hour of violence is upon us.

MARIO
Hour of violence?

DANTE
Il Comandante had so many women calling he had to declare nine o'clock the hour of violence! If a woman came after nine, she was there to "chiavare." [fuck.] *(makes a sexual gesture)* So beautiful. Full women. One time, only once, I got one. Il Comandante had double booked, so he put one in my room and....

FINZI enters from PAGE 159, EMILIA's room.

FINZI
What are you doing?

DANTE
Standing in my gondola.

FINZI
What were you talking about?

DANTE
We are not talking, we are listening.

FINZI
You were talking, Dante.

DANTE
Look, Mario! How does he do that? The Capitano's walking on the water.

FINZI
Get down!

MARIO cautiously gets down.

DANTE
(to MARIO) I did not tell you about the crocodiles in the canal.

FINZI
What does it mean? Nothing...like your gondola. Get down, Dante.

DANTE
I don't swim so well. *(gets down)*

FINZI
Get out, Mario. I'll deal with you later.

MARIO exits to the Servants' Hall where he has a brief scene with EMILIA, PAGE 172.

DANTE
Care for a little drink, Capitano?

He takes a drink of vodka and crosses to FINZI where he spits on FINZI's boots. FINZI trips him and kicks him in the groin. DANTE continues on PAGE 173. FINZI exits to EMILIA's bedroom, PAGE 173.

SCENE 145

THE SERVANTS' HALL

MARIO leaves the Kitchen, PAGE 171, and finds EMILIA in the servants' hall. EMILIA is from PAGE 159, her bedroom.

    EMILIA
You're all right! I...I told Finzi...about —

    MARIO
What?

    EMILIA
— that, that we were lovers.

MARIO kisses her.

Can I come to you?

    MARIO
Give me an hour. I think I drank too much.

    EMILIA
I'll have to make an excuse to Il Comandante.

    MARIO
Make a choice. Him or me.

    EMILIA
Wait for me.

MARIO exits quickly to his room and INTERMEZZO. To follow him into the second day, see DANTE's introduction to Act Two, PAGE 179. As he slams his bedroom door shut, FINZI appears from the Kitchen, PAGE 172.

FINZI

Emilia, get me some castor oil. I think it's time Mario learnt a lesson.

EMILIA

No, Aldo.

FINZI

Get it.

EMILIA

(coyly) And what about me? My lesson. Twice today you've left me waiting. Come on. Tonight it's free. Come.

FINZI

(smiling and allowing himself to be led into EMILIA's bedroom) Oh, I will. I will.

They enter the bedroom, closing the door behind them. Their INTERMEZZO begins. See DANTE's speech, PAGE 179, to follow them into the second day.

SCENE 146

KITCHEN AND HALL

DANTE moans on the floor of the Kitchen and slowly gets up. He takes his empty vodka bottle and slowly walks into the hall. MARIO, EMILIA and FINZI's audience find themselves standing in the hall, out of all the servants' rooms, as DANTE enters.

DANTE

Signore, Signori. I'd like to propose a toast....it's empty....*(holds up his bottle and sees that it's empty; throws it down — it shatters)* Andiamo. I've got a secret supply upstairs. Shhh. Not a word. If Signor de Spiga hears us, there won't be anything left to drink. *(leads his audience upstairs and into the Dining Room)* Sssh. Il Comandante is making one of his speeches. I'd advise you to tiptoe. His behaviour is sometimes unpredictable.

He will stay with the audience throughout INTERMEZZO. He begins Act Two on PAGE 179.

SCENE I47

THE ORATORIO

d'ANNUNZIO sits up on the funeral bier and notices de SPIGA, who has watched LUISA leave and has stopped playing the piano. He motions for de SPIGA to bring him some cocaine. de SPIGA complies by pouring a line of cocaine out on the bier.

de SPIGA

Women, love—no one is true and nothing is pure; except this...and it is always faithful.

As d'ANNUNZIO snorts the cocaine, de SPIGA exits to PAGE 155, the Side Hall. d'ANNUNZIO finishes snorting the cocaine; he glances up and sees the statue of San Sebastian.

d'ANNUNZIO

(examining the dagger) Yes...Luisa said, "To you, chosen by God to radiate the light of renewed liberty throughout the world, we, the women of Fiume and Italia, religiously offer this holy weapon, this blessed bayonet, so that with it you may carve the word victory into the living flesh of our enemies." *(appears to be crying)* And I thought of San Sebastian...and told the crowd about the women who had tended his body, washing it, pulling out the arrows of his enemies one by one, and I said, "I want to believe, my brothers, my sisters, that this blade was made from the metal tips of the first and last arrows which struck San Sebastian down. For he cried out as he fell, 'I die in order not to die.' He cried bleeding, 'Not enough! Again!' Oh! The immortality of love, the eternity of sacrifice, the blood of the hero is inexhaustible. This is the meaning of this gift! *(mounts a pulpit)* Are you prepared to join me, to sacrifice your lives for this great enterprise? Then this is not the time to talk but to do, not the time to think but to act, and to act in the Roman way! *(snorts more cocaine)* If it is considered a crime to incite the citizens to violence then I...here...now, boast of that crime. If instead of words I could throw weapons to all of you, I wouldn't hesitate! I'd do it without remorse! For every excess of force is permissible if by it we prevent the motherland from falling. You can and must prevent a handful of ruffians and good-for-nothings from imperiling and losing Italia! Whatever action is necessary is absolved by the true laws of Roma. Listen to me! Hear me! Treason is today obvious. Not only do we smell the terrible smell of treason but we already feel its opprobious weight."

SCENE I48

THE ORATORIO

AÉLIS enters after PAGE 156, the Side Hall.

d'ANNUNZIO
Treason lives in Roma! In the city of the soul, in the city of light!

AÉLIS
You promised there'd be no more speeches.

d'ANNUNZIO
(quietly) It was nothing new.

AÉLIS
(crossing to pulpit) That's irrelevant —

d'ANNUNZIO
It's more relevant than it ever was. *(comes down the pulpit steps and goes to AÉLIS)*

AÉLIS
(hugging him) Our house is tied to your silence!

d'ANNUNZIO
Shhh! I've taken a vow of silence...at least for tonight.

d'ANNUNZIO kisses AÉLIS. He begins exiting the Oratorio. As he passes his tomb, he spits on it.

AÉLIS
(following d'ANNUNZIO to the Oratorio doors, then turning to the audience)
Ladies and gentlemen, after what you just witnessed, I'm certain you'll understand that Il Commandante needs his privacy. If you will follow me, I have asked Dante to lay out some refreshments for you.

AÉLIS guides d'ANNUNZIO and the audience into the Dining Room. d'AN-NUNZIO and AÉLIS exit as soon as they can from the Dining Room and head for their own INTERMEZZO. To find out where they begin Act Two, turn to DANTE's speech, PAGE 179.

INTERMEZZO

A Vittoriale degli Italiani 10 Gen 1927
In Honour of the Arrival of Tamara de Lempicka
Intermezzo
"Tamara" Cocktail
Perrier Jouet Champagne

Antipasto

Caponata

Sicilian Eggplant with Tomatoes,
Green Olives and Capers on Grilled Baguette Slices

Primi Piatti

Prime Filet of Beef Carved on Buffet
Served with Green Peppercorn Sauce

Curried Breast of Chicken "Le Cirque"
with Crème Fraîche, Celery, Apples,
Roasted Peanut and Coconut Garnish

Pasta Primavera "Le Cirque"
Fusilli with Snow Peas, Tomatoes and Mushrooms
tossed with Basil, Parmesan, Garlic and Pine Nuts

Green Beans with Hazlenuts

Insalata "Vittoriale"

Green Salad with Champagne Vinaigrette
Black Olives,
Basket of Fresh Vegetables,
Basket of Bread, Crackers, Breadsticks

Dolci

Basket of Fresh Strawberries
Assortment of Italian Cookies
Crème Brulée "Le Cirque"

Presented by Le Cirque
Designed by Chef Daniel Boulud and Catered by Remember Basil
Tamara Cocktail by Seagram/Champagne by Perrier Jouet

AUTHOR'S NOTE: *While the guests enjoy this lavish buffet they have an opportunity to mingle and exchange the information they have gathered from following various members of the household.*

ACT TWO

SECTION J

SCENE J49   DANTE and FINZI introduce the audience to the second
Page179   day.

SCENE J50   FINZI interrogates an audience member.
Page 181

SCENE J49

DANTE
(standing on chair in the middle of the Dining Room) Attenzione, per favore, attenzione. Presto, presto, we are all waiting for you. Buon giorno, Signore and Signori. *(waits for response from audience)* Ahh! You have been eating and drinking. You have more strength than that. Let us try one more time. Buon giorno!

This time, a larger response from the audience. He sees FINZI.

Ahh! The smiling Capitano.

FINZI
Your passport please?

He picks out a female in the audience near him. When a missing passport is found during the First Act it is given to FINZI and he uses that name if it is a woman.

What did I tell you when you came in here?

Audience response is usually that they should hold on to their passports.

What's the date?

Audience response is usually the actual date.

All right. I told you that it was January 10, 1927. Good for forty-eight hours.

Audience member responds with "right."

Capice? What's the date?

Audience usually responds with January 10, 1927.

No, Signora, that was yesterday. Today is January 11, 1927. Come with me!

FINZI leads audience members into the hall, where he questions her, PAGE 181.

DANTE
Everyone say ciao to the signora. Ciao, Signora. Signore. (pointing) Signore,

the Signora, she is with you? Do not worry, we will find you another signora. Unlike Capitano, I need no informers to find out what is going on in this building. Like any good valet I can tell you who is doing what to whom and in what room they are doing it. I will prove it to you. But first, Il Comandante has asked me to remind you when you enter a room, please go all the way to the far side of the room, stand against the wall, do not talk, do not get in the way, do not go wandering about on your own, and most important do not stand in front of a door; someone is going to open the door and hit you in the back. We do not want to have anyone hurt. Grazie. Now, you are such lovely guests that Il Comandante has asked me to extend an invitation to all of you. At the conclusion of tonight's activities you are welcome to come back here to join us for some café, dessert and conversation, just in case there may be one or two little things that you may have missed during the course of the evening.

From out in the hall we hear the female audience member who went with FINZI scream and then FINZI yells: "Let that be a lesson to you, January 11, 1927."

(motioning to female audience member's companion) Signore, what is your Signora doing to the Capitano? I'd recognize that scream anywhere. Now, for today's activities Il Comandante has instructed me to tell you he wants you to feel at home here; and now that you know your way around the villa and know its rules, he suggested that I simply tell you where the others are and let you go to follow them; so I suggest you quickly decide who you wish to follow. But before you leave here, if you would do Dante a favour, per favore; do not take any food or cups with you. Nothing, just your sweet little selves. And one other thing...it's important that we all leave here together, so wait until I say the word....Now where is everyone? I know Signorina Barra, the young ballerina, is down the hall in the Oratorio with Signora Luisa Baccara and Tamara — I don't remember her last name — the Polish one. *(PAGE 196)* Il Comandante? Well, since I didn't wake him, no doubt he's in his quarters with Aélis complaining about me. *(PAGE 191)* Who else? Signor de Spiga, I saw him going into the dining room and there's Capitano Finzi. *(PAGE 188)* That's everyone except of course for us servants. As soon as I finish here I'm going downstairs to wake Mario and we'll get Emilia to make us some breakfast. *(PAGE 183)* Everyone ready? *(pause)* Andiamo.

SCENE J50

FINZI

(to audience member) Did you follow Mario? *(pause for reply)* Did you notice anything unusual, anything out of the ordinary? *(pause for reply)* Thank you for your information. I'll make certain Roma hears of the valuable work you've done on behalf of the party. Now, so that your friends suspect nothing, I'm going to ask you to scream, scream as loud as you can. Scream.

Audience member screams.

Let that be a lesson to you, January 11, 1927. *(quietly)* You should get back. Tell no one of our talk. No one.

FINZI exits back to the Atrium, then heads to his office, PAGE 188.

SECTION K

THE FOLLOWING SCENES HAPPEN SIMULTANEOUSLY:

SCENE K51   MARIO is joined by DANTE in his room. EMILIA enters at
PAGE 183   the end of this scene.

SCENE K52   de SPIGA and FINZI are in FINZI's office.
PAGE 188

SCENE K53   AÉLIS and d'ANNUNZIO are in d'ANNUNZIO's room.
PAGE 191

SCENE K54   LUISA, TAMARA and CARLOTTA are in the Oratorio.
PAGE 196

SCENE K51

MARIO'S ROOM

DANTE enters MARIO's room and finds a nude MARIO, just wrapping himself in a towel, combing his hair.(Note: EMILIA enters on PAGE 187.)

MARIO
You all right?

DANTE
Six hours up, six hours down, that's a Venetian. Like the tide.

MARIO
Finzi was watching my room. I couldn't come back.

DANTE
Why didn't you save me from the crocodile?

MARIO
I was scared.

DANTE
You were in the war, you know how to fight.

MARIO
Hc is the law.

DANTE
Not here. Il Comandante is the law.

MARIO
Finzi reports...to Roma.

DANTE
Words....Il Comandante writes a better report.

MARIO
I'm new.

DANTE
It is my way to be pleasant, Mario. When a tourist pretends to be a marquess, I

call him a marquess. Venezia is the city of dreams. But here, Mario, you cannot pretend with me.

MARIO
I don't pretend.

DANTE
No, my friend, you lie. You think me a silly man. I am not. Last night, I was
drunk. Vodka is not from the grape. It is clear. To know a building in a town
you say you've never been to, to quote Shakespeare, to know the name of a
Soviet minister: that is a lot for a mere chauffeur to know…and it's too much
for any cousin of Emilia's.

MARIO
I read the papers!

DANTE
Si, you told me, but you see, Mario, Chicherin's visit wasn't in the papers. He
came secretly from Geneva for one day. The press knew nothing.

MARIO doesn't reply.

You should leave now.

MARIO
I can't.

DANTE
What can you hope? d'Annunzio is old; he'll stay.

MARIO
If he knew of our movement, how organized we are—

DANTE
Now you are organized! Where was your great Communist organization in
1921? There was a chance then, before the Fascists seized power.

MARIO
The party was involved in internal struggles with the Socialists.

DANTE
He's done with politics. Go. He's happy here.

MARIO
How can he find joy in Italia?

DANTE
Cocaine.

MARIO
What about the poor?

DANTE
There's no joy.

MARIO
And you?

DANTE
I miss Venezia, love Emilia, hate Finzi, serve Il Comandante and think little of myself.

MARIO
Then think of others.

DANTE
Who should I think of? My father, thirty-three years head of our union, killed by Fascist thugs?

MARIO
Yes, think of your father, and all the others!

DANTE
I think only of those who stood by; his friends stood by and did nothing. They are the others, young Mario. Don't dream of mass resistance! People want the black shirts. Soon, the locks will be back on the ghetto doors.

MARIO
And why? Because men like d'Annunzio have seduced them with a childish fantasy which has no form, no ideology, no morality, no thought but one: "Make Italia strong again." Without morality you have only the strength of muscle.

DANTE
You mustn't speak like that to Il Comandante. If you talk, say you have always admired his political insight. Tell him that as a man of action, he must know in

his heart that now is the time for action. Flatter him. What do you want, exactly?

MARIO
How can I trust you?

DANTE
Trust my love for Emilia; if she wasn't involved I would have turned you in when you came.

MARIO
We want to take him abroad, to have him denounce the British for supporting a regime that does not have the support of the Italian people.

DANTE
Where?

MARIO
England.

DANTE
He likes the British, loves their dogs. Remind him about the dogs; the Waterloo Cup is next month.

MARIO
It won't be a holiday.

DANTE
Not for you, but if he goes....

MARIO
Will you help me?

DANTE
I will not betray you.

MARIO
No help?

DANTE
That's help enough. If he leaves with you, then you can have my job, you can get him up every morning and tell him how great he was and I will return to Venezia to take care of Mamma.

EMILIA comes out of her room and crosses the hall to enter MARIO'S room.

EMILIA
(to MARIO) Are you coming for breakfast?

MARIO
Dante knows —

EMILIA
(running and lunging at DANTE) Bastard! You told him.

MARIO
Told who?

EMILIA
Finzi.

MARIO
Did you?

DANTE
No.

MARIO
What do you suggest?

DANTE
Are you wanted? Do they have your name?

MARIO
Si.

DANTE
(to EMILIA) What did Finzi say?

EMILIA
He said that he knew Mario wasn't my cousin.

DANTE
Is that all? Emilia?

EMILIA
I told him we were lovers.

> **DANTE**
> Are you?

> **EMILIA**
> I made up a story.

> **MARIO**
> Nothing else?

> **EMILIA**
> You must leave, Mario.

> **DANTE**
> Finzi is slow but very methodical. You have two days, maybe three.

Enter FINZI from PAGE 191, his office.

> **FINZI**
> Mario, do you recall our little chat?

> **DANTE**
> Capitano, we were just going to have some breakfast. Won't you join us?

> **FINZI**
> Emilia, get this ass some oats.

EMILIA and DANTE exit to the Kitchen. PAGE 208 begins. MARIO and FINZI remain behind, PAGE 203.

SCENE K52

FINZI'S OFFICE/ THE DINING ROOM

FINZI enters his darkened office from the Atrium with his audience. He sits in his armchair. de SPIGA, with a drink in one hand, flips on the room light. He has been in the office waiting for FINZI.

> **FINZI**
> What?

de SPIGA
Why didn't you come up? I was waiting for you.

FINZI
I was up all night watching Mario's room.

de SPIGA
That was very commendable of you!

FINZI
There's a note on my desk for you.

de SPIGA
(goes to the desk) "Nario not Emilia's cousin!" I assume you mean Mario. *(crosses to FINZI)* The letter "M" is composed of two humps — just think of Luisa's buttocks next time.

FINZI
Don't—

de SPIGA
(kicking FINZI's leg) I say don't! I run this operation. You do as I tell you and when I say don't, you don't. Is that clear?

FINZI
If I did what I was told, we would do nothing. Go ahead and drink, Francesco. It's you who doesn't see clearly. I told you the first day Mario was a subversive. I know politics; you should stick to music.

de SPIGA
You just continue to observe — nothing else. I make the decisions.

FINZI
(going to his desk) There's no time. Speed. How do you think we came to power? While the Communists and the Socialists argued about the rules, we crossed the finish line. Speed.

de SPIGA
"We came to power because we had the strength to do absolutely nothing." Mussolini, stolen from Shakespeare. I remind you, Aldo, the party made a decision about d'Annunzio in 1924. Surely you recall Mussolini's words on the subject? What were they?

FINZI
"If one has a tooth that hurts, you either pull it out or fill it with gold."

de SPIGA
Very good! I forgot you actually admire Il Duce. But remember the point he was making. It is more important that the people believe d'Annunzio supports us than to get rid of him and risk civil war. He harms no one here.

This scene moves into the Dining Room as de SPIGA searches for a drink.

FINZI
The man is waiting for the moment to act!

de SPIGA
And so will you! Understood? Question Mario once again. Keep it routine this time...you know, former address, last employer, etc. And Aldo, don't use any muscle. We intend to drive to Gardone this morning to lunch at the Grand Hotel. When I get there I'll wire Roma....And Emilia — she's the one who told you?

FINZI
I had to use force.

de SPIGA
That doesn't interest me. Will she warn Mario?

FINZI
She's too frightened. He tried to convince me they were just lovers but there's no way he's working class.

de SPIGA
I'm sure I can recognize my own kind. Just keep your inquiries confined to my outline. And stay out of my sight. If you ever sit at this table —

FINZI
Three years ago, you begged to sit at my table. "Under-secretary Aldo Finzi will see you now, Signore." And you walked in like a scared cat. I took you and introduced you when they wouldn't even let aristocrats into Roma. Why? Because you were funny. Because you said the right things. And now that I'm no longer in a position to advance your career, you take every opportunity to abuse me. Why? Luisa? I've courted Luisa for two years. Francesco, why do you do this to me?

de SPIGA
We have to work together because Mussolini wants us to, not because I want

to. In the meantime, you obey my orders. We'll do a good job, a clean one, and we'll see it right through to the end. *(finishing cognac)* I think I've earned another cognac, don't you?

FINZI salutes de SPIGA then heads for MARIO's bedroom, PAGE 188. de SPIGA returns FINZI's salute and watches him leave. When FINZI is safely out of sight, de SPIGA goes to the phone.

Roma 3135. *(pause)* Luciano, is he there?...Benito? Francesco...de Spiga. *(laughs)* Do you like the concerto? *(pause)* I thought it was time you became a bit more adventurous. *(pause)* Some of the fingerings in the allegro may be a bit awkward — the violin is not my instrument, after all, but we can make adjustments...true...don't concern yourself with the harmonics just yet, they're a nice effect, but not essential. *(pause)* Yes, but not military precision, Benito. *(laughs)* Five/four's not march time. *(laughs; pause)* No. I'm not getting much done....Gabri's not the problem, it's Finzi. He's developed an obsession with Mario Pagnutti...he's a...you do know everything. *(laughs, then suddenly serious)* Should I take action or...uh...I understand....*(pause)* What! Mario, son of the Duke of Milano. A Communist? But the duke's a Fascist. Extraordinary! Yes. Yes. Safe passage to Nice. How do you propose I get him there...and if he refuses? *(pause)* Done. Now, I think I'll go drink some more of Gabri's cognac...yes, your cognac, of course. *(laughs)* Ciao. *(hangs up the telephone and holds up his empty snifter)* How obsequious we've become.

de SPIGA exits to the Oratorio, PAGE 216.

SCENE K53

d'ANNUNZIO'S ROOM

d'ANNUNZIO is lying on his bed. He is wearing a housecoat. AÉLIS enters with a handful of invoices, eating an apple.

AÉLIS
Good morning.

d'ANNUNZIO
You make that sound like a curse, Aélis.

AÉLIS
That imbecile, Dante, didn't wake me. I missed exercising with Carlotta.

d'ANNUNZIO
I didn't sleep at all.

AÉLIS
Were you writing or was it your insomnia?

d'ANNUNZIO
I want thicker glass in all the windows...kept hearing traffic...but it didn't seem to be going anywhere...just the sound of engines running...men shouting orders...there were lights at the end of the drive.

AÉLIS
You were probably dreaming about the war.

d'ANNUNZIO
No. It was reality seeping through the cracks. Do you remember when we could still dream, Aélis? My dream was to write just one volume of prose, which would be a war cry for the Latin people.

AÉLIS
You have.

d'ANNUNZIO
No. There was a spark at Fiume, perhaps some fire...but now, it's all smoke. *(taking the invoices out of AÉLIS's hand)* You bring me bills....*(looking through them)* Did I pay that much for the dress she wore last night?

AÉLIS
We haven't paid it yet.

d'ANNUNZIO
Fortunny wants money for his fabric—

AÉLIS
It's five months overdue.

d'ANNUNZIO
Murinni...don't pay this, the vase was broken. Pratesi—

AÉLIS
Did you talk to Mussolini?

d'ANNUNZIO
Aélis, I told you to pay this last month—

AÉLIS
We have no money.

d'ANNUNZIO
I've spent my most fabulous nights of love on these sheets—

AÉLIS
They are 10,000 lire.

d'ANNUNZIO
Order another two dozen.

AÉLIS
Gabri—

d'ANNUNZIO
(pause) Listen to me now! Just seven years ago I led three hundred men to Fiume. I took the land which the British had promised us for entering the war, land which our diplomats at Versailles were afraid to demand...and on that land, and in the hearts of its people, I built a new order based on heroism and genius...not wealth, or blood, or power. I gave the people a constitution —

AÉLIS
(with d'ANNUNZIO)...which guaranteed the equality of women, care for the aged, free medical insurance.... Can we not begin a day without this litany?

d'ANNUNZIO
How should I begin? Do you want them to say in a hundred year's time: "d'Annunzio...ah yes, now there was a great interior decorator!"

AÉLIS
(calming him with an embrace) Gabri...I was there....Now is not your time....You must wait....What's that phrase of yours? "Blessed be he who waiting and trusting wastes not his strength, but preserves it, with a warrior's discipline."

AÉLIS and d'ANNUNZIO kiss. As d'ANNUNZIO begins getting too excited, AÉLIS breaks their embrace.

No, no, no, Gabri, I have work to do.

d'ANNUNZIO
Have Defelice brought up to the house, and show her that new trick you do
with your tongue.

AÉLIS
Don't tell me you've given up on Tamara already.

d'ANNUNZIO
I don't know...her uncertainty irritates me. And you? What about Carlotta?

AÉLIS
(coyly) I had a delicious kiss last night but I won't get anywhere with her unless you give her that recommendation.

d'ANNUNZIO
I cannot compromise my aesthetics just so that you can get into bed with her.

AÉLIS
And why not? You'll sit for a portrait just to —

d'ANNUNZIO
A girl like Carlotta shouldn't go to Paris.

AÉLIS
She's good.

d'ANNUNZIO
Goodness has no place in dance. She should become a missionary. A girl like
her should always be seen in the company of starving negroes. It's not a recommendation she needs, but a halo.

AÉLIS
Gabri, please. Isabelle needs your recommendation.

d'ANNUNZIO
(gets out of bed, removes his housecoat and puts on a shirt and sweater) So
that's what this obsession is about...Isabelle.

AÉLIS
I meant—

d'ANNUNZIO
You sadden me, Aélis. I'd thought you'd stop looking for Isabelle in every vir-
gin that strays past our gate.

AÉLIS

I have. There are some physical similarities, I admit, but Carlotta is completely different.

d'ANNUNZIO

Isabelle is dead. A love dies and that is a sacred thing; you belittle her memory by seeing her in Carlotta.

AÉLIS

I don't see her in Carlotta. It was a slip of the tongue....

d'ANNUNZIO

I don't believe in slips of the tongue as you call them, though I suppose with your proclivities they're essential.

He exits, followed by AÉLIS.

(walking to the Oratorio) Now I'm going to watch this silly girl dance. Let us hope her brains are in her toes.

AÉLIS

You're jealous...afraid that if you give her the recommendation I'll go with her to Paris.

d'ANNUNZIO

I rely on you. This is your home.

AÉLIS

And I'll stay. There's no going back. Just a few days —

d'ANNUNZIO

And it's over?

AÉLIS

Over. I promise.

d'ANNUNZIO

(arriving at the Oratorio) And now the hard part begins.

AÉLIS and d'ANNUNZIO enter the Oratorio, PAGE 216.

SCENE K54

THE ORATORIO

TAMARA is sketching CARLOTTA in charcoal. CARLOTTA is exercising as LUISA enters.

TAMARA
Bonjour.

LUISA
(smiles at TAMARA, then turns to CARLOTTA) Up early.

CARLOTTA
In my family, early means before sunrise. Are we still going to Gardone?

LUISA
If Francesco ever wakes up.

CARLOTTA
Uncle Guido was like that. Sleep, sleep, sleep. He used to tell me sleeping was the only true act of genius. What does that mean? Funny Uncle Guido. It was terrible when he died. I thought he was just sleeping. I kept shaking him, shaking him. "Wake up, Guido, wake up!" Poor Uncle Guido.

LUISA
(after a pause, looks over TAMARA's shoulder to see what she has been sketching) Madame de Lempicka has been sketching you.

CARLOTTA
Tell her not to.

LUISA
You should be honoured. She is very good.

CARLOTTA
Tell her to stop!

LUISA
I can't speak French.

CARLOTTA rips page off and looks at it.

TAMARA
Vous pouvez l'avoir si ça vous plait. [It's yours if you like it.]

CARLOTTA
Don't you hate foreigners, Luisa? *(rips the paper)*

LUISA
Carlotta!

TAMARA walks away.

You tore up her art.

CARLOTTA
I hate foreigners.

LUISA
Why go to Paris?

CARLOTTA
Study.

LUISA
Do you think you can learn from people you hate?

CARLOTTA
I hated my ballet master in Roma — a Jew.

LUISA
An Italian Jew, or a foreign Jew?

CARLOTTA
Luisa, you are peculiar!

LUISA
Have you discussed this with Finzi?

CARLOTTA
What's there to discuss? All Jews are foreigners.

LUISA
What a hateful child you are. It must be difficult to dance with so much hate on the brain. I thought country girls like you were free of that.

CARLOTTA
(now exercising en pointe) I'm not a country girl! I'm a modern woman.

LUISA
That's only too apparent. Tell me, Signorina Barra, how does the modern woman reconcile art with intolerance? Why move the body if the mind stands still?

LUISA grabs CARLOTTA causing her to fall to the floor.

CARLOTTA
I don't understand. You are upset. I don't understand.

LUISA
Who? Me? Tamara? Jews? Who don't you understand?

CARLOTTA
You're yelling at me.

LUISA
Do you want to understand?

CARLOTTA
(near tears) Isn't it so? Papà says Jews drive down interest rates. They're bad for our banks. I understand. Papà cannot earn only six percent and send me to Paris.

LUISA
And what do the Polish do to interest rates?

CARLOTTA
Luisa, please don't be upset. Why is it wrong to dislike foreigners? We are Italiano. Is not Italia the greatest country in the world?

LUISA
Caesar is dead.

CARLOTTA
But Il Comandante lives, and Il Duce and the Pope.

LUISA
(picks up a piece of the torn sketch) You'll never be a modern dancer. Oh, you can move, but you're not free. There's a border around you. You can't learn or communicate if you tear the world into scraps of paper.

CARLOTTA
(crying) Why are you so cruel to me, Luisa?

TAMARA comforts her.

LUISA
Whose kindness led you to think so ill of others? The nuns? Carlotta, you have a chance to be great, an opportunity I had once; take it. You have your art. Stop looking for gods to serve and devils to hate.

CARLOTTA
I don't, I don't!

LUISA
Then don't talk to me about Il Comandante or Mussolini. If you dance, dance. Not for Italia, or any country, but for dance.

CARLOTTA
Il Comandante writes for Italia.

LUISA
What? Tell me what has he written in five years? Ten? You're too young to understand. I gave up my career to join Gabri in Fiume. Young people always join movements, but movements keep on marching— you wake up one day, abandoned...old, and alone. So now, when I play, there are fingers on keys...*(quietly)* but there's no music. It's too late for me, maybe it always was....Father was so Italian I couldn't play Bach in the house. Poor Gabri thinks I can play Debussy. I wanted to study in Paris, but my father threatened to disown me.

CARLOTTA
Papà wants me to go.

LUISA
As long as you say, "I am Italian" before you say, "I am a dancer," there's no sense in going. Pavlova isn't a Russian dancer, she is a dancer. I didn't want to be an Italian pianist or a woman pianist, just a pianist. *(to TAMARA)* Don't you agree? Oh! You don't understand.

TAMARA
Comment? [What?]

LUISA
Uh. Don't you know any French, Carlotta?

CARLOTTA
Just dance terms.

LUISA
(trying to speak in French) Une artiste etre, non, est une artiste, si, oui? [An artist to be, no, is an artist, yes?]

TAMARA
Naturellement. Oui....[Naturally, yes.]

LUISA
Ce n'est pas un...what is the word? Ce n'est pas une question. [It is not a....It is not a question.]

TAMARA
Question?

LUISA
Oui, une question de...nationality.

TAMARA
La nationalité. Non, je suis Polanaise. J'habite à Paris. Maintenant, je suis en Italie. Pour l'artiste, le monde entier est sa patrie et sa patrie est son art. C'est un pays que l'on appelle liberté. Vous comprenez? [Ah, nationality. No. I am Polish. I live in Paris. Now, I'm in Italy. For the artist, the whole world is her country and her country is her art. It is a country called freedom. You understand?]

LUISA
Oui, non. *(indicates that she has understood a little)*

CARLOTTA
What did she say?

LUISA
I'm not sure.

CARLOTTA
See, you can't talk to foreigners. Papà says for too long they have stolen from us. Now we must get back what is ours.

LUISA
Culture is not doll's clothing, Carlotta. You can't ask Liszt to take the Italian flavour out of his "Pelerinages."

CARLOTTA
His what?

LUISA
All I'm saying is that your first responsibility is to dance.

CARLOTTA
No. First to our Lord Jesus, then to Papà, then to dance.

LUISA
Let's stop talking. *(goes to the piano)* Just dance.

LUISA plays approximately four and a half measures of "La Marseillaise" to honour TAMARA, then segues into Chopin's Waltz Op. 70, #2. CARLOTTA begins dancing to the Chopin.

Frederic Chopin — Polish.

This scene continues, PAGE 216.

SECTION L

THE FOLLOWING SCENES HAPPEN SIMULTANEOUSLY:

SCENE L55   MARIO and FINZI in MARIO's room.
PAGE 203

SCENE L56   DANTE and EMILIA talk in the Kitchen.
PAGE 208

SCENE L57   AÉLIS, d'ANNUNZIO and de SPIGA join CARLOTTA,
PAGE 216   LUISA and TAMARA in the Oratorio. MARIO, FINZI,
                 DANTE and EMILIA will enter near the end of this scene.

SCENE L55

MARIO'S ROOM

FINZI and MARIO have just come from the hall, PAGE 188. MARIO dresses while he speaks with FINZI. FINZI is looking about the room while he speaks with MARIO.

FINZI
Mario, you do recall our chat? I tried last night to get in touch with your last employer, the Principessa d'Avignon.

MARIO
She winters in Capri.

FINZI
It seems she doesn't have a phone. Now, Mario, that is your real name, Mario?

MARIO
Si.

FINZI
I need to know, Mario, and you must answer this question honestly: Are you now, or have you ever been, a member of the Communist party?

MARIO
No.

FINZI
You should know, Mario, that I insist all my friends call me Capitano. A man must always be identified by his rank...or party. I ask again: are you a Communist?

MARIO
No, Capitano.

FINZI
Have you ever known a Communist?

MARIO
No, Capitano.

FINZI

Three times you answer no. *(pause)* I want you to write down for me your name in full, the address of your family, your father's occupation, and what rank you held in the war. *(holding out the book and pencil)*

MARIO

(coming out from behind the dressing screen) I don't know how.

FINZI

No schooling?

MARIO

No, Capitano.

FINZI

You speak very well for someone who has never been to school.

MARIO

My Capitano in the army was a Visconti, it's his voice you hear.

FINZI

The address of your family is....

MARIO

Quindice [Fifteen] Via Emanuelle Filiberto, near Santa Scala. Do you know Roma?

FINZI

The British Embassy is near there, correct?

MARIO

Most of the the embassies are near there, but you can't see much from our basement.

FINZI

Father's occupation?

MARIO

He was a baker.

FINZI

Dead?

MARIO
Two years ago.

FINZI
Your mother still lives at this address?

MARIO
Si, Capitano.

FINZI
Your rank?

MARIO
Corporale.

FINZI
And you were discharged when?

MARIO
1917, a shrapnel wound.

FINZI
Would you fight for Italia again?

MARIO
I will always fight to save Italia. *(pause)* Were you in the war, Capitano?

FINZI
That's not important. And now this Visconti....

MARIO
My capitano in the war.

FINZI
He was killed?

MARIO
Si.

FINZI
His first name was...?

MARIO
I told you —

FINZI

Tell me again! *(pause)* Some think me slow; I'm not slow, Mario. I double check. Now what was Capitano Visconti's first name? Army records list three Viscontis.

MARIO

His name was Mario.

FINZI

Same as you.

MARIO

That's how we met. Someone said, "Mario," and we both answered. After that, we flipped a coin; I lost. So they called me by my last name, Pagnutti.

FINZI

Why didn't they call him Capitano?

MARIO

He wouldn't allow it. He never forgot his men.

FINZI

And how did he die?

MARIO

Court-martial.

FINZI

This is the man you looked up to?

MARIO

He saved my life!

FINZI

Nothing to take pride in. He disobeyed an order!

MARIO

Our position was exposed. He pulled us back to the first line of trenches.

FINZI

There's no excuse for retreating.

MARIO
Our line held! *(calmly)* If you'd ever been at the front, you'd know he did the right thing.

FINZI
(calmly) Answer this: how did this dead Capitano Visconti recommend you for a job with the Principessa d'Avignon?

MARIO
I was out of the army before he went to trial.

FINZI
Isn't it strange, Mario, that your Capitano Mario Visconti never went to trial? He escaped?

MARIO
My name is Mario Pagnutti.

FINZI
And the police are now looking for this same Mario Visconti in connection with a bombing in Padua and a bank robbery in Turin.

The servants' bell rings.

MARIO
They want me upstairs. *(exits)*

FINZI
(following him into the hall) And where else?

MARIO
You have my papers.

FINZI
(walking away from MARIO) And they are being checked and when they return, I'll have them rechecked.

FINZI exits to the Oratorio, PAGE 219.

MARIO returns to the room, puts his gun in a new hiding place, then gets his cap and exits to the Oratorio, PAGE 219.

SCENE L56

THE KITCHEN

DANTE and EMILIA are in the Kitchen. They are from PAGE 188, MARIO's room.

DANTE
I'll leave, Emilia; I will. Or kill him. Why does Il Comandante put up with him? We managed without him.

EMILIA
Finzi's here to stay.

DANTE
Not I! Why can't it be like Venezia?

EMILIA
Always Venezia with you, Dante. The canals stink. The rats are bigger than the cats. Every disease in Europe starts in Venezia. And what did we make? The pay's better here.

DANTE
I wouldn't know. I don't have your equipment. Can't make bonuses.

EMILIA
Il Comandante will want you upstairs.

DANTE
Is he up?

EMILIA
Shave before you go.

DANTE
(takes his shaving equipment off a shelf and fills the bowl with water) I remember when you cried, Emilia.

EMILIA
Not since I was born.

DANTE
Money didn't matter. When you came, you had only one dress. Aélis wouldn't

have you, remember? But you got the job because Dante told His Highness
that you had eyes like a Roman high priestess.

EMILIA
Don't remind me.

DANTE
Everyone wants to forget around here. There were good days before.

EMILIA
Who forgets? We're surrounded by the past. You and Il Comandante live it.
Things have changed. Change, Dante.

DANTE
I've still only one outfit, Emilia. *(lathers his face)*

EMILIA
Watch it. You're shaking.

DANTE
How can you let Finzi touch you?

EMILIA
Sit down. Let me. *(takes DANTE's straight-edge razor and sits down to shave
him)* I need the money.

DANTE
A Fascista.

EMILIA
What difference — men are pigs.

DANTE
We could have married.

EMILIA
I'm Catholic, not Jewish.

DANTE
There was a time when you would have converted, before you became a
whore.

EMILIA
(showing him the razor) Watch it, this is a razor!

DANTE
The first time you shaved me, you almost slit my throat.

EMILIA
You coughed.

DANTE
A cold. It was you who wanted me to swim the Grand Canal.

EMILIA
Like Il Comandante.

DANTE
Must everything be like Il Comandante?

EMILIA
Who was the one who wanted me to shave his head?

DANTE
A drunk!

EMILIA
No, you weren't.

DANTE
I confess.

EMILIA
I remember the poetry you used to write me.

DANTE
None of that, Emilia!

EMILIA
(laughing)
"Your breast sailed so smoothly
like the gondolas of San Marco...."

DANTE
I taught you how to walk in shoes.

EMILIA
(continuing)
"My hand outstretched
You left, I retched."

DANTE
I'll retch again if you don't stop.

EMILIA
You were so funny.

DANTE
Both of us were...inexperienced. A man grows older. I wanted to be wise, like my father. Did I become wise?

EMILIA
No.

DANTE
No, I suppose not. If wise men are happy, then I am...a fool. Things seemed possible then. We thought for sure we could become a conte and contessa.

EMILIA
I still do.

DANTE
By sleeping with Finzi?

EMILIA
Dante, I don't have a choice. He knows about Mario.

DANTE
Bastard! *(pause)* Why bring Mario here? Il Comandante won't go.

EMILIA
I don't know what he wants. They said it was just to talk.

DANTE
He wants Il Comandante to go to England.

EMILIA
And us! What about me? My job.

DANTE
Aiding his escape — a serious charge.

EMILIA
Defelice said it was just to talk.

DANTE
Il Comandante's personal whore is a Communist! Who else?

EMILIA
I don't know anything. They said it was just to talk! Il Comandante won't go.
Dante?

DANTE
Watch my nose!

EMILIA
I can't do this.

*EMILIA throws the razor down on the table. DANTE wipes the remaining
lather off of his face. EMILIA takes out a bottle of wine from her hiding place.
She opens it and drinks.*

What are we going to do?

DANTE
....you going to do?

EMILIA
If he goes, you won't have a job.

DANTE
Venezia is best this time of year. If Finzi knows about the money, Mario's
finished.

EMILIA
Dante, help me!

DANTE
Wait...that's all you can do.

EMILIA
If I tell Baccara?

DANTE
You're finished.

EMILIA
I'll tell Finzi everything!

DANTE
As long as Finzi doesn't know about the money, nothing will happen. It never does.

EMILIA
He's not going to let up this time.

DANTE
Will he tell Baccara? The story about you and Mario being lovers?

EMILIA
No...I...not if I sleep with him.

DANTE
Il Comandante, Finzi, who else? What if Aélis finds out — will you sleep with her too?

EMILIA
I hate them all! *(drinks)*

DANTE
A bit more of that and you'll forget all about them.

EMILIA
I won't forget them. And I don't forget the girl I was. We were never happy, Dante. I know what I was — a peasant.

DANTE
Now you're a woman of the world.

EMILIA
I want our daughter to be a lady.

DANTE
By putting her in a convent!

EMILIA
Si, until I can make a better life.

DANTE
Where is she? You never tell me. A man has a right to know. We had a chance, Emilia. Things would have worked.

EMILIA

For the daughter of a gondoliere. What would she have to look forward to? Do you think I've forgotten your mother? Waiting every night for your father to come home. Praying those Fascist thugs hadn't got him.

DANTE

The union takes care of her.

EMILIA

Don't lie to me, Dante! I know Il Comandante sends her money. That's why you stay here, isn't it? It's not for me.

DANTE

It wouldn't be like that for us.

EMILIA

No, worse. Much worse.

DANTE

Anything would be better...than being a whore.

EMILIA

I have a chance. Yes, I suffer, but I won't cry for myself. Somehow I'll get out. I'll hook a rich man.

DANTE

And what of Caterina? If you hook a rich man, what of her? Will he take her in? Will he give her his name? You'll never be anyone's wife. Who comes here except a few old Fascists?

EMILIA

(crying) I don't care how old he'd be. If he's ninety, I'll be a child.

DANTE

And when this is over? When black is no longer fashionable except for widows?

EMILIA

The money will be mine.

DANTE

And our daughter? My Caterina! Do you think she'll want your legacy? A Fascist inheritance!

EMILIA
At least she'll have money.

DANTE
Blood money.

EMILIA
I'm doing it for her!

DANTE
Keep saying it.

EMILIA
Everyone's a whore, Dante. Stop walking on water. Look at Il Comandante —
Il Duce owns him. And Tamara — she'll screw him to paint his picture.

DANTE
Your world is ugly.

EMILIA
There's only one world.

*DANTE goes to EMILIA and kisses her. DANTE takes a lemon out of a basket
of vegetables and cuts it.*

DANTE
Here. It'll hide your breath.

They each bite into a slice of lemon.

Bitter?

EMILIA
Not as much as me.

They kiss.

DANTE
Let's go.

DANTE and EMILIA head upstairs to the Oratorio.

Will the sun be out today?

EMILIA
(laughing) Remember...Caterina used to ask you that every morning.

DANTE
She thought it was my trick —

EMILIA
(imitating a child) Papà make the sun shine.

DANTE
It was a good trick. Every night she'd go to sleep and when she woke up, the sun was shining.

EMILIA
And then it rained for a month.

DANTE
But she still loved me; even if I wasn't much of a magician. *(pause)* I can't make the sun shine, Emilia, but I love you; marry me, please.

EMILIA walks ahead and turns as she's about to enter the Oratorio. She looks at DANTE but does not answer him. They enter the Oratorio, PAGE 220.

SCENE L57

THE ORATORIO

TAMARA, CARLOTTA and LUISA are in the Oratorio continuing from PAGE 201. de SPIGA enters from FINZI's office, PAGE 191. d'ANNUNZIO and AÉLIS enter from PAGE 195. LUISA stops playing when d'ANNUNZIO enters.

d'ANNUNZIO
So! The angel of enchantment has descended to dance.

CARLOTTA
Now? You want me....I can....Now? You want me to dance. Oh! Comandante! *(hugs him)* Forgive me. *(embarrassed by the breach of decorum, she curtsies)* I am excited. Finally! What shall I do? Luisa, will you play for me?

LUISA
Yes.

d'ANNUNZIO
(to TAMARA) And like Orfeo, I have descended to find my Eurydice in this underworld.

de SPIGA
I gather you've yet to find her in her underwear.

d'ANNUNZIO
Shut up, Francesco! You know how I hate the sound of men's voices in the morning.

de SPIGA
(to LUISA) What is she wearing?

LUISA
Jodhpurs...very chic.

d'ANNUNZIO
(to TAMARA) Certaines femmes ont laissé une impression, une image, une trace. Vous seriez la première à laisser un portrait. [Some women have left an impression, an image, a residue; you are the first to leave a portrait.]

AÉLIS
Of course, Gabri, she's a portrait painter.

d'ANNUNZIO
Don't state the obvious, Aélis. *(to TAMARA)* Le portrait, Madame?

d'ANNUNZIO and TAMARA go to exit.

AÉLIS
Comandante, the dance.

d'ANNUNZIO
Yes, of course. La petite veut danser pour moi. [The little one wants to dance for me.]

CARLOTTA
Luisa, will you play "The Miracle" for me?

d'ANNUNZIO
Sit down, Aélis. Over there. Luisa, to your piano, and you, Francesco, find another perch.

de SPIGA sits on the tomb. d'ANNUNZIO turns to TAMARA and whispers to her in English. At several points in the following brief speech, LUISA interjects "Dites non."

d'ANNUNZIO
Perhaps you were right to keep me waiting.

LUISA
Dites non.

d'ANNUNZIO
There is a point when waiting is the yeast of love...

LUISA
Dites non.

d'ANNUNZIO
...but there is another, no less discernable...

LUISA
Dites non.

d'ANNUNZIO
...when waiting can become a stale, flaccid hell.

d'ANNUNZIO walks over to LUISA and grabs her by the hand.

(whispering) I'll break it if you don't desist! *(turning to CARLOTTA)* Ready, Carlotta? *(goes and stands next to TAMARA)*

CARLOTTA
(doing a last-minute exercise) Si, Comandante!

d'ANNUNZIO
Luisa, back to your piano.

LUISA plays two bars, fast, of "Soeur Anjelico" by Puccini (adapted by Schallert).

CARLOTTA
Wait, Luisa.

LUISA
(stops playing) I can't play it! *(gets up)* Francesco, play.

CARLOTTA
Luisa, you promised.

LUISA
I can't.

d'ANNUNZIO
Luisa, don't make us endure Francesco's thumping.

de SPIGA
(tenderly) Go sit down, Luisa; I'll do the cruel deed.

CARLOTTA
But you promised.

LUISA
Why is it that only artists are expected to keep promises? Francesco, play.

de SPIGA goes to the piano.

AÉLIS
Shall we begin?

CARLOTTA
Grazie, Signore. Grazie. This is the story of the miracle of St. Catherine of Siena.

de SPIGA sits down at the piano and begins to play. At this point, approximately, FINZI and MARIO have entered from PAGE 207. Upon seeing FINZI enter, he stops playing and sings an upbeat version of the Fascist song "Giovinezza, Giovinezza!"

All laugh except AÉLIS and CARLOTTA.

Signor de Spiga, this is very important to me. You receive many commissions, have important friends....

AÉLIS
Comandante! Please. Do something!

de SPIGA
I'm sorry, dear Carlotta. I was overwhelmed by the sight of the black shirt.

(If FINZI has not arrived by this point, de SPIGA will say:) "Carlotta, I keep forgetting that not all cultural events have to begin with that anthem."

By this time, LUISA has gone over to the cognac and poured herself a drink. Looking at TAMARA, she dramatically rips her own necklace off and drops it in her drink. She then crosses over to near the end of the piano, taking her drink with her. TAMARA has noticed all of this.

d'ANNUNZIO
Une plaisanterie personnelle. [A private joke.]

CARLOTTA
Thank you. The miracle of St. Catherine of Siena.

Finally CARLOTTA begins to dance to de SPIGA's piano solo of "The Miracle." Approximately ten measures into the dance, TAMARA will abruptly rise and run out of the Oratorio and into the Dining Room. d'ANNUNZIO will follow. PAGE 222 will begin.

CARLOTTA's dance is one of almost virginal naivety, which is played straight for a resoundingly comic effect. Throughout the dance LUISA continues to drink.

As the dance ends, EMILIA and DANTE enter from the Kitchen, PAGE 216. The scene continues on PAGE 225.

SECTION M

SCENE M58   TAMARA and d'ANNUNZIO in the Dining Room.
PAGE 222

SCENE M59   TAMARA has a brief monologue in the hall.
PAGE 223

The rest of the characters (LUISA, FINZI, MARIO, AÉLIS, de SPIGA) are in the Oratorio watching CARLOTTA dance, except DANTE and EMILIA who will enter sometime during the dance.

SCENE M58

THE DINING ROOM

TAMARA has walked out on CARLOTTA's dance, PAGE 220, the Oratorio.
d'ANNUNZIO has followed.

d'ANNUNZIO
What is it? What's wrong? Her dance?

TAMARA
I can't stand the way you torment Luisa.

d'ANNUNZIO
She torments herself. Believe me, it has nothing to do with us.

TAMARA
She gave up her art to be with you and now that you've used her up you keep
her here in this...this museum.

d'ANNUNZIO
I use her? Isn't that what you're doing to me? You came here to paint the
portrait of a great man, hoping to find your fame in the shadow of my own.

TAMARA
I admit...no. That's not the real reason. I was honestly hoping to find in you
someone who shared my....I don't want to say philosophy — someone who
feels, who understands what I try to paint. Who —

d'ANNUNZIO
Let's not undertake a philosophy of art. For me it is enough to say: the history
of culture can be summed up in a word — Yessss! I love that word.

TAMARA
No. Man has gotten to where he is because he has said no. Civilization is
standing up and saying no to the darkness.

d'ANNUNZIO
(pressing TAMARA against the Dining Room door) Yes. Let's quit these dark
halls. Let me take you to bed where we can bask in each other's light.

TAMARA
(tired of his insistence) No. Haven't you heard a word I've said?

d'ANNUNZIO
If you didn't want me you would have left last night. So what is the real
reason? Are you afraid of getting pregnant? Don't laugh. In Africa, I learned
the secret of the pygmies: orgasm without ejaculation. I feed my life fluids into
my work. Open my books, they smell of blood and sperm.

TAMARA
(pushing him away) I wouldn't want to get syphilis.

She exits to the hallway, PAGE 223.

d'ANNUNZIO
Syphilis! You dare speak to me of syphilis!

d'ANNUNZIO begins to rave; PAGE 225, the Dining Room, begins.

SCENE M59

TAMARA alone in the hallway.

TAMARA
Are we all so vain? I hurt his pride — but what of mine? Can't he understand
that I can't crawl into a bed that's still warm — I don't care if they haven't
been together for years — I can't find pleasure knowing she's suffering and
now I'm suffering and he's suffering and on and on. I feel like I'm trapped in
an Italian opera.

She re-enters the Oratorio just as CARLOTTA's dance ends, PAGE 225.

SECTION N

THE FOLLOWING SCENES HAPPEN SIMULTANEOUSLY:

SCENE N60   d'ANNUNZIO is alone in the Dining Room.
PAGE 225

SCENE N61   Group scene in the Oratorio.
PAGE 225

SCENE N62   AÉLIS and d'ANNUNZIO in the Dining Room.
PAGE 231

SCENE N60

THE DINING ROOM

*d'ANNUNZIO is left alone in the Dining Room after TAMARA exits. d'AN-
NUNZIO is from PAGE 223.*

d'ANNUNZIO
Syphilis — to Gabriele d'Annunzio! I, who with word and deed cleansed the
phallus which is Italia of all the rot and provincialism which has infected it for
five hundred years. I, who held Italia in my hands and spent its semen, its
youth, my semen, my youth on propagating a new order, erecting a new Italia
pure and proud, pulsating with the forgotten passion of empire. I, who made
Europe fall to her knees at the sight of such an awesome member throbbing
with such singular intention and strength. She dares to suggest to me, whose
progeny is a nation, that I am infected! Aélis! *(pause)* Does she think me some
Moslem sheik weaned on harem girls? I who stand as the paragon of discern-
ing seducer, who brought Dionysius to the drawing room and bed chambers of
the most distinguished women in Europe. Aélis! Aélis!

AÉLIS enters from the Oratorio, and the scene continues, PAGE 231.

SCENE N61

THE ORATORIO

*CARLOTTA's dance ends as TAMARA re-enters the room. Everyone applauds.
CARLOTTA does not acknowledge the applause. TAMARA has come from
PAGE 223, the hallway.*

AÉLIS
Wonderful, Carlotta! I had no idea. You're better than Rubenstein.

TAMARA
Monsieur d'Annunzio a un mal de tête affreux. [Mr. d'Annunzio has a headache.]

AÉLIS

A headache? But he never gets — Je verrai ce que je peux faire. [I'll see what I can do.] Merci, madame.

CARLOTTA

You said he'd watch — how will I ever get my recommendation to Diaghilev?

AÉLIS

You'll get it, Carlotta, but first I must attend to Il Comandante's headache.

CARLOTTA

I can cure it!

de SPIGA

Not only does she dance, she does miracles.

AÉLIS

Don't you want to put on your new dress? We're lunching at the Grand Hotel in Gardone. Be ready in five minutes.

AÉLIS exits to d'ANNUNZIO in the Dining Room, PAGE 231.

CARLOTTA

Are you lunching with us, Capitano?

FINZI

I'm afraid I have a report to send.

CARLOTTA

I was hoping to hear what you thought of my dance.

LUISA

I'm surprised you care about Finzi's opinion, Carlotta.

CARLOTTA

I value the opinions of friends more than strangers.

LUISA

But according to you he is a stranger, or a foreigner.

FINZI

Why are you drinking, Luisa?

No response.

CARLOTTA
I never said anything but kind things about —

LUISA
He's a Jew, Carlotta. Didn't you tell me that all Jews were foreigners? —

deSPIGA
Is this necessary? Come and sit down, Luisa....

LUISA doesn't move.

FINZI
You should get changed, Signorina.

LUISA
(quietly) Tell her. Tell her or I'll scream.

FINZI
I've never denied it. Have I, Dante?

He looks to DANTE, who has been watching the scene. DANTE does not respond.

I am a Jew.

CARLOTTA
(quietly to FINZI) We kissed...why, why did you lead me on?

LUISA
What leads you on is hate.

FINZI
Luisa, please.

LUISA
I was the same way, Carlotta...but there's still time for you to change. Change, Carlotta.

CARLOTTA
(quietly) I should get ready for lunch.

CARLOTTA exits to a room off the hall for a quick change and returns just before AÉLIS and d'ANNUNZIO re-enter, PAGE 235.

The remainder of SCENE N61 is a triplet scene. MARIO, EMILIA and DANTE are together near the tomb, PAGE 228, below. LUISA goes to pick up her cognac, pursued by FINZI, PAGE 229. de SPIGA turns to talk to TAMARA, PAGE 230. All scenes play simultaneously.

1 — DANTE, EMILIA AND MARIO.

EMILIA
(to DANTE) Your buttons.

DANTE looks, to find his fly open.

(whispering) How can you be so calm?

MARIO does not respond.

(to MARIO) Finzi knows more than you think.

MARIO
What?

EMILIA
You'd better go now.

MARIO
You betrayed me.

DANTE
Keep your mouth shut.

MARIO
I'll talk to Il Comandante and go, tonight.

EMILIA
You lied to me!

DANTE
(loudly) Of course I lied! I didn't want you to make a fuss about my birthday.

EMILIA
You're taking him to England.

DANTE
(loudly) A shirt from England!

MARIO
We paid you —

DANTE
You paid too much!

LUISA
(across the room) Dante, if you must yell, do so in your own quarters.

DANTE
Si, Signora Baccara.

EMILIA
What about me? I'll end up in jail.

MARIO
(to EMILIA) Do as you're told and we'll all live.

DANTE
(whispering) I'll turn you both in if you don't stop.

*d'ANNUNZIO and AÉLIS enter from PAGE 233, the Dining Room. The group
scene continues, PAGE 235.*

2 — LUISA AND FINZI

*LUISA and FINZI talk, unheard by the others. This happens simultaneously
with the above scene.*

FINZI
Luisa, what is it, I've never seen you like this.

LUISA
(drinking heavily) We're all so terribly polite. Il Duce talks about chaos but it
won't be chaos that kills us...we'll die over tea, Aldo. We'll say yes signora
just a little milk and sugar and a bullet in my brain.

FINZI
What are you talking about?

LUISA

Carlotta chatters on about Jews and foreigners as if she was talking abut the weather. No one sees it. Not even Tamara. She thinks she's free, but already Gabri has drawn her into his web....Why can't I go...I just want to go.

FINZI

Luisa, I'm on to something. Something which will clip Gabri's wings and make me colonello. We'll go to Roma together, Luisa. You and me.

LUISA

Together? Between you, Gabri and Francesco, I'll go mad. I just want to go...alone....I hate this house! These hands!

FINZI
Calm down, Luisa.

d'ANNUNZIO and AÉLIS enter from PAGE 225, the Dining Room. The group scene continues, PAGE 235.

3 — de SPIGA AND TAMARA.

TAMARA
Is Luisa all right?

de SPIGA
A slight "contretemps." Now, tell me about the portrait; have you decided on a pose?

TAMARA
No.

de SPIGA
I'm sure, in time....

TAMARA
Unfortunately, I must be in Nice next week—

de SPIGA
Nice?

TAMARA
Yes. There's a possibility of a commission, no one so grand as a poet; a doctor, I think. One must work.

de SPIGA
Talk to me before you go; I have friends there. The Duke of Milano, for one.

TAMARA
Visconti?

de SPIGA
You know him?

TAMARA
I painted his wife.

de SPIGA
And the rest of the family?

TAMARA
Non, non, she was staying in Zurich with friends, I never met the others.

de SPIGA
Ah...you know what you might do is to ask Gabri if Mario could drive you to Nice for a few days, to see this doctor, and then you could return.

TAMARA
I can only think of one portrait at a time, monsieur.

de SPIGA
I see.

d'ANNUNZIO and AÉLIS enter from PAGE 233, the Dining Room. The group scene continues, PAGE 235.

SCENE N62

THE DINING ROOM

d'ANNUNZIO is alone in the Dining Room. Enter AÉLIS, from the Oratorio. d'ANNUNZIO is from PAGE 225 and AÉLIS is from PAGE 226.

d'ANNUNZIO
Do you know what she said?

AÉLIS
It was cruel of you to walk out on Carlotta.

d'ANNUNZIO
I can't believe it. No one —

AÉLIS
You said you'd watch her! You broke her heart, Gabri.

d'ANNUNZIO
Aélis, are you listening to me?

AÉLIS
I'm listening. I'm listening.

d'ANNUNZIO
She had the nerve to say to me, Gabriele d'Annunzio, that she is afraid of getting syphilis! I, who've had my choice of every titled woman in Europe!

AÉLIS
She said that to you?

d'ANNUNZIO
Did Rubenstein say it? Or Duse....

AÉLIS
No one, no one, Gabri.

d'ANNUNZIO
Or Bernhardt, Nike, Isadora Duncan? Emma Visconti?

AÉLIS
No one, Gabri.

d'ANNUNZIO
And the words, Aélis. You should have heard the beautiful words...the gifts—

AÉLIS
You've spent 150,000 lire on her already. The woman's a professional.

d'ANNUNZIO
No, she's, she's...more than that!

AÉLIS
She's perverse!

d'ANNUNZIO
(happy with the word) Perverse. I must go tell her. Perverse.

AÉLIS
You'll do nothing of the kind. You'll go back to the Oratorio and tell Carlotta she was marvelous.

d'ANNUNZIO
Marvelous? The girl is hopeless.

AÉLIS
I don't care, Gabri. Tamara said you had a headache, and instead of saying she hoped it kills you, Carlotta begged me to let her come and massage you. Now come and tell her she was wonderful, so we can get to Gardone in time for lunch.

d'ANNUNZIO
What am I going to do about de Lempicka?

AÉLIS
Whatever you do, Gabri, please do it soon. I'm tired of having the whole house hang by her pubic hair. *(pause)* Now, if you make Carlotta happy...let me emphasize the word if.... *(goes to a vase with a rose, takes it out and hands the rose to d'ANNUNZIO)* I'll get a letter from Dottore Barzini saying that you are clean.

d'ANNUNZIO
Aélis, you're wonderful.

AÉLIS
Say it to Carlotta. Come.

They exit and head for the Oratorio, PAGE 235.

SECTION O

THE FOLLOWING SCENES HAPPEN SIMULTANEOUSLY:

SCENE O63   AÉLIS and d'ANNUNZIO enter the Oratorio. All are
PAGE 235   present.

SCENE O64   MARIO, de SPIGA, FINZI, LUISA and TAMARA prepare
PAGE 236   to leave for Gardone.

SCENE O65   d'ANNUNZIO and DANTE, alone briefly in the Oratorio.
PAGE 239

SCENE O66   AÉLIS and CARLOTTA exit to the automobile. They join
PAGE 241   LUISA, de SPIGA, then TAMARA. The five drive to Gar-
                 done.

SCENE O67   MARIO returns from the automobile in time to see
PAGE 242   TAMARA give EMILIA a note.

SCENE 063

THE ORATORIO

Enter d'ANNUNZIO, carrying a flower for CARLOTTA. He is accompanied by
AÉLIS. They are from PAGE 233, the Dining Room. TAMARA, CARLOTTA,
MARIO, DANTE, EMILIA, LUISA, FINZI and de SPIGA are from PAGE 231,
the Oratorio.

d'ANNUNZIO
Who has a headache? The pain is in the world, not me.

CARLOTTA
Comandante, you're better?

AÉLIS
Emilia, get our wraps. Mario, the automobile.

MARIO exits to the automobile and PAGE 237. EMILIA exits to the Side Hall
and helps with the coats and hats as the various individuals exit the Oratorio,
PAGE 236. FINZI also follows MARIO out to PAGE 237.

d'ANNUNZIO
It was nothing. I was so overcome with the beauty of your dance, that's all.

CARLOTTA
Will you recommend me?

d'ANNUNZIO
If I can find the right words—

de SPIGA
If I can find the right music....

CARLOTTA
Grazie, Comandante. My papà will be so proud.

d'ANNUNZIO
(giving CARLOTTA the flower and paying no attention to TAMARA) My letter
of recommendation to you....I should pin this on you. But where?

d'ANNUNZIO goes to put the flower in her cleavage but AÉLIS intervenes.

AÉLIS
(taking the flower) Allow me, Comandante. *(pins the flower on CARLOTTA)*
We should be off.

AÉLIS and CARLOTTA exit to the Side Hall, PAGE 241.

LUISA
Yes, let's go.

LUISA exits and TAMARA follows behind her to PAGE 236 (this page).

d'ANNUNZIO
Francesco, what's bothering the Barracuda? She never drinks.

de SPIGA
...surprised you noticed.

d'ANNUNZIO
Francesco, I invited you here to get Luisa interested in music again, not to turn
her into an alcoholic.

de SPIGA
Then let me take her away from here, away from you.

d'ANNUNZIO
Never. Just take her to lunch. I want her sober when she returns. And Francesco, have your pharmacist prepare another package for me. *(gestures the
snorting of cocaine.)*

*de SPIGA exits to PAGE 237. d'ANNUNZIO remains behind with DANTE,
PAGE 239.*

SCENE 064

THE FRONT DOOR

*EMILIA helps LUISA put on her coat. TAMARA puts on her own and stands to
the side.*

EMILIA
It's much too early to be drinking, Signora Bacarra.

LUISA
It's much too late.

Enter de SPIGA from the Oratorio, PAGE 236.

de SPIGA
There'll be plenty to drink at the restaurant, Luisa. You don't have to bring
your own. *(takes the glass and puts it on a sidetable)*

LUISA
I want to go to the airfield....Francesco, let's take Tamara to the airfield. We'll
fly away.

de SPIGA
I doubt an airplane could get you any higher.

Enter MARIO from outside. He is from PAGE 235.

Mario, isn't it?

MARIO
Si, Signore.

de SPIGA
(taking the keys) I'll drive today.

MARIO
I should show you how to work the clutch; it's sticking.

*They exit to the automobile as FINZI enters from outside. He is from PAGE
235.*

LUISA
(taking a drink from her cognac on the sidetable) Aldo, I want my gun back.

FINZI
No, you —

LUISA
I won't go without it.

FINZI
(takes out a small revolver and hands it to her) All right. Now put it in your purse. And put down that drink.

LUISA
Bang, bang. *(exits to the automobile, helped by FINZI)*

TAMARA is just finishing a note to d'ANNUNZIO, with a piece of charcoal. The note reads:

"...Allons, mon frère. Cédons à nos bons instincts et embrassons-nous, puisque nous souffrons, tous les deux, pitoyables....Tamara." [Come, brother, a good impulse, let's embrace, since we both suffer....Tamara.]

TAMARA
(handing note to EMILIA as MARIO enters from the automobile) Pour Monsieur d'Annunzio. [For Mr. d'Annunzio.]

EMILIA
What?

TAMARA
Pour Monsieur d'Annunzio. [For Mr. d'Annunzio.]

EMILIA
Ah....Si, Signora. *(takes the note)*

TAMARA
Merci...Grazie. [Thank you.]

de SPIGA, AÉLIS, CARLOTTA, LUISA and TAMARA drive off to Gardone. AÉLIS and CARLOTTA reappear on PAGE 268, the Atrium. The others return on PAGE 270, the Atrium.
FINZI will wait outside and watch LUISA drive off with the others. He will then usher the audience back inside and close the doors behind him. MARIO approaches EMILIA on PAGE 242, the Atrium. FINZI sees MARIO talking to EMILIA, and as MARIO exits to the Oratorio, he calls out to EMILIA, PAGE 253.

SCENE 065

THE ORATORIO

d'ANNUNZIO and DANTE are talking.

d'ANNUNZIO
Dante.

DANTE
Si, Comandante.

d'ANNUNZIO
You didn't wake me this morning.

DANTE
I was…Mario and I were trying to decrease the amount of vodka in the world.

d'ANNUNZIO
You two were drunk last night?

DANTE
It's the best way to see Venezia.

d'ANNUNZIO
Tell me about Mario.

DANTE
Comandante?

d'ANNUNZIO
People don't fool you, Dante. I know you have the misfortune to see reality as it is. So, tell me who Mario really is.

DANTE
That he didn't reveal, but he seems anxious to talk to you.

d'ANNUNZIO
Only talk?

DANTE
He means no harm, Comandante. I ask you, per favore, please listen to him, and let him go…for Emilia's sake.

d'ANNUNZIO
Emilia?

DANTE
Si.

d'ANNUNZIO
Why this deception about their being cousins? Why would she help?

DANTE
Money. Perhaps if you'd paid her wages for the last five months this wouldn't have happened.

d'ANNUNZIO
But we are famiglia.

DANTE
I understand, Comandante, but you know how Emilia is, she likes to shop, buy dresses, wants to look like Signora de Lempicka.

d'ANNUNZIO
She's a peacock in heat.

DANTE
Bella.

DANTE makes a sexual gesture, indicating her curvatures. d'ANNUNZIO slaps his face in a friendly manner.

d'ANNUNZIO
Eh! Enough. Now, be off to your canals...and Dante, clean my room.

DANTE exits and goes to PAGE 257, D'ANNUNZIO's room.

MARIO will enter from PAGE 238, the Atrium. PAGE 245, the Oratorio, begins with d'ANNUNZIO.

SCENE 066

THE HALL

AÉLIS and CARLOTTA on the way to the automobile. They are from PAGE 236, the Oratorio.

AÉLIS
Wasn't that a wonderful gesture of Il Comandante to give you that flower?

CARLOTTA
Aélis, do you think you could get Il Comandante to write down his recommendation?

AÉLIS
As soon as we get back. And then —

CARLOTTA
I just want to go home.

AÉLIS
What is it, Carlotta? I thought you'd be happy to have your recommendation.

CARLOTTA
It's what father wants.

AÉLIS
And you?

CARLOTTA
Capitano Finzi is a Jew, Aélis. Did you know that?

AÉLIS
Of course. What has that to do with...did he say something to upset you? I'll speak to Il Comandante if—

CARLOTTA
No. It's...what we were talking about last night.

AÉLIS
Passion? Love? Is that what you're talking about?

CARLOTTA
I'm talking about....God, I don't know what I'm talking about. Everything's so confused. St. Catherine, help me. *(runs out to the automobile)*

AÉLIS
Oh, God. There are so many nuns in this country, can I not have just one? *(exits to the automobile)*

AÉLIS and CARLOTTA drive off with TAMARA, LUISA and de SPIGA to Gardone. CARLOTTA and AÉLIS return on PAGE 268.

SCENE O67

THE ATRIUM

MARIO and EMILIA are from PAGE 238, the front door.

MARIO
(calling and then running to EMILIA) Emilia! Emilia!

EMILIA has by this time moved in to the Atrium.

You have a note from Madame de Lempicka. I saw her give it to you.

EMILIA hesitates.

Give it to me.

EMILIA
No.

MARIO
Emilia, I lied to you to protect you. Please. This is my chance, and then I'll go.

EMILIA
Take me with you.

MARIO
I can't.

EMILIA
Finzi forced me to tell him about Defelice.

MARIO
Christ—

EMILIA
(frightened) We're all going to be arrested —

MARIO
No. I'll take you with me. But you'll have to trust me if we're going to get out.

EMILIA
Anything you say.

She hands him the note.

MARIO
Take care of Finzi. Just give me five minutes with d'Annunzio.

He kisses EMILIA, puts the note in his pants' pocket and goes to the Oratorio, PAGE 245. As MARIO enters the Oratorio, FINZI will call out to EMILIA, PAGE 253.

SECTION P

THE FOLLOWING SCENES HAPPEN SIMULTANEOUSLY:

SCENE P68   MARIO and d'ANNUNZIO are in the Oratorio. This scene
PAGE 245   defines the length of time of this section.

SCENE P69   FINZI and EMILIA in the Atrium, and then in the servants'
PAGE 253   hallway.

SCENE P70   DANTE is alone in d'ANNUNZIO's room.
PAGE 257

SCENE P71   FINZI is in the Atrium and DANTE is above on the stairs.
PAGE 258

SCENE P72   EMILIA searches MARIO's room.
PAGE 260

SCENE P73   FINZI enters MARIO's room.
PAGE 261

SCENE P74   FINZI makes a brief phonecall in his office.
PAGE 262

SCENE P75   DANTE enters to find EMILIA in MARIO's room just after
PAGE 263   FINZI exits to the Side Hall.

SCENE P76   MARIO leaves the Oratorio where he encounters FINZI in
PAGE 265   the Side Hall. Upon hearing their argument, d'ANNUNZIO
                   calls after FINZI.

SCENE P68

THE ORATORIO

MARIO enters the Oratorio, from PAGE 243, the Atrium, and comes to attention at the bottom of the north aisle.

MARIO
(loudly) Comandante!

d'ANNUNZIO, who is from PAGE 240, the Oratorio, is examining some of his books on one of the pedestals.

d'ANNUNZIO
Quiet!

d'ANNUNZIO motions for MARIO to come to attention and to face away from him. MARIO does and then remains quiet for a few moments.

I thought he would go back to work.

MARIO
What are you talking about, Comandante?

d'ANNUNZIO
There's a worm in my house. Spying on me. I sit down and put pen to paper, and he's there.

MARIO
Finzi?

d'ANNUNZIO
No. *(laughing)* A bookworm. *(slowly crosses to a pedestal with a book in a large jar)*

MARIO follows.

He's gone through my Catullus, Sextus Propertius, Ovid...thought Petrarch would stop him, stopped me. The man's a mortician...went right through him! I thought I could confine him to the study, now he's out here too. *(crossing to another pedestal)* But he won't get my Machiavelli. Hermetically sealed...a first edition of *Il Principe,* published by Antonio Blado, Roma, 1532.

MARIO
(following d'ANNUNZIO) It's safe in the jar?

d'ANNUNZIO
You think not?

MARIO
What if the worm is inside?

d'ANNUNZIO
In the jar? You don't know Machiavelli.

MARIO
A book is to be read, yes?

d'ANNUNZIO
Mine are lived.

MARIO
Then what I ask is this: what good is a book in a jar?

d'ANNUNZIO
It's a first edition.

MARIO
There is only one?

d'ANNUNZIO
Thirty-seven.

MARIO
If I was in the jar, I die, yes?

d'ANNUNZIO
Morto.

MARIO
I think this house...is a big jar.

d'ANNUNZIO
So is the world.

MARIO
You're lucky you only have bookworms to worry about. I had a capitano in the

war, a writer. Once Austrian guns pounded us for twelve hours. He could think of nothing else, so he wrote about the guns; their guns stopped.

d'ANNUNZIO
(still wandering about the room, he stops at another pedestal and picks up a book) d'Annunzio does not write about worms!

MARIO
(following d'ANNUNZIO) If you are against something—

d'ANNUNZIO
I denounce it.

MARIO
At any price?

d'ANNUNZIO
I am an Italian.

MARIO
I'm just a chauffeur.

d'ANNUNZIO
Just a chauffeur? Mario. *(putting his arm around MARIO and guiding him to the front of the tomb)* Do you know why I have the *Puglia* moored behind the villa?

MARIO
It was one of the boats used for your raid on Split.

d'ANNUNZIO
The capitano of the *Puglia* was my friend. Tommaso Gulli. He was wounded on the raid. At the hospital he asked to look at his wounds. When the doctor told him he would bleed to death if the bandages were removed, he resolutely ripped them off. Let this action be an example to you, Mario, an example to all Italia, to uncover the wounds and face them without flinching.

MARIO
Did he survive?

d'ANNUNZIO
He was not afraid to die.

MARIO
He's dead.

d'ANNUNZIO
(angered) Yes. Yes, you fool, he's dead. One of the lucky ones.

MARIO
But you have other friends, Comandante. Your picture is always taken with Il Duce. Il Duce likes you. He quotes your poems.

d'ANNUNZIO
My friends are dead.

MARIO
Are you willing to uncover the wounds?

d'ANNUNZIO
(does not respond; he opens a book he is carrying; there is a gun inside it which he draws and points at MARIO) I am too tired to continue leaping about in metaphors as if they were rocks in a brook. What do you want?

MARIO
Comandante, Madame de Lempicka asked me to give you a note.

d'ANNUNZIO
You are a Communist. You are not a chauffeur. You are not here to kill me. So I ask again, what do you want?

MARIO
My name is Mario Visconti and I want your help.

d'ANNUNZIO
Your father is the Duke of Milano.

MARIO
Yes.

d'ANNUNZIO
And your mother is Emma.

MARIO
I'm sure you know each other quite well, but I'm running out of time. Finzi knows.

d'ANNUNZIO

She is very beautiful, Emma. Yes. Yes. I can see the resemblance. The eyes. *(sits on the tomb and places the gun down beside him)* Marchese Mario Visconti. So, what would you have me do?

MARIO

The people who sent me want you to leave Italia.

d'ANNUNZIO

Why?

MARIO

(sitting next to d'ANNUNZIO) You have a voice. They want you to go to England. Your friend is the Duke of Connaught. He's in the House of Lords; he has influence with the Cabinet. Together we can help stop the British loans which float Mussolini's regime.

d'ANNUNZIO

Your mother is English; you know these people. Why do you need me?

MARIO

They don't talk to Communists.

d'ANNUNZIO

So you are a Communist.

MARIO

Are you willing to join our fight?

d'ANNUNZIO

For freedom, no doubt. *(rising and walking slowly around the tomb)* I tell you this, Mario, freedom is a very overrated vice.

MARIO

In Italia it is an underrated virtue.

d'ANNUNZIO

(crossing to MARIO) And when would our freedom crusade begin?

MARIO

(rising) Tonight.

d'ANNUNZIO

Impossible.

MARIO
Tonight.

d'ANNUNZIO
People are always asking me to lead the way. Every year, a new cause, a new movement. This is my home, young Mario. My house of glass. The air is clean.

MARIO
Why does it make me sick?

d'ANNUNZIO
(grabbing MARIO by the shoulder, angrily) Why must every son mount the cross! I despise you young men.

MARIO
(backing away) I'd meant to take my time, to draw you out slowly, but there is no time. Finzi is filing his report. Since you hired me, it might be assumed that you are working with the Left once again.

d'ANNUNZIO
(sitting on the tomb) I do not involve myself in politics.

MARIO
Finzi might convince them otherwise.

d'ANNUNZIO
I am quite capable of dealing with Roma.

MARIO
That's why the Fascist Finzi's in the hall?

d'ANNUNZIO
A man of my importance needs protection.

MARIO
From whom? From whom? Remember August 13, 1922? Four months before Mussolini seized power you were about to begin your own march on Roma, but some Fascist pushed you off a balcony!—

d'ANNUNZIO
I fell! I lost my balance.

MARIO
Or was it your courage?

d'ANNUNZIO
I've given enough! I can't give anymore!

MARIO
You have given nothing. You "artistes" keep crying you can't give anymore. Qu'est-ce que vous avez donné? C'est du faux! C'est de la merde! You inspired a nation with words, filled it with thoughts of grandeur and mythic glory. "Make Italia strong!" you shout. And you feed us on an exotic diet of old Roma, new ports, and trains that run on time. Yet Italia is starving. For you have given nothing! Your words hypnotize, but they don't feed. What you've written Italia will forget.

d'ANNUNZIO
I have the power to have you shot.

MARIO
(angrily) You have nothing but what the Fascists give you!

d'ANNUNZIO
I have this gun.

MARIO
Yoo. And you can take my life, if you want. But you cannot take my conscience. It's time to make a choice. A choice must be made. Say yes....Look, four weeks ago, Antonio Gramsci —

d'ANNUNZIO
Another Communist!

MARIO
...a freely elected member of Parliament, was arrested. My friend. Every day freedoms are curtailed. The only laws passed are those which restrict liberty. You know these things. This is not the new Italia you dreamed of. Because I was there on the thirteenth of May, the day before we entered the war. You spoke from the balcony of the Capital. You decried the government. You called them "Clowns rigged out in tri-colour shirts, whose turds defile the sacred soil of Italia." Isn't that what Mussolini is...a clown?...I'm preaching to you. I wasn't sent here to. I leave tonight. I must have your answer.

d'ANNUNZIO
Do you think the British would listen to me?

MARIO
Yes!

d'ANNUNZIO
After all the insulting things I said about Lloyd George?

MARIO
Baldwin's in power now.

d'ANNUNZIO
True. Eleonora Duse sent me a telegram just before the war, urging me to abandon art for politics. It said simply, "You must change your wings." I miss flying, Mario. I was planning a trip to Japan, but I think England would be a better destination.

MARIO
(pulling out the note from his pants' pocket) I was to give you this note, from Madame de Lempicka.

d'ANNUNZIO
Read it.

MARIO
(translating the note) "Come, brother, a good impulse, let us embrace, since we both suffer "—

d'ANNUNZIO
...for Italia! *(embracing MARIO)* Until tonight, young Mario.

MARIO
Comandante.

MARIO salutes as he exits to his room. As he leaves the Oratorio, MARIO encounters FINZI, PAGE 265. d'ANNUNZIO, upon hearing their argument, calls after FINZI, PAGE 265.

SCENE P69

THE ATRIUM and THE SERVANTS' HALL

FINZI and EMILIA, alone in the Atrium. As EMILIA slowly crosses to FINZI, she picks up a basket of oranges and playfully tosses one in the air. FINZI is from PAGE 238, the automobile. EMILIA is from PAGE 243, the Atrium.

FINZI
What were you and Mario talking about?

EMILIA
Dante's asked me to marry him again.

EMILIA and FINZI kiss. EMILIA slides her hand down FINZI's crotch. EMILIA giggles and heads downstairs. FINZI catches up to her at the base of the stairs. They embrace again. Suddenly FINZI slams his fist into EMILIA's stomach. She falls to the floor.

FINZI
Emilia, what did you say to Mario? Unlike your Comandante, I don't cringe when it comes to striking women.

EMILIA
Only men frighten you.

FINZI
Now, what did you tell Mario?

EMILIA
I told him to leave.

FINZI
Do you want to ruin me? He can't leave! He's the biggest thing that's ever happened to me. Roma! Does your brain understand what I'm saying? Roma.

EMILIA
(sitting up) Roma. Venezia. I don't care about you men and your cities!

FINZI
Roma isn't a city, it's my future!

EMILIA
If Mario stays, I won't have a future.

FINZI
You don't have a choice, Emilia. I'm your future. Whether he stays or goes has nothing to do with it. You brought him in. I'll take him out...when I'm ready. What happens to you? That depends....

EMILIA
And Aélis, Baccara...are you going to make us starve in the street to pay your fare to Roma?

FINZI
I've asked Luisa to come with me.

EMILIA
You can't afford to have her piano tuned.

FINZI
(pointing at the oranges on the floor) Clean it up! Did Mussolini have money? Power begets money. d'Annunzio has his money, but no power. She will come.

EMILIA
(picking up oranges which are scattered about the room) He has power here.

FINZI
Here. In the garden.

EMILIA
And Aélis?

FINZI
She will be deported back to France.

EMILIA
And....

FINZI
You, Emilia? If you go free, settle down with Dante. It's what he wants, the best you could hope for.

EMILIA
(standing) I don't need Dante.

FINZI
(shoving her against the wall) What does he know?

EMILIA
Nothing.

FINZI
I think, more than you.

EMILIA
You're wrong.

FINZI
They were drunk last night.

EMILIA
Dante's drunk every night.

FINZI
I walked in on them. Conspirators. I'm sure of it. I'll get him later.

EMILIA
(caressing FINZI) He doesn't know. Leave him out, Aldo. He thinks Mario's my lover. We fought about him this morning.

FINZI
(shoving her once again against the wall) Your lies are as weak as Il Comandante's knees.

EMILIA
If you question Dante, he'll go to d'Annunzio.

FINZI
(picking up an orange and peeling it) I can handle him. How long will he take to clean Il Comandante's room?

EMILIA
Why? *(pause)* I don't know.

FINZI
You're too stupid to be coy. How long?

EMILIA
Ten minutes, I don't know.

FINZI
I want you to search Mario's room.

EMILIA
What if Mario walks in?

FINZI
I'll be waiting for him. *(tossing orange peel at her)* Go.

EMILIA
He'll be back in a minute.

FINZI
I can have you arrested in less than that. *(tosses more orange peel at her)* Go.

EMILIA
What am I looking for?

FINZI
(tosses third orange peel at her) Go!

EMILIA
Where should I look?

FINZI
You're the thief.

EMILIA
I wouldn't hide anything of value in my room.

FINZI
(throws the entire orange at her) Go!

EMILIA runs into MARIO's room, PAGE 260, and FINZI, after picking up another orange, heads upstairs to his office. While crossing the Atrium, he sees DANTE sitting on the stairs, PAGE 258.

SCENE P70

d'ANNUNZIO'S ROOM

THE STAIRS OVERLOOKING THE ATRIUM

DANTE on the way up the stairs to d'ANNUNZIO's room sees EMILIA and FINZI kissing.

DANTE
(to himself) When she kisses him I know she's thinking how much she hates him. And he kisses her as if he was beating her — and me — I do nothing because I love her. How did the world get turned upside down?

DANTE enters d'ANNUNZIO's bedroom from the Oratorio and begins straightening out his desk and picking up scraps of writing paper which have been crumpled and thrown on the floor. When he puts a fountain pen away in the desk drawer, he pauses.

Il Comandante's gun is missing. *(searches the desk)* For six years I've cleaned this room, he's changed the furniture twice — the books come and go, but the gun is always loaded and in this drawer — So where is it? It was here yesterday. Why did it disappear today? Mario. Mario, he's the only one who would have taken it. Il Comandante says it's sacred and won't touch it. He says it belonged to a defeated Austrian general, but that's not the real reason he keeps it...the gun is there so that he can...how did he put it... *(lapses into an imitation of d'ANNUNZIO)* "So that I can choose the time to die...when the words no longer greet me...when the women turn their backs....on the day I no longer believe the lies you tell me about how great I am...on that day, I'll pull the trigger." *(snaps out of his imitation)* Only the rich can think of suicide. He wants to choose the time to die — how could I ever find a time when my responsibilities would end? How many times have I thought I can't go on with this pain: watching Emilia with other men, not seeing my daughter Caterina...but I'll go on, with or without them. I must. Even when there is no reason there is still God, still the memory of my father. He never gave up. When the steamboats came, he fought them for all the gondolieri. And when the Fascists came he fought them, even though he knew he'd lose, that one night they'd get him. *(pauses and goes to make the bed...sits down and hugs a pillow)* Papà, remember you used to say: "Life is the struggle, Dante. Pain...happiness come and go with the tides. What matters is that we drink from whatever cup our Lord offers us." Il Comandante refuses to drink. He lies in this soft bed and feels nothing. And Papà, I keep seeing you naked on that cold slab of marble, your body bruised and bloated from two days in the canal. Rabbi Levi sprinkled you first with hot water, then with cold — but you did not move. We wrapped you in a sheet; then put on your prayer shawl…and one by one I undid its four knots; finally you were free of your responsibilities…to God, and to all of us. But mine go on. *(brief pause)* Enough. Today I'll forget to make the bed.

DANTE exits to the stairs where he begins to sing the folksong "Tumbalalaika."

Tumbala, Tumbala, Tumbalalaika, Tumbala, Tumbala, Tumbalalaika, Tumbalalaika, Shpiel Balalaika, Tumbalalaika, Fraylach Sol Zine Shate ah Bucher, Shtate und Tracht, Tracht un Tracht ah Gonzor Nacht. Vemin Tsu Nemin une nit Fer Shemin. Vemin Tsu Nemin unc nit Fer Shemin.

[Strum balalaika, strum balalaika, play balalaika, let there be joy. Stands a student, stands and thinks, thinks and thinks, a whole night long. Whom shall I choose and not be ashamed of, whom shall I choose and not be ashamed of.]

FINZI arrives in the Atrium.

SCENE P71

THE ATRIUM

DANTE is sitting on the steps singing "Tumbalalaika," as FINZI crosses the Atrium on his way to his office from Intermezzo area.

FINZI
Behold, the romantic gondoliere. He sits on the steps above and sings to the canals of Venezia below. That would be "Tumbalalaika" that you sing, si?

DANTE
(stops singing) And where does a Fascist learn "Tumbalalaika?"

FINZI
From my Jewish mother, Dante.

DANTE
Did the Capitano's mother teach him to dance when he was a little boy?

FINZI
Sing, Dante.

FINZI starts to dance in a grapevine step with a black handkerchief in one hand and the orange in the other. He suddenly stops.

It reminds me of a long time ago. Si, I remember. The old way, Dante. But what did it get us? A few folk songs? We didn't dance our way out of the ghetto in 1848. We had to fight. If the Jews hadn't financed Garibaldi, Italia would still be just be a collection of city-states owned by the aristocrats and the church. And why did we fight? Because we had no loyalty to the aristocrats or to the church. We were the first true Italians, Dante.

DANTE
But to Signorina Barra you're still just a Jew.

FINZI
She's young. So far the church has succeeded in supressing the history of the Jews, but fascism will soon change that. We are entering a new era, Dante.

DANTE
And in this new era of the Capitano's, does he see an end to the hate which has broken our beloved country?

FINZI
Perhaps, perhaps when we have rid ourselves of the troublemakers.

DANTE
That depends on who is making troubles for whom — on which side of the fence you stand.

FINZI
And those who sit on the fence, Dante? What about them?

DANTE
It is you who sit on the fence, Capitano, half Fascist, half Jew.

FINZI rips the orange in half and throws half to DANTE. DANTE catches it and kisses it.

Grazie, Capitano.

FINZI turns to leave.

Capitano, I too have a small gift.

FINZI, cautious, reaches for his gun.

Something to remind you of the old days. *(throws FINZI a Yarmulke)*

FINZI
(near tears) Shalom Alechim, Dante.

DANTE
Alechim Shalom, Aldo.

FINZI exits to MARIO's room, PAGE 261. DANTE resumes singing. He will slowly walk to MARIO's room and PAGE 263.

SCENE P72

MARIO'S ROOM

EMILIA has been forced to search MARIO's room by FINZI, PAGE 256, Atrium area.

EMILIA
Ten minutes....Oh, Mario, that didn't work at all. Who does Finzi think he is here? I don't want to look...but I have to; forgive me, Mario....*(begins her search)* What am I looking for...socks ...pants...shirts....*(taking a shirt off the hanger)* It's ripped....I should sew it for him....Nothing but worn out clothes...and I kept saying I'd fall in love with a rich man who wore silk shirts and had a tailor in Milano, like Il Comandante. *(drops the shirt and goes over to the bed; under the pillow she finds a black stocking)* So that's where I left it...and he keeps it here under his pillow, that must mean something. *(pause)* He loves me...well, at least part of me. *(resumes searching the room)* Good. Nothing there. Mario, you're too smart for Finzi! I knew you wouldn't hide anything in your room. Bene. Nothing. *(finds a gun)* Comandante's gun! Mario, how could you be so stupid? Did you think Finzi wouldn't search; or force me to? You say "trust me." I trusted you to be smart, to get me out of here. When Finzi finds this gun I'll — No, he's not going to find it....I'll hide it...say there's nothing here. *(hides the gun behind a dresser)* Oh, Mario, I wish I could hate you, betray you and finish this....God if this is love, I hate it, I hate it.

SCENE P73

MARIO'S ROOM

FINZI enters from PAGE 260, the Atrium.

> **FINZI**
> So, did you find anything, Emilia?

> **EMILIA**
> *(trying to be calm)* No, Capitano. I looked everywhere. I finished the search and there is nothing.

FINZI starts to tear the room apart.

> **FINZI**
> *(opening trunk)* Did you look in here, Emilia? *(tosses clothes out)*

> **EMILIA**
> Si, Capitano. I looked and there is nothing. You see?

> **FINZI**
> *(going through the closet)* Here?

> **EMILIA**
> Si.

> **FINZI**
> *(ripping the pillows off a chair)* What about here?

> **EMILIA**
> Si, Capitano. I looked everywhere.

> **FINZI**
> Did you look in Mario's bed, Emilia?

> **EMILIA**
> Capitano, please leave his bed alone. I already looked and there's nothing.

FINZI tears up the bed, one cover at a time.

FINZI

Did you look under the pillow? *(throws it in her face)* Did you look under the mattress, Emilia?

FINZI throws the mattress onto the floor and on the box spring he finds a huge cache of 1,000-lire notes, amounting to about 130,000 lire.

EMILIA

I didn't lift up the mattress, Capitano...I....It's just his savings...he was always very frugal.

FINZI

There must be over 100,000 lire. *(gathers up the money)*

EMILIA

Maybe the Principessa d'Avignon gave it to him. Maybe —

FINZI

Communists robbed the Banco Ambrosiano in Turin last month, this money might be from there....This is very serious, Emilia.

EMILIA

Capitano, I didn't know about this...you have to believe me.

FINZI

This room is a mess, Emilia. Clean it up!

FINZI exits to his office with the money, PAGE 262. EMILIA begin to clean as DANTE enters, PAGE 263.

SCENE P74

FINZI'S OFFICE

FINZI enters his office and puts the money in his desk. He then picks up the phone and dials the operator.

FINZI

Garda Barracks, please. *(pause)* Corporale Tittonni....Tittonni, Capitano Finzi here....Are your men dug in at the gates? Good...and have your people found

Defelice....Good....No...I'll be right there, this means Roma for me...and a promotion for you too....Now, see if you can locate a list of serial numbers for the money taken from Banco Ambrosiano last month...in Turino....Si....Ciao. *(hangs up)*

FINZI exits to PAGE 265, the hallway.

SCENE P75

MARIO'S ROOM

EMILIA is cleaning MARIO's room. She is from PAGE 262. DANTE is coming from PAGE 260, the Atrium stairs.

DANTE
(looking around) Why are you searching his room, Emilia?

EMILIA
Finzi made me. *(continues cleaning up the room)* Now leave before he finds you.

DANTE
There's a gun missing from Il Comandante's quarters. Did you find it?

EMILIA
No.

DANTE
Telling Finzi won't help you. Where is it, Emilia?

EMILIA
There's nothing here.

DANTE
Where is it? *(throws mattress)*

EMILIA
I hate you! Everything I do is wrong. I'm doing what's best for Caterina.

DANTE

For our child? No, leave the child out of it. Let's not lie. I'll stop with Venezia and you with Caterina. Va bène?

EMILIA

(crying) Everything is so complicated. I don't want to tell but...Dante, I told Finzi about Defelice and now if he finds the gun, I—

DANTE

The gun will be back in Il Comandante's room! No one will know. When Mario is gone, we can leave. Maybe we should go to Palestine. Mamma knows people in Jerusalem.

EMILIA

Now it's Jerusalem.

DANTE

Anywhere. China. Just you and me and Caterina. She'll be nine years old next month.

EMILIA

Stop stabbing me with dreams. There's no way out. If Mario goes or not, Finzi owns me. He won't let me leave.

DANTE

Get fired. Steal Baccara's earrings.

EMILIA

I already have.

DANTE

Then get caught!

EMILIA

(laughing) Never stop, do you?

DANTE

A Jew learns how to survive. Now, where's the gun?

EMILIA takes the gun from the hiding place behind a dresser.

EMILIA

Hurry.

DANTE
You ask a gondoliere? *(takes the gun, kisses EMILIA on the cheek and exits slowly)*

EMILIA
Hurry! Presto!

DANTE
Clean up.

DANTE exits and runs upstairs to d'ANNUNZIO's room. He then comes downstairs to PAGE 268. EMILIA begins to clean up once again as MARIO enters, PAGE 282.

SCENE P76

THE SIDE HALL and THE ATRIUM

MARIO bursts out of the Oratorio, PAGE 252, where he finds FINZI waiting for him. FINZI is from PAGE 263, his office.

FINZI
What were you two talking about?

MARIO
(ignoring FINZI and crossing into the Atrium) I gave him a note from Madame de Lempicka.

FINZI
(following MARIO into the Atrium) What did it say?

MARIO
It was in French. Ask Il Comandante.

MARIO continues through the Atrium and heads down to his room. Upon entering he finds EMILIA cleaning it, PAGE 282.

d'ANNUNZIO has heard this short conversation from the Oratorio, PAGE 252, and upon seeing FINZI, yells out at him.

d'ANNUNZIO
Finzi! Finzi!

FINZI stops in the Atrium and waits for d'ANNUNZIO. As d'ANNUNZIO approaches, FINZI notices that d'ANNUNZIO has the note given to him by MARIO. FINZI holds out his hand expecting d'ANNUNZIO to give the note to him.

Here. Read it.

Instead, d'ANNUNZIO stuffs it in FINZI's mouth.

d'ANNUNZIO laughs and heads to the Leda singing "Rule Britannia." After entering the Leda, d'ANNUNZIO continues to sing while he takes off his jacket and shirt, then puts on a kimono. He then practises a few poses in which to be found on the bed by TAMARA, until the sound of AÉLIS' shouting brings him back into the hall, PAGE 269.

FINZI
Love notes — *(rips up the note)* Does he think I'm a fool? It won't be his affairs they'll be reading about — I can see the headlines now — "Capitano Aldo Finzi uncovers Communist cell led by Gabriele d'Annunzio."

FINZI heads for his room but is interrupted when CARLOTTA bursts in through the front door screaming. She is followed by AÉLIS, PAGE 268.

SECTION Q

THE FOLLOWING SCENES HAPPEN SIMULTANEOUSLY:

SCENE Q77   The return of those who left for Gardone.
PAGE 268

SCENE Q78   de SPIGA and FINZI help the wounded LUISA to the
PAGE 270   Oratorio.
                   NOTE: This scene determines the timing in this section.

SCENE Q79   CARLOTTA runs to her room in a state of panic.
PAGE 276

SCENE Q80   DANTE enters CARLOTTA's room to help her pack. They
PAGE 277   are joined by AÉLIS.

SCENE Q81   DANTE monologue.
PAGE 282

SCENE Q82   MARIO enters his room to find EMILIA cleaning up the
PAGE 282   mess from FINZI's and DANTE's search.

SCENE Q83   DANTE interrupts MARIO and EMILIA in MARIO's room.
PAGE 286   DANTE and MARIO continue in the hall.

SCENE Q84   TAMARA, after first going to d'ANNUNZIO's room, meets
PAGE 289   him in the Leda.

SCENE Q85   AÉLIS and CARLOTTA coming up one stairway, and
PAGE 293   MARIO and DANTE coming up the other, meet FINZI in
                   the Atrium.

SCENE Q77

THE ATRIUM and THE SIDE HALL

FINZI is heading for his office with the note d'ANNUNZIO has just stuffed in his mouth, PAGE 266, when CARLOTTA bursts in through the front door. She is followed by AÉLIS.

CARLOTTA
(screaming) Capitano! Capitano, hold me! *(hugs him)* She's drunk! She tried to kill me!

FINZI
Who? Who tried to kill you? Carlotta, calm down.

AÉLIS
(enters out of breath and sees CARLOTTA in FINZI's arms) Carlotta! He's the one who is responsible.

CARLOTTA
(breaking away from FINZI) What am I doing? You tricked me into showing my affections.

FINZI
Carlotta, you must understand —

CARLOTTA
Stay away from me, Jew!

CARLOTTA runs sobbing down the stairs to her room, PAGE 276.

AÉLIS
(yelling after her) Carlotta…wait…Carlotta. *(seeing DANTE coming down the stairs after returning the gun to d'ANNUNZIO's room, PAGE 265)* Dante, help Signorina Barra pack, and tell Mario to take her to the Grand Hotel.

DANTE exits to CARLOTTA'S room, PAGE 277.

FINZI
What was she saying? Who tried to kill her?

d'ANNUNZIO
(entering from PAGE 266) Aélis, what's going on? Did you get me the letter from Dottore Barzini?

AÉLIS
Gabri, there are soldiers at the gate....Luisa's been shot —

d'ANNUNZIO
My Barracuda, dead?

AÉLIS
Non. The bullet just grazed her.

FINZI
Where is she? *(goes toward the door)*

d'ANNUNZIO
Finzi, why are there soldiers outside?

FINZI
Extra security is needed to deal with the present situation.

AÉLIS
What situation? Are we in danger?

d'ANNUNZIO
So you dare to do battle with me? You're finished here, Finzi....You'll die the bureaucrats' death, not the soldiers': death by telephone.

AÉLIS
Why are we surrounded by troops?

d'ANNUNZIO
Aélis, we're surrounded not by troops but by possibility! Today — this moment, I can do anything.

AÉLIS
Then have Finzi removed from this house.

d'ANNUNZIO
I'll phone Roma...but first, Tamara. Sex before battle, Aélis. *(exits to the Leda, PAGE 289)*

de SPIGA and TAMARA, propping up the drunk and wounded LUISA, enter from outside.

FINZI
Luisa! My God, Luisa! *(runs to LUISA and pushes TAMARA aside)* Get away from her!

TAMARA heads upstairs to d'ANNUNZIO's room. Since he's not there, she heads back to her room, PAGE 289.

AÉLIS
I'm not going to pick up the pieces anymore! Do you understand, Luisa? I run this house and I won't put up with it. What you did was intolerable. Intolerable! Everything!

AÉLIS exits to CARLOTTA's room, PAGE 277.

de SPIGA
Come along, Luisa.

LUISA
I'm back, we're here again!

de SPIGA and FINZI help the wounded LUISA to the Oratorio, PAGE 270, below.

SCENE Q78

THE ORATORIO

de SPIGA and FINZI enter the Oratorio with the wounded LUISA. They help her to sit on the tomb. FINZI gets some pillows for LUISA's head.

LUISA
Francesco, you said we were going to fly away. I feel sick.

de SPIGA
Don't worry, Luisa, we'll leave soon.

FINZI
Luisa, what does he mean, leaving?

de SPIGA
Luisa has decided to move in with me, finally.

FINZI
She's drunk.

de SPIGA
Very. I had planned a wonderful meal — pasta, veal—

LUISA
Insalata.

FINZI
What happened?

LUISA
Bang!

de SPIGA
I stopped at the gate to get the mail.

LUISA
Let's leave!

FINZI
Be quiet, Luisa! *(kneeling by LUISA)* ...I'm sorry...I...didn't mean to yell at you.

de SPIGA
There must be a whole regiment outside the walls.

LUISA
I feel sick.

FINZI
Close your eyes, Luisa. Put your head back. *(to de SPIGA)* It's a precaution.

de SPIGA
You had no authority!

FINZI
There was no time.

de SPIGA
Luisa started talking to one of the soldiers. The man turned out to be a marksman.

FINZI
(goes to de SPIGA) What was his name?

de SPIGA
I don't know his name.

LUISA
(rises) Vitto, Vitto, "No-toe."

de SPIGA
Said he'd accidentally shot off his baby toe in the war.

LUISA
"All-doe," "No-toe," were you in the war?

FINZI
(going to LUISA) Luisa!

LUISA
Don't say my name like that, "All-doe."

de SPIGA
The point is, and underline this, fool, the man was a marksman. Fine. Things had proceeded "andante con motto." I wasn't in a rush, so I let Luisa talk to him. Suddenly she was shouting at him. Then Aélis tried to drag her into the automobile with Carlotta's help. And next thing, everything was "presto vivace." Luisa took out your toy and—

LUISA
Fortissimo!

de SPIGA
Bang! I thought it was the automobile until I saw the blood.

FINZI
The guard shot her?

de SPIGA
No, she tried to shoot the guard.

LUISA
I tried to shoot myself.

FINZI
Luisa, I don't understand what's happened to you.

de SPIGA
She's been shot!

FINZI
That's apparent!

de SPIGA
Evident. I had to reveal myself to prevent her from being arrested. Fortunately Aélis was too busy trying to calm Carlotta to notice, but I think Tamara —

FINZI
I don't care about you —

LUISA
(singing) No more octaves.

FINZI
Why, Luisa? Why did you drink? *(to de SPIGA)* She doesn't drink. *(to LUISA)* You don't drink. In a few days, we'll be away. Roma.

de SPIGA
Luisa has decided to live with me. We will leave once her hand has healed.

FINZI
I don't believe you. Luisa, listen to me. He's worse than Il Comandante. You don't know what he's capable of doing. Luisa. Think. Give me a...few more days....

de SPIGA
I understand Il Capitano hopes to win a promotion. No doubt you will, Aldo. You'll end up a generale and I'll be sent to prison.

LUISA
I'm going by myself.

FINZI
Luisa!

LUISA
If I stay here, I'll kill Il Comandante, and if I leave with one of you, I'll kill myself.

de SPIGA
Luisa, you can't survive on your own.

FINZI
He's right, Luisa.

LUISA
I could go to America. They love bad pianists.

FINZI
Luisa, stay here. For Italia.

LUISA
I don't want to play music for Italia.

de SPIGA
Then come with me to Asolo.

LUISA
To forget? There's nowhere left to hide, Francesco. Even drunk, I feel it. *(sits on the tomb)* I want to sleep. I can't sleep. It's numb.

FINZI kneels by LUISA.

de SPIGA
(to FINZI) Get some water.

FINZI hesitates.

The water, Finzi.

FINZI exits, slowly, to the Side Hall where there is a pitcher of water and a glass.

Luisa, let's get out of this house. I have a quiet house. There are two grand pianos — you could play music again. You make everything I write sound so much better.

LUISA
Shhh!

de SPIGA
I wrote a song for you. Let me play it for you now.

de SPIGA goes to the piano and plays Schallert's "Song for Luisa." As he starts, FINZI enters with the water. He crosses very slowly to LUISA. He puts the pitcher and glass next to her and slowly removes his gloves. He dips one glove in the water and gently caresses LUISA's forehead. FINZI kisses LUISA's hand and slowly exits to PAGE 293, the Atrium.

(finishing the song, he goes over to LUISA) I wrote it in five minutes. The melody overwhelmed me like a dream. There was a breeze last night.

LUISA
Luisa has turned to lead. Why isn't Luisa dead? Francesco, why didn't the guards take me away? I should have gone to prison. That's where they put free men, isn't it? What did you say to that guard? You showed him something.

de SPIGA
(crossing away) It never fails to amaze me how the sight of a 5,000 lire note can induce temporary blindness in even the most dedicated policeman.

LUISA
Don't. Stop clowning.

de SPIGA
What can I say? Luisa, how can I respond to what you've done, what you're doing to yourself, to me? I love you, can help you....

LUISA
No. Not I. Me. It's my hands you want. I don't want to be an organ-grinder's monkey. I'm no good to you now, or Gabri. *(holds up her hand)*

de SPIGA
(going to LUISA) Luisa, it will heal.

LUISA
Never. *(slaps him)* Never.

de SPIGA backs away and pulls a letter out of his coat pocket.

de SPIGA
I think I will deliver the mail.

de SPIGA exits to PAGE 301, the Leda. LUISA waits alone after de SPIGA has left.

LUISA
Gabri, it's all true now. Remember your poem? *(recites)*
In a dream
Stands enticing
The mutilated woman.
In a dream
Erect and motionless
Lives the terrible woman
With the severed hand.
And beside her
The pool is red with blood.
And within it
Is her hand
Still living.
But unstained by a single drop.

AÉLIS and DANTE enter the Oratorio via the Dining Room entrance. This scene continues, PAGE 297.

SCENE Q79

CARLOTTA runs to her room in a state of panic. She has just returned from Gardone, PAGE 268.

CARLOTTA
(crossing herself as she walks) I am covered in soot from standing too close to the flames of hell. St. Catherine, please answer me. Why does God test me so? I cannot walk unmolested forever amongst so many snakes in human form. Catherine, why would our Lord tempt me to fall in love with Capitano Finzi? He seems a good man...but underneath he's still a Jew. No. It couldn't have been our Lord, it was the devil himself tempting me. Yes. This house and everyone in it has been a test for me...but I won't lose my faith, Catherine. That's why the devil made Luisa shoot at me, he was angry because I wouldn't

sin...and that is why God must save me...save me so I can save my soul. Bless you Catherine for answering my call.

She crosses herself and enters her room as DANTE catches up with her. He is from PAGE 268, the Atrium.

SCENE Q80

CARLOTTA'S ROOM

DANTE
Signorina Barra —

CARLOTTA
Go away!

DANTE
Signorina Barra, Aélis told me to help you.

CARLOTTA
Only God can help me now...the devil tried to kill me.

DANTE
Aélis, Signorina?

CARLOTTA
She wanted to shoot me. Called me....I am not hateful. I love Italia.

DANTE
Who wanted to shoot you?

CARLOTTA
Luisa!

DANTE
Signora Baccara?

AÉLIS enters from PAGE 270.

AÉLIS
(hugging CARLOTTA and sighing with relief) Oh, Carlotta, thank God....When the gun went off and you ran away....You had me so frightened....I thought you would be wounded or bleeding....If Luisa had shot you I —

CARLOTTA
Don't mention that devil's name...she's possessed. It's this house, it's....*(throwing clothes to DANTE)* Dante pack these!

AÉLIS
Luisa didn't mean to —

CARLOTTA
She pointed the gun right at my foot!

AÉLIS
It was an accident.

CARLOTTA
And you defend her! I should have known better than to trust a Frenchwoman.

AÉLIS
I'm not defending her, Carlotta, it was unspeakable; but Luisa's not well...it's an illness —

DANTE
This is true, Signorina.

AÉLIS
She was trying to shoot herself.

CARLOTTA
By aiming at my foot.

DANTE
Maybe Signora Baccara thought the ricochet would eventually kill her?

AÉLIS
Shut up, Dante.

CARLOTTA
(seizing a sweater that Dante is packing) That's not how you fold it.

CARLOTTA attempts to fold the sweater as AÉLIS talks.

AÉLIS
But what about your recommendation?...Il Comandante's writing it—

CARLOTTA
Burn it.

AÉLIS
Your recommendation to Diaghilev?

CARLOTTA
The devil aimed at my toe, that is an omen telling me to renounce dance.

AÉLIS
You can't mean that?

CARLOTTA, frustrated by her folding, throws the sweater into the suitcase and the lid drops shut. DANTE seems impressed.

CARLOTTA
I do.

AÉLIS
Carlotta. Why don't we take a trip together, just the two of us. Verona is lovely in the offseason. Isabelle and I went there all the time. We —

CARLOTTA
I'm leaving tonight.

AÉLIS
Then at least stay at the Grand Hotel for a few days. You'll have a chance to think this through.

CARLOTTA
I must tell my family of my decision.

AÉLIS
But there's no train tonight.

DANTE
There is, Signora Mazoyer.

AÉLIS
There isn't.

DANTE
We're on the winter schedule now so...*(looks at his vest watch)* you'd have to leave right away, Signorina Barra. It departs in twenty minutes.

AÉLIS
Dante! Get Mario and take her bags to the Grand Hotel.

CARLOTTA
Aélis, I'm leaving.

AÉLIS
Dante! Get out!

DANTE exits with CARLOTTA's bags to MARIO's room, PAGE 282.

AÉLIS
You can't run away from it, Carlotta.

CARLOTTA
I'm not.

AÉLIS
This has nothing to do with Luisa, it's us. That's what frightens you.

CARLOTTA
(confused) Aélis, I'm not afraid of you.

AÉLIS
No, you're afraid of what you are. As I was, until Isabelle showed me, allowed me, helped me to feel the special love between women.

CARLOTTA
The...what?

AÉLIS
You felt it last night. Admit it. My hand on your thigh, the way we kissed ...that's what you were trying to tell me last night. Wasn't it?

CARLOTTA

No...no...Aélis. The devil has taken your soul. He's making you sin in ways I'd never imagined. You must pray for salvation.

AÉLIS

I don't want salvation, I want you just as you want me.

CARLOTTA

No.

AÉLIS

Stop trying to deny it. I felt it in your lips just like that first time with Isabelle.....*(kisses CARLOTTA.)*

CARLOTTA breaks away.

CARLOTTA

(slapping AÉLIS) Only the love of God is pure, everything else is sin.

CARLOTTA gathers up her crucifix and a picture of St. Catherine of Siena and exits upstairs. She is pursued by AÉLIS.

AÉLIS

Carlotta, I know what I'm saying. Prayers aren't going to keep you from temptation.

CARLOTTA

This house is possessed by unnatural desires. *(walking upstairs)* Papà says that within a few years fascism will rid Italia of evil. It's foreign influences which have corrupted us. Even I almost fell in love with that Jew, Finzi.

AÉLIS

Finzi! You can't mean that. Carlotta, you mean so much to me. I can't....*(goes to touch her)*

CARLOTTA

Don't touch me! I spit on your soul, Aélis Mazoyer. Frenchwoman. Foreigner!

AÉLIS

Non, Carlotta. I love you. Everything I do is for love of you.

CARLOTTA

You do the devil's work.

At this point CARLOTTA and AÉLIS have arrived in the Atrium, PAGE 293.

SCENE Q81

THE HALLWAY

DANTE, after leaving CARLOTTA's room, exits to the hallway with her bags. Here he pauses for a quick drink.

DANTE
Up the stairs, down the stairs...everyone yelling and screaming...Signora Baccara firing a gun.... Aélis and Carlotta, I don't know what's going on...it's all too much. Things used to be quiet around here....We could keep the gate locked and let the world fall apart...but now...Dante...it's just not worth it. As long as you're waiting for Emilia she'll tell you to wait — it's time to get out. *(drinks)* I've got to force her to take me seriously. I'll tell her I'm leaving in two days — with or without her. This is the last chance I'm giving her...if only I could say it...but the words would never come out....I'd stand there with my mouth open — and then take another drink of vodka — Enough. *(enters MARIO's room, PAGE 286)*

SCENE Q82

MARIO'S ROOM

EMILIA is hurriedly cleaning up MARIO's room when he enters. EMILIA is from PAGE 265, MARIO is from PAGE 265.

MARIO
What are you doing here?

EMILIA
Mario, I didn't have a choice, Finzi sent me.

MARIO
(closes the door) I trusted you.

EMILIA
He...he found the money.

MARIO
And the gun?

EMILIA
I just want to run away from here.

MARIO
(searching) Where is it? Where, Emilia?

EMILIA
Dante took it.

MARIO
Who else was here? Are you giving guided tours?

EMILIA
If Finzi had found the gun here, he'd have had us shot. He already thinks the money came from a bank robbery in Turina. He knows what you are, Mario. He's just waiting to find out how Il Comandante is involved. If Il Comandante goes, he'll catch you. Mario, he told me he wants you both. This is his big chance. We have to leave now.

MARIO
I leave tonight.

EMILIA
And me? You promised to —

MARIO
I can't jeopardize my life, and the lives of others, for someone who can't keep anything to herself!

EMILIA
(crosses to MARIO) My life! Is that too much? I lied to get you in, gave you a week to talk to Il Comandante, told you when Finzi was on to you, let you into my bed.

MARIO
No, you came to me.

EMILIA

You are the one who lied! If you and Il Comandante leave without me, I go to jail. That is what communism means to me! You call Fascists thugs. Finzi beats me, but I know what he wants.

MARIO goes to hit her with a fist. EMILIA flinches.

MARIO

Is this what you want? *(walks away)* I waited for you last night, Emilia. A man underground is used to waiting. Waits for a knock, a letter, orders, but never for love. You spend your time on code books, clean your gun, memorize your new identity. There's no place for thoughts of warmth, your hand is always clutching steel. These hands have pulled the cord tight on Fascists' throats, pulled the trigger on betrayal, and never shook. Last night, waiting for you, they began shaking.

EMILIA

Finzi forced me.

MARIO

Was he shaking when he held you?

EMILIA

(sits up) It wasn't like us —

MARIO

It was. Because he and I are the same. A different cause, but men who fight are the same.

EMILIA

No, I wanted you.

MARIO

Why?

EMILIA

I wanted to hold someone. Hold. No money. Not because they paid me. Si, they pay. I try to pretend I'm a lady but I'm just a whore, Mario. I have no school, can't read Il Comandante's books, I try to teach myself. I have a daughter, Caterina. Next month, she'll be nine. Is it wrong to want good for her? I know what you do is right. Dante wants to marry me, maybe that too is right. Sixteen years. I worked since I was fourteen and only dream of my reward for me and my Caterina....*(pause)* I shouldn't say these things.

MARIO
(sits on the bed) Why? Because it makes you weak? It takes strength to dream, Emilia.

EMILIA
I need to be with you.

MARIO
What about Dante?

EMILIA
I'll have to tell him.

MARIO
No. He's already too involved.

EMILIA
But —

MARIO
No. Tell him you'll marry him —

EMILIA
I can't lie to him.

MARIO
If he suspects you're leaving he'll try to stop us.

EMILIA
It's his daughter Caterina he wants, not me.

MARIO
Where is she?

EMILIA
She's safe....I'll get her when we get to where we're going. Where are we going?

MARIO
Last month I got a message from a comrade. He had been detained, because he had a gun, but they still let him go. He met my father. Twice my father said he would be in Nice for January. Twice.

EMILIA
Will we go to him?

MARIO
Emilia, my father is the Duke of Milano, a Fascist. He runs the party in Milano and tells people that his son died for fascism.

EMILIA
And your mother?

MARIO
My mother...Emma Visconti....*(continues packing)* I was raised by maids, Emilia.

EMILIA
Your family is wealthy?

MARIO
We have money, but we're very poor.

EMILIA goes to MARIO. She kisses him.

Soon we will all be free.

They embrace and kiss. Enter DANTE from CARLOTTA's room. The scene continues, PAGE 286, below.

SCENE Q83

MARIO'S ROOM and THE SERVANTS' HALL

DANTE enters MARIO's room from CARLOTTA's room, PAGE 282, to find MARIO and EMILIA kissing.

DANTE
Mario, I —

MARIO
Dante!

DANTE
(stares at EMILIA) Signorina Barra is leaving. I...I was told to...I'm sorry to come in, I —

MARIO
Just a kiss good-bye. And, of course, congratulations. *(shaking DANTE's hand)* Congratulations.

DANTE
For what?

MARIO
You mean she hasn't told you? I'm the first to know?

EMILIA
Mario!

MARIO
Emilia is accepting your proposal.

DANTE
Emilia, you're going to marry me? You're going to convert? Do you know how long I've waited for this girl, Mario? Eleven years!

EMILIA
Carlotta's leaving?

DANTE
I've forgotten. This is too much excitement. Carlotta claims that Luisa tried to kill her. She's hard to follow, but there was some kind of accident. I can't...what are we doing here? Hurry up, Mario, you're to drive her to the train. Ciao. Come on, Mario.

DANTE kisses EMILIA and exits. MARIO exits reluctantly, looking at EMILIA all the time. MARIO and DANTE gather CARLOTTA's luggage in the hall and walk upstairs. EMILIA stays in MARIO's room, PAGE 307.

Mario.

MARIO
What is it, Dante?

DANTE
Mario, you've got to go now. Finzi has soldiers stationed at the gate. You

won't get out with d'Annunzio. I advise you to drive the ballerina to the train station and then you get on the train, too. Forget Il Vittoriale. Forget Il Comandante.

MARIO
You put the gun back in Il Comandante's room, didn't you?

DANTE
Minus the bullets.

MARIO
(affectionately slapping DANTE) You're good, Dante.

DANTE
Unlike you, I'll do what's necessary to protect Emilia.

MARIO
It wasn't supposed to be like this.

DANTE
But it is. You think I was fooled by that show back there?

MARIO
Dante, we —

DANTE
I know her. I see that she loves you. But perhaps in time her love will return to me.

MARIO
It never left....she'll stay with you.

DANTE
You see, Mario, I am a Jew. That's never meant much to me, but as things get worse, I realize it's all I have. Emilia will have to convert. I —

MARIO
Dante, Caterina needs a family.

DANTE
Si, Mario. Go with God.

DANTE and MARIO enter the Atrium where FINZI is talking to AÉLIS and CARLOTTA who have just come up the other stairs from PAGE 282. PAGE 293, the Atrium now begins.

SCENE Q84

THE LEDA

TAMARA enters from PAGE 270, the hall/Atrium, to find d'ANNUNZIO on her bed.

TAMARA
Gabriele —

d'ANNUNZIO
Tamara, I've been waiting.

TAMARA
Luisa's shot herself in the hand.

d'ANNUNZIO
A flesh wound, nothing more. Aélis will send for a doctor.

TAMARA
You know about the soldiers. Why are they here?

d'ANNUNZIO
Those soldiers at the gate tell me I am alive.

TAMARA
What?

d'ANNUNZIO
Tamara, every day I hope for a sign, something to say I am still a threat. I sit here a silent volcano and the Fascists pray I won't erupt like Vesuvius.

TAMARA
You must escape before it's too late. A year after the Bolsheviks took power, they came to arrest my husband and they found us sitting in bed, sipping champagne. Get out now, if you still can.

d'ANNUNZIO
Yes, we'll leave, not to flee but to fight.

TAMARA
We are surrounded by armed men.

d'ANNUNZIO

This tongue is my weapon, it is a feather and it is a sword. At Fiume, they sent regiments to force me to surrender, but as soon as I opened my mouth — the government soldiers laid down their weapons and joined me.

TAMARA

Those soldiers aren't going to pause to listen to a speech before they pull the trigger. They will kill you.

d'ANNUNZIO goes to comfort TAMARA.

d'ANNUNZIO

We have to have the courage to believe we can make a difference. Remember what you said this afternoon — we must stand up and say no to the darkness.

TAMARA

Maybe you're right, perhaps when the world has become so brutal and insensitive, we should start touching each other with knives and guns instead of books and portraits.

d'ANNUNZIO

No, you must paint and I must write as if our brushes and pens were bullets and knives. *(begins to kiss TAMARA)*

We'll drive through the gate and the soldiers will jump to attention.

TAMARA

And Luisa?

d'ANNUNZIO

What about her?

TAMARA

We'll take her with us —

d'ANNUNZIO

Let's not talk of Luisa. She's always having accidents.

TAMARA

No, she held the gun like this. She knew what she was doing. She tried to shoot off her hand.

d'ANNUNZIO

What artist would want to shoot off their own hand? Did Van Gogh cut off his hand? No. And why? Because cutting off his ear was a way of cutting off the world, but to shoot off a hand is to cut one's self off from the only things which really matter: art and touch.

TAMARA
She wants to kill herself. Do you feel nothing?

d'ANNUNZIO
Francesco will take care of her.

TAMARA
de Spiga's one of them — I saw him giving orders to the soldiers.

d'ANNUNZIO
I know what he is — Mussolini's worm.

TAMARA
You know and you let him spy on you?

d'ANNUNZIO
He loves her. Luisa will be safer with him.

TAMARA
In the arms of the secret police. It's not just her love for you that's driving her to suicide. It's this world that kills anyone with any sensitivity. If she stays, she'll pull that trigger again.

d'ANNUNZIO
Every day for five years I too have thoughts of pulling the trigger. For five years I've let Mussolini pay my bills — buy my silence. I tried to convince myself I'd be free to create. And what have I created? Nothing! Nothing! Mario made me see it. That's why we are going with him to England.

TAMARA
With Mario Visconti?

d'ANNUNZIO
Yes.

TAMARA
Now you align yourself with Communists. They're worse than Fascists. Go on your own. You say you have the power. Or have you sold yourself to the highest bidder?

d'ANNUNZIO

Tamara, we can change history — you will sit in the gallery of the House of Lords and hear me denounce Mussolini — there's history. There's your portrait.

TAMARA

Whenever I hear someone talking like that I know people are going to get kill-ed and the first sacrificed will be Luisa. She believed your words. I too wanted to believe them. Believe they were the words of someone who understood love.

d'ANNUNZIO

You talk to Gabriele d'Annunzio of love? I have given everything for love of my country. But who will love me? Who? Can I sleep in the arms of a nation? Dante worshipped his Beatrice and Napoleon his Josephine.

TAMARA

I won't be your Luisa.

d'ANNUNZIO

An artist needs his inspiration. We artists, we leaders, we stand alone on the peaks calling out to each other. We are the lonely gods on Olympus.

TAMARA

I'm just a human being.

d'ANNUNZIO

You are an artist. Our destiny is to be the summits the people aspire to reach, and their fate is never to touch us. If you want to love people, then you can only turn to other artists, like myself.

TAMARA

You love only yourself. You look at me and see only breasts. I have a heart; it beats and screams and cries for compassion, as does Luisa's. But you feel only the impotent heat between your thighs and use your words, the one gift God granted you, to gain a moment of selfish pleasure — a moment in history. You're not a leader, you're not an artist, you're not a man — You wanted me to paint your portrait — here it is, monsieur. *(grabs the blank canvas)* Gabriele d'Annunzio alone on his snow-capped peaks. Here it is!

They are suddenly interrupted by de SPIGA, PAGE 301.

SCENE Q85

THE ATRIUM

FINZI enters from PAGE 275 the Oratorio, just as AÉLIS and CARLOTTA come up the stairs from PAGE 282, DANTE and MARIO enter from the opposite staircase, PAGE 288.

FINZI
Are you leaving, Signorina Barra?

CARLOTTA
Si, Capitano. Mario is driving me to the train station.

FINZI
That won't be necessary. Allow me, it will give me the opportunity to clear up any misunderstandings.

CARLOTTA
You may drive me, Capitano, but I have nothing more to say to you.

FINZI
Carlotta...your rosary. I fixed it for you. *(hands it to her)*

AÉLIS
Carlotta, please...let's not part like this....

FINZI
(to DANTE) Dante, take her bags to the automobile. Mario, stay here.

DANTE and MARIO exchange glances. DANTE exits out to the automobile.

(to CARLOTTA) The accident was most regrettable, Carlotta.

CARLOTTA
God meant it to happen, Capitano. He wanted to warn me. If I'm to save my soul, I must give up dance, and all other unnatural acts.

AÉLIS
Carlotta, I beg you, please give me another day.

CARLOTTA

If Italia is to be safe, Capitano Finzi, all Italians, even the Jews, must help rid her of these godless foreigners.

CARLOTTA salutes FINZI and exits to the automobile, never to return. FINZI returns the salute.

AÉLIS

Finzi!

FINZI stops at top of stairs in the Side Hall.

You have no authority to turn this house into a prison.

FINZI

Events will prove my authority. Defelice has just been arrested for subversive activity.

AÉLIS

Prostitution?

FINZI

Communism!

MARIO

Should I inform Il Comandante, Signora Mazoyer?

AÉLIS

Oui, oui, tell him at once.

FINZI

(smiling) Si, Mario, tell him.

MARIO exits to d'ANNUNZIO's room, PAGE 309.

AÉLIS

(to FINZI) I won't have you destroying my house. Il Comandante will phone Roma and you'll be finished here. Finished!

FINZI

Many will soon be finished here, but I will not be among them. I understand there are many pretty young ballerinas in France, Signora. Perhaps you'll have better luck there.

DANTE
(re-entering from the automobile) Capitano, Signorina Barra asks you to hurry.

FINZI exits to the automobile and returns on PAGE 312.

AÉLIS and DANTE move on to PAGE 297, the hall and Oratorio.

SECTION R

THE FOLLOWING SCENES HAPPEN SIMULTANEOUSLY:

SCENE R86   AÉLIS and DANTE begin in the hall and head for the
PAGE 297   Oratorio where they meet LUISA. DANTE leaves shortly
                 after arriving.

SCENE R87   A brief scene with de SPIGA interrupting TAMARA and
PAGE 301   d'ANNUNZIO in the Leda.

SCENE R88   de SPIGA and TAMARA in the Leda.
PAGE 302

SCENE R89   TAMARA monologue.
PAGE 305

SCENE R90   DANTE gives a monologue in the Kitchen.
PAGE 306

SCENE R91   EMILIA gives a monologue in MARIO's room and in her
PAGE 307   own bedroom.

SCENE R92   MARIO has a monologue in d'ANNUNZIO's bedroom.
PAGE 309

SCENE R93   d'ANNUNZIO meets MARIO in his bedroom.
PAGE 310

SCENE R94   DANTE heads back upstairs for a brief scene with FINZI
PAGE 312   who is just coming in the front door after returning from
                 Gardone.

SCENE R95   de SPIGA monologue.
PAGE 313

SCENE R96   MARIO encounters de SPIGA outside d'ANNUNZIO's bed-
PAGE 314   room door.

SCENE R86

THE HALL and THE ORATORIO

*AÉLIS and DANTE are in the hall. They are from PAGE 295, the Atrium.
AÉLIS rushes into the Oratorio while DANTE follows. LUISA is sitting, alone,
on the tomb. She is from PAGE 276. DANTE sits in a chair.*

AÉLIS

Never, never, never! Will I never be rid of him? Another night. Why must we
endure him? Luisa, you're pushing me to the edge! I have to wake up knowing
Finzi is already crawling about the house, dirtying my rugs. And now, you
decide to abandon me to the luxury of drunkenness! Finzi's looking for spies
in the fishbowl, you get drunk and almost kill yourself and Carlotta, Gabri is
blind to everything but the thighs of the Polish woman, Mario seeps around
the house trying to be mysterious, Emilia is nowhere to be found and Dante
(seeing him) sits....Stand up, Dante! *(pulls DANTE out of the chair)* Luisa, I
warn you, I'll leave. If you don't start helping out, you'll find yourself alone.
Oh! Carlotta, Carlotta....

LUISA goes to AÉLIS and gently comforts her.

(gaining her composure) Dante, don't you have something to do?

DANTE

Si. I'm getting married, Signora Mazoyer. To Emilia.

AÉLIS

What do you mean? You know Il Comandante won't allow it.

DANTE

Our plan is to leave.

AÉLIS

Do you think I'm going to service Il Comandante every night? I won't let you
leave. Do you hear me? You can't leave.

DANTE

Watch me! *(turns and walks out, heading for the Kitchen, PAGE 306)*

LUISA

Bravo! *(clutching her hand)* Oh! My hand.

AÉLIS

Dante...Emilia...Carlotta. *(pause)* Don't leave me, Luisa.

LUISA

Aélis, I'll do anything you ask, just don't start about Aldo; I won't go with him or Francesco, or...I just want to sleep.

AÉLIS sits next to LUISA.

The bullet didn't work. Aélis, I'm so numb. *(crying)* Sometimes I kiss Aldo to try and throw up. I let him take me from behind and Aélis, I want to hate, to love him, to hate myself, but there's nothing, not even disgust! Aélis, I...Gabri took everything. There's nothing...why couldn't he...Aélis! There's nothing! Why can't I feel anything? I haven't been to the toilet for days. My period has stopped. There's nothing! Aélis, I don't want you to be mad, I just want to feel. Aélis! Aélis!

AÉLIS takes LUISA in her arms.

AÉLIS

I'm sorry. I'm sorry, Luisa, please. Luisa, don't. I love you. Luisa, you can't block everything out....

LUISA

(clutching at AÉLIS) Don't you understand? There's nothing to block out, nothing inside. A nun, a whore— what do they want?

AÉLIS

Stop talking about them.

LUISA

Keys! Keys! Everything: black and white. I hate pianos. I hate....if only I could hate...Men invented pianos...their songs, their music, their games, their damnable Italia. I'm going to throw up.

AÉLIS

(gets up and reaches for the water pitcher) Luisa, please; Luisa, calm down. Here. *(putting the pitcher in front of her)* Let it out.

LUISA

(tries but nothing comes) I can't. I can't. There's nothing.

AÉLIS

Put your finger in your mouth.

LUISA
(tries; still nothing) It won't let go. *(again)*

AÉLIS puts the pitcher down. She takes LUISA in her arms and rocks her.

You're so strong. *(pause)* I don't want to surrender. You don't give up. I'm sorry, Aélis. About Carlotta. I'm sorry.

AÉLIS
(whispering) Sister, sleep. *(rocks her)*

LUISA
I wanted her to understand. She thinks it's her face in the mirror. But it's mine. We get old, teach children our fairy tales, and they believe the world holds its breath for Italia. Every new generation picks up the flame of the last, until the whole world is on fire. Gabri, Il Duce, they're old men who fell asleep smoking in bed. Now, the fire is everywhere. Aélis, I'm so hot, and there's no one to put out the flames.

AÉLIS
Luisa, Luisa. This house is our world. We're safe. There's no flames except the flames of Gabri's desire. Things will run their course, we can't change that. What we must do is try to be happy, whatever happens. Carlotta is gone, but I'll survive...the same way I did when Isabelle died. We have to keep hope to persist. Look at Gabri, with "La Polonaise." The minute she gives in the honeymoon is as good as over.

LUISA
No. Tamara's not like us; she'll leave.

AÉLIS
If she does, she'll be the first woman in my years of service to do so.

Enter TAMARA from the Leda, PAGE 306, carrying her luggage.

TAMARA
Je dois partir. [I have to leave.]

AÉLIS
Ce soir? Ne soyez pas si pressée, Madame de Lempicka. Je suis sûre que le Comandant veut que vous restiez. Vous n'avez même pas commencer le portrait! [Tonight? You shouldn't be so hasty, Madame de Lempicka. Il Comandante will be down soon. I'm sure he wants you to stay. And you haven't even begun the portrait!]

TAMARA
Ça ne l'interesse pas. [He's not interested in that.]

LUISA
Let her go, Aélis.

AÉLIS
(to LUISA) She'll go when Gabri tells her to go, not before.

AÉLIS exits to PAGE 319, d'ANNUNZIO's room. The scene continues, with LUISA trying to coax TAMARA to leave. Because they speak different languages, the scene is half French, half English with plenty of frustration and mime included.

TAMARA
Ça vous fait mal? [Does it hurt?]

LUISA
Tamara.

TAMARA
Oui.

LUISA
Go while you can. Go. It's too late for me. Go, find freedom. Libre!

TAMARA
Liberté. Pour vous et pour moi. [Freedom, for you and me.]

LUISA
Yes. You could go to London, Paris, Zurich, Berlin....

TAMARA
Oui. Je connais un médecin à Zurich pour vous. [I know a doctor in Zurich for you.]

LUISA
Zurich?

TAMARA
Oui. Vien Luisa, vite. [Yes. Come Luisa, quickly.]

LUISA
(laughing) Hong Kong, Tokyo, New York.

TAMARA
Ça ne fait rien—allons-y. [It doesn't matter. Let's just go.]

Finally, LUISA picks up TAMARA's luggage and the two of them head for the front door, PAGE 317.

SCENE R87

THE LEDA

TAMARA and d'ANNUNZIO continue from PAGE 292. Enter de SPIGA from PAGE 276, the Oratorio.

d'ANNUNZIO
Get out, Francesco!

de SPIGA
(to TAMARA) You must forgive my intrusion. In the confusion this afternoon, I forgot to give you this letter I picked up at the gate. It must be from your husband.

d'ANNUNZIO
I said get out, Francesco!

de SPIGA
Gabri, don't get upset, you'll start to sweat.

d'ANNUNZIO
(to TAMARA, ignoring de SPIGA) You humiliate me, Madame. I offered you my words, my flesh. But you mock my tongue, molest my body, spit on my sensibilities and scorn my soul. Francesco, you will leave by tomorrow! You do not amuse, you abuse my hospitality. Baccara stays. I say again: she stays, you go.

d'ANNUNZIO exits to his room, PAGE 310.

SCENE R88

THE LEDA.

de SPIGA and TAMARA continue from PAGE 301.

TAMARA
You seem to be able to open any door, Monsieur.

de SPIGA
It was open. I hope you'll accept my apologies, not only for walking in on what was obviously a private moment, but also for Gabri's rude remarks. Your letter. *(holds it up)*

TAMARA
Men have nothing to say to me.

de SPIGA
Not even your husband?

TAMARA
The last thing of importance my husband said to me was: "I do." And that was a lie.

de SPIGA
And Gabri? Does he lie also?

TAMARA
(begins packing) Monsieur d'Annunzio drowns me in words as if I were a child and he a senile priest performing a baptism. He speaks as if truth were a dizzy mystic language, but it isn't. It is a hard straight line which stabs you like a knife.

de SPIGA
I find your directness refreshing.

TAMARA
Another lie. I frighten you. You must truly be weak to fear a coward such as I.

de SPIGA
It seems I always speak too soon. I don't follow —

TAMARA
No, you lead. Those guards at the gate knew you, one of them even saluted. Why?

de SPIGA
A formality.

TAMARA
I'm leaving, Monsieur, because this house and its inmates have built a prison of lies and illusions which will destroy them all. Monsieur d'Annunzio believes he is free. He's trapped, not by your guards, but by his own words. And you, why do you do it? For your career?

de SPIGA
That's one reason.

TAMARA
Just because you get work, Monsieur, that does not mean you have art to give.

de SPIGA
Naivete does not become you, Madame. But since you seem bent on hissing ugly truths, let me explain —

TAMARA
I've heard all the explanations. I lived through the Russian Revolution, Monsieur. I saw how the second rate rose to the top and sacrificed a culture, in the name of politics.

de SPIGA
Music has no politics. I'm just a humble Italian composer.

TAMARA
Patriotism and art...you're stretching skin on a drum, Monsieur; one day it will crack.

de SPIGA
My work is uncompromising.

TAMARA
And your life!

de SPIGA
I'm free to say or do whatever I wish.

TAMARA
In public?

de SPIGA
Yes. Don't you see the beauty of it? Since my allegiance is secret I can publicly denounce the government and still they let millions hear my music.

TAMARA
That's true. But finally, history will plug her ears.

de SPIGA
Enough. The fact that you have to copulate to win your commissions annuls your feeble attempts at morality.

TAMARA
My art stands on its own!

de SPIGA
Not in Italia. Go. Take all of Gabri's gifts, paid for by the Italian government, and leave!

TAMARA
I am!

de SPIGA
But...not yet. You'll wait here until I come for you around midnight. There will be no goodbyes. Mario will drive you to Nice. Do we understand each other?

TAMARA
How many Fascists does it take to guard an old man against Mario Visconti —

de SPIGA
Who?

TAMARA does not reply.

(grabs her hand) You said a name.

TAMARA
Let me go.

de SPIGA
How do you know him?

TAMARA
I don't!

de SPIGA
(pushing TAMARA against the wall) Think harder.

TAMARA
(frightened) He...I recognized him from a photograph....I saw it when I was painting his mother's portrait in Zurich.

de SPIGA
(gripping her hand tightly as if to break it) Isn't it interesting how all that practising makes a pianist's hands so strong? Did he say why he's here?

TAMARA
No.

de SPIGA
Just...curious. *(tightens grip)* You know, a woman once told me that the reason men use knives is that they do not menstruate.

TAMARA
He's a Communist. That's all I know. I swear —

de SPIGA
Please don't. *(lets go of her hand)* You have a piece of knowledge, Madame. I suggest you drop it. For a piece of knowledge is more dangerous than a piece of broken glass. It cuts deeper.

de SPIGA exits, heading for d'ANNUNZIO's room. Realizing that MARIO is with d'ANNUNZIO, he lingers outside waiting for MARIO, PAGE 313.

SCENE R89

THE LEDA

TAMARA
I hate these modern men. These men who claim to love their country, love politics and power and anything else as long as it's abstract — d'Annunzio

says he does it in the name of humanity; what is that, but one person plus another and another?..and de Spiga sees the world as so many notes on a musical score, but he forgets to play them one at a time. Played together those notes are nothing but a scream — a horrible scream — *(goes to take her art and throws it down violently)* No, Luisa.

TAMARA grabs her bags and runs to the Oratorio to say goodbye to LUISA, PAGE 299.

SCENE R90

THE KITCHEN

DANTE enters the Kitchen from the Oratorio. On his way down to the Kitchen, DANTE finds one of his many hidden vodka bottles in the Side Hall. He is from PAGE 297.

DANTE
Emilia...Emilia...*(knocks on her door)* Emilia? Where is she? Emilia. *(entering the Kitchen he finds his gondoliere hat and puts it on)* I've spent six years in this house. This was my Venezia, a place where my mind could row back into time, back to Fridays in Mamma's kitchen, the scent of herbs and pasta, the smell of clean sweat, the sound of women working in the kitchen. Mamma showing Emilia how to make "challah," Caterina crawling on the counter....Oh, Emilia, where is my daughter? I want my child. *(drinks)* When Papà would come home, Mamma would light the shabbat candles and Papà would take Caterina in his arms and say, "May you be like Sarah, Rebecca, Rachel, and Leah." Emilia! Wasn't there joy then? Papà would recite the Kaddush and later he would read from the Torah and when I tried to talk you'd cut me off and insist that Papà continue. You were family, Emilia. And it could be that way again. It's not easy, it never is when you're poor. *(drinks)* Mario says he fights for us, Finzi says he fights for us. They fight for power, power over us. If they don't kill each other, they'll end up like Il Comandante, old men who beat their servants because the world beat them. No longer. For too long I've said, "not yet." Not yet to my God, not yet to my people, not yet to freedom. *(drinks)* I've stayed with Il Comandante because he took care of Mamma, because you stayed; no more, I am taking charge now. You look at Mario and think he is strong; what am I? Weak, afraid, and a fool? No. *(drinks)* I may not be in the hills, but I'm fighting. Fighting for my wife and

my child because a man's first responsibility is to his family. *(slams the bottle down on the table; vodka spills out onto his hand)* No more drinking or dreaming, *(throws his hat onto the floor)* or living in the past! I see this room and say; no more. This is not my house. The only thing left for us is tomorrow. Not next year in Jerusalem, but tomorrow. I will get Mario out. Not for the revolution, but to save you and our daughter. We'll get Mamma and go to Palestine. We'll be safe there. *(pause)* And Finzi, if he fails as a Fascist, maybe he'll learn to win as a Jew.

DANTE exits upstairs where he meets FINZI coming in from the front door, *PAGE 312.*

SCENE R91

MARIO'S ROOM and EMILIA'S ROOM

EMILIA
I'm going with him. I'm leaving! "Work, work harder and die." No, Caterina — not for us. No more. If Il Comandante comes we'll go to England. Mario will introduce us to all the important people. We'll even meet the King....Oh, Caterina, the one time your mamma falls in love it's with the son of a duke, a marquess! When I was your age, old Peppino would sit outside the taverna and tell his fairy stories, and everyone laughed at me for believing them...but I always knew in my heart that there had to be a happy ending. God couldn't have made me just to watch me suffer. And he didn't give you to me just to let the neighbours gossip....Everything has a purpose...no matter how foolish I've been I can see now....It was meant to end this way...You see, Caterina, there is a God. *(takes a sheet off the bed and wraps it around her shoulders)* We'll have fur capes, big white ones...and wear diamond tiarras as we sail down the canals....I bet the canals in England are even bigger than the ones in Venezia...and we'll have our own gondoliere....*(pause)* Dante...what will I tell him?...Mario says he's not to know but I can't just leave....I have to explain...but I can't....As long as Finzi believes Dante didn't know anything about Mario and me then he's safe....Il mio Dante....

EMILIA drops the sheet and exits to her room. As she enters she turns on the radio, the last forty-five seconds of Verdi's La Traviata *Act Two, Scene Two is playing. NOTE: The radio will be left on and Act Three will play as background music for the final scene.*

EMILIA

Dante...do you remember....No, don't start, Emilia....I just want to tell him I'm going. Mario loves me and I'm leaving with him....All my life you've protected me, Dante....Whenever I feel tears, you have a story. When I get into trouble you lie for me. When I steal, you cover up. No more. *(pause)* I know you've always tried to do what's right, but I learned when I was pregnant with Caterina that I have to do what's right for me. Me. A woman feels her child kicking and knows that only she can really feel it. The womb grows, fills up, but instead of feeling there's someone else inside, you feel more and more alone; because no one can share it. No one. Oh Dante, I want to tell you all this and I know you'd say you understand, like a papa tells his child...he understands....But I'm not dreaming now....I know it won't be a fairy tale but it's the ending I want....Mario loves me....I feel him the way I felt Caterina kicking inside me....Dante let me go....You're not even here and I feel you pulling me in....We can't hold on to what we once were....It's dead....I tried so hard to love you....So many nights I dreamt of you beside me and Caterina in her crib...the way it was...but it can't be that way. I love you, Dante...but I need more....Mario...I know I hardly know him...but win or lose...he's my only chance for freedom....This locket's for you....*(puts it on her bed; notices a cross on her wall; kneels and prays)* Dear Lord, forgive me for the suffering I cause Dante and hear my prayers that you will comfort him in his sadness....I ask for no blessing for myself, but pray that you keep Caterina healthy and happy, and that Mario grows to love her as his own. Amen. Now, where's my special suitcase....*(looks under the bed and pulls out a very elegant hand-crafted suitcase)* It's been under here for three years. Dante said I'd never use it because I'd never leave, but a lady needs proper luggage....When the Marchessa Cassatti arrived she had twenty-four pieces...she left with twenty-three....Didn't even miss it. I guess when you're really rich you don't have to know how to count. *(begins to pack some clothes)* Why take these? Mario will take care of me, now...*(dumps the clothes on the floor)* what a mess. Maybe I could hire Aélis and say to her, "Pick that up, will you, Aélis." It would be worth it just to see the look on her face...and ...*(picks up the clothes)* I should take these so I never forget...just to remind me....*(packs the clothes then picks up a book)* I'll put this book back in the Oratorio. When I learn to read I'll buy brand new books....I should find out if he's coming with us or not. Poor Comandante, he'll go insane watching me in Mario's arms....

EMILIA exits with her suitcase and heads upstairs to the Oratorio, PAGE 317.

SCENE R92

d'ANNUNZIO'S ROOM

MARIO bursts into d'ANNUNZIO's room from PAGE 294, the Atrium.

MARIO
Comandante? *(checks the room)* He's probably downstairs with Tamara. *(checks the door which leads to the Leda)* The old satyr couldn't resist a last kiss. *(pause)* And me? Can I go to Emilia and hold her just once again? No...never again. There's no plan to get a woman out. We'll just be two sailors heading for Genova, our ship...what was it? The *Helen* bound for Marseilles. Where is he? Finzi will have to go to the top to get permission to arrest one of d'Annunzio's staff. I've got an hour, maybe two. And then if I fail? The public will never hear that d'Annunzio has joined the resistance, there'll be no speeches. They'll keep him quiet here with extra guards at the gate and a few more grams of cocaine...and they'll let me have an accident...and Emilia? Christ, why can't he hurry? I hate this waiting...it's the silence before the barrage starts. *(looking at some of d'ANNUNZIO's war memorabilia)* At Caparetto I remember looking down the line and thinking: which ones will the guns kill?...No, please, not him, he has a family....God not him, he's so young...and on and on until the guns began to pound us and then finally, every thought was crushed. There were no individuals, no comrades, just death and terror....You're leaving Emilia behind. An innocent woman will go to jail for her part in this...if I could just convince myself she only did it for the money, or for the cause like Defelice....I have to...I have to....She'll get a few years in jail, that's all...and Dante will wait for her. If I take her she could be killed....It's not in the plan...the capitano of the ship would never let her board. At least this way she'll live...she'll.... Christ, she loves me. *(pause)* I...love her. Love. I do my duty for the good of the cause. But then, after I've sacrificed everything for the good of the cause...where is the cause? What is it...if not love? Stop it. Think of all the others. My job is to get d'Annunzio out...after that....No...get him out...do your duty and then it's over...just one act...just one. Hurry up. Hurry.

The scene continues on PAGE 310.

SCENE R93

d'ANNUNZIO has entered his room from PAGE 301, the Leda.

d'ANNUNZIO
So many judges. Do you know what that woman said to me?

MARIO
There is no time for women! Defelice's been arrested.

d'ANNUNZIO
Defelice? She's one of you!

MARIO
We're everywhere. Comandante, we must leave now.

d'ANNUNZIO
(sitting at his desk, beginning to write a letter) Why do you fight, Mario? To free the oppressed?

MARIO
We've had this discussion. Let's go.

d'ANNUNZIO
And who are they? The whores! The Emilias and Defelices...let's not use old words sterilized and reused! Left, right, left, right — everyone marches and grunts to the same tune. I look at the world and I am alone.

MARIO
You close your eyes and think you are alone? Italia is full of men who stand alone against fascism. They're waiting for a leader.

d'ANNUNZIO
No more apostles!

MARIO
You chose the path and men followed. You still know the road to Roma. Are you coming with me?

No reply.

To stop, to give up here and now, is to abandon a nation.

d'ANNUNZIO
Mussolini leads them—

MARIO
In circles. His government is worse than any Roman senate. You know what date this is? On January 10, 49 BC, Caesar crossed the Rubicon.

d'ANNUNZIO
The tenth was yesterday. I'm old.

MARIO
Now you fall back on the convenience of age. Five minutes ago, you were doing your best to seduce a woman twenty years your junior —

d'ANNUNZIO
Thirty.

MARIO
If a man is still sexually active, he should be politically active. Love Italia again.

d'ANNUNZIO
What would I be in England?

MARIO
The voice of the true Italia.

d'ANNUNZIO
A dirty old man. Go back. Tell your leaders as I told Mussolini. Tell them all to let me die! It's over.

MARIO
Everything? Words? Books? Deeds?

d'ANNUNZIO
Everything. It's over. Mussolini owns all my words. He took them and turned them around like words in a mirror. He took my slogans, my uniforms, even my men! Finzi once followed me! How do you expect me to call out when Mussolini has taken my voice? His gestures, the way he reaches up for a word as if it were a chalice from heaven. That's mine! He keeps me here as if I were the King's miter, and visits only to refresh himself, to make sure he's gotten the correct intonation on a word, that his pause is in the right place. He even shaves his head! *(shaking with anger)* The march on Roma was my idea! He

said it would never work. And I, I who have built my career on reading the minds of the Italian people, listened to him. Jesus had his Judas, but mine won't let me die.

MARIO
(*crossing behind d'ANNUNZIO*) Jesus died for a cause. In three days we could be in England. Action is the only way to find salvation.

d'ANNUNZIO
I wrote this introduction to the Duke of Connaught....(*holding up the letter he's just finished*)

MARIO
You or nothing! (*doesn't take the note, but pulls a knife out and puts it to d'ANNUNZIO's throat*) If you do not come, my orders are to eliminate you.

d'ANNUNZIO
Please let me die in uniform.

MARIO backs away. d'ANNUNZIO goes to put on his uniform. MARIO takes the note and goes to exit.

But your orders are to kill me.

MARIO
I'll leave it to history.

MARIO exits the room and is intercepted by de SPIGA, outside. PAGE 314 begins. d'ANNUNZIO continues, PAGE 319.

SCENE R94

THE FRONT DOOR

DANTE arrives upstairs via the servants' stairs from PAGE 307. He sees FINZI coming in the front door. FINZI was last seen on PAGE 295. He has just come from driving CARLOTTA to the train.

DANTE
Who are you? What are you doing here?

FINZI
Don't try me, Dante.

DANTE
They'll try you all right. Name? Who let you in? Where were you last night? From now on I ask the questions. No; better...you don't even exist. *(suddenly surprised)* Where did he go? The Fascist is gone! *(seeing FINZI as if for the first time)* Now who is this nice Jewish man? It's Aldo Finzi. I remember him now...you used to hide in the back row of the synagogue.

FINZI
Enough games, it's over, Dante. Defelice has signed a statement....As soon as I get through to Roma...Mario will be arrested.

DANTE
And Emilia.

FINZI
I'll do what I can.

DANTE
Just let me take her away.

FINZI
I have to telephone Roma. *(turns and walks away, then turns back)* No promises.

FINZI exits to his office, PAGE 326. DANTE pauses for a moment and then sees MARIO heading to his room. He follows MARIO to PAGE 323.

SCENE R95

OUTSIDE d'ANNUNZIO'S ROOM

de SPIGA after leaving TAMARA in the Leda heads upstairs to await MARIO, outside d'ANNUNZIO's room.

de SPIGA
(examining the letter from TAMARA's husband) Now what would her husband want to send her? *(opens the letter and begins to read)*

My Dearest,

It's three in the morning and no I've not been drinking, I spent the evening sitting in your studio. You're always saying you want to hear what I think of your work and I'm always making excuses not to go and look at it — well, I went this evening and on the table beside your easel there was a well worn volume of Goethe's poetry. I opened it to this one... (translates from the German)

Gehe
Verschmahe
Die Treve
Die Reve
Komnt nach

I've forgotten my German — "Gehe Verschmahe," (in English) Go then, scorn faith....No, that's not it, it's "Go then, scorn fidelity, remorse will follow."

Of course, I thought of my own indiscretions, but then I thought of just how much I've tried to discourage you from painting, because I wanted you out socializing with me and it struck me that that was like asking you to be unfaithful to your art. You must paint, Tamara. I hope your visit to this d'Annunzio will renew your faith in art and that this letter will renew your faith in me.
Love you
Tadeusz.
(stops reading the letter) She should have read it. (puts it in his pocket)

SCENE R96

OUTSIDE d'ANNUNZIO's ROOM

After leaving d'ANNUNZIO's room, PAGE 312, MARIO encounters de SPIGA.

de SPIGA
Mario, you are wasting your time with Gabri, he has nothing left to say or do.

MARIO
Why do you tell me this?

de SPIGA
It is enough that I tell you. Now, I'm going to save your life.

MARIO

You know me? *(pulls out a knife and threatens de SPIGA)*

de SPIGA

There are people, people in high places who want you, Mario Visconti, to go abroad, to leave here, alive. Don't ask questions, just leave. Your father wants to see you. He's dying, Mario. Go to him. He's in Nice. Mussolini has assured him we'll guarantee your safe passage. I have arranged for you to drive Madame de Lempicka to Nice later this evening…after everyone has retired. Do we understand each other? We keep d'Annunzio, you leave.

MARIO

Will Emilia be safe?

de SPIGA

No harm will come to her. Now, put away that knife.

MARIO puts his knife away.

That's better.

MARIO goes downstairs to his bedroom, PAGE 323. de SPIGA runs into TAMARA, LUISA and EMILIA in the hall outside the Oratorio, PAGE 317.

SECTION S

THE FOLLOWING SCENES HAPPEN SIMULTANEOUSLY:

SCENE S97   EMILIA meets LUISA and TAMARA in the Oratorio. They
PAGE 317   are joined briefly by de SPIGA.

SCENE S98   de SPIGA monologue.
PAGE 318

SCENE S99   AÉLIS rushes to d'ANNUNZIO's bedroom.
PAGE 319

SCENE S100   DANTE comes to warn MARIO.
PAGE 323

SCENE S101   FINZI phones Roma.
PAGE 326

SCENE S102   EMILIA and TAMARA help LUISA upstairs.
PAGE 326

SCENE S103   FINZI and de SPIGA meet in FINZI's office.
PAGE 328

SCENE S104   de SPIGA has a monologue in the Oratorio.
PAGE 330

SCENE S97

THE ORATORIO

EMILIA arrives outside the Oratorio from PAGE 308. She puts down her suitcase and peers in just as TAMARA and LUISA are leaving. They are from PAGE 301. LUISA is carrying TAMARA's luggage. She trips and falls to the floor.

EMILIA
Are you all right, Signora Baccara?

LUISA
(laughing) Everything in Italia falls down. The Coliseum, the government, even Francesco.

TAMARA tries to assist EMILIA in helping LUISA up, but LUISA pulls her down.

TAMARA
Luisa.

LUISA holds TAMARA's face in her hands. TAMARA and LUISA laugh.

LUISA
Dites non...Gabri.

TAMARA
Oui. Oui.

EMILIA
Let me help you to your room, Signora.

LUISA
Shhh! We're escaping.

Enter de SPIGA from PAGE 315, outside d'ANNUNZIO's room.

de SPIGA
(gently helps TAMARA up, then brutally throws her in a chair) Je déteste me répéter. J'ai dit demain, Madame, demain. Rentrez dans votre chambre! [I hate to repeat myself. I said later, Madame. Later. Get back to your room!]

LUISA
(to de SPIGA) You? You too....God! God! Let someone go free.

de SPIGA grabs LUISA's hands.

EMILIA
Signore, she's not well.

de SPIGA
This doesn't concern you, Emilia.

LUISA
We were other people once, Francesco. But we were...people.

de SPIGA puts his arm around LUISA and turns to TAMARA.

de SPIGA
Montez avec elle, Madame. [Take her upstairs, Madame.] Sleep, Luisa. Sleep. Emilia, help her upstairs and then see that Madame de Lempicka's luggage is put back in her room.

EMILIA
Si, Signore.

de SPIGA exits to the Dining Room, PAGE 318, below. TAMARA and EMILIA help LUISA up to her room, PAGE 326.

SCENE S98

THE DINING ROOM

After leaving LUISA, EMILIA and TAMARA, de SPIGA pauses in the Dining Room on his way to FINZI's office.

de SPIGA
If Finzi hadn't posted guards at the gate...why must Roma force me to associate with such stupidity and bad taste? Luisa need never have known. Everything I've tried to do has been to shelter her — protect her from this.... Perhaps she'll have forgotten it all by the time she wakes in the morning. If

not I could probably convince her it didn't happen. After all — Tamara will be gone, Finzi will have arrested Emilia so this little incident in the hall need never come to light and I'm sure Aélis was much too preoccupied with Carlotta to have noticed what happened at the gate and — listen to yourself. What did Luisa used to say, "Francesco, you're much too logical to ever be a great composer." *(pause)* She's not going to forget— *(he exits to FINZI's office, PAGE 328)*

SCENE S99

d'ANNUNZIO'S ROOM

d'ANNUNZIO is alone in his room after MARIO's departure, PAGE 312.

d'ANNUNZIO
(pulls a gun out of his desk and crosses to Duse's veiled bust) Eleonora...my veiled witness. My mentor, and memory. My youth. *(pause)* Do you remember how we used to scream no? No! No to everything that was second-rate. We vowed to raise our hammers and shatter the marble of mediocrity. *(pause; pulls veil off)* And now we are stone. We surrrender, say yes...and are afraid. *(pause)* There's only one "No" left...death. I'm so frightened that if I open my mouth to scream, not a sound would be heard, and the flies would rush in.

d'ANNUNZIO bends down and kisses the statue and slowly raises the gun to his temple. Enter AÉLIS from PAGE 300, the Oratorio.

AÉLIS
Non! Non!

d'ANNUNZIO
Let me go, Aélis.

AÉLIS
Like this!

d'ANNUNZIO
You said this morning it was not yet my time. It is my time. Leave me to it.

AÉLIS
Don't turn your phrases on me!

d'ANNUNZIO

Fine. Let's not say a word. Leave....Suicide is a selfless act, it demands solitude. Leave. Leave!

AÉLIS

(starts to exit, then stops) Selfless — you wrote the book on selfishness, and even that you kept locked in a drawer! Go on, curse us all, and die. Die! *(goes to exit)*

d'ANNUNZIO

No, Aélis. Wait. No. Understand this....I do this for Italia! For everything she has become, because of me. I led a nation "to the wolves and the wasteland." I must die. If you kill the root...you kill the tree.

AÉLIS

(mocking) You're doing this for your wayward children?

d'ANNUNZIO

Yes. Finally. You'll tell the world?

AÉLIS

I'll tell them. I've written it all down! For twenty years I've kept a diary, devoted to you, Gabri. I'll tell the world. I'll tell it that without your women, you would have been nothing. I'll tell the world how you crawled inside "your beloved" Eleonora Duse and ransacked her heart and soul, as a beast would a nursery, turning her suffering into "a great novel." I'll tell the world how your wife, Donna Maria, has tried twice to kill herself; about Nike, whose fortune you spent and left destitute. *(goes to d'ANNUNZIO)* My list is endless. I'll tell the world about Luisa.

d'ANNUNZIO

No! No! Everyone accuses me! I never wanted her to love me!

AÉLIS

But she does! All of Italia loves you.

AÉLIS tries to grab the gun from d'ANNUNZIO. They struggle and d'AN-NUNZIO pulls the trigger. Nothing happens. He pulls the trigger several more times. Nothing. They laugh.

d'ANNUNZIO

They plug their noses and leave the leper to rot. Even Mario refused to do his duty. The stench, Aélis! The horrible smell!

AÉLIS

(suddenly concerned) What do you mean, Mario refused to do his duty? What do you mean about Mario?

d'ANNUNZIO

He was supposed to kill me if I didn't go—

AÉLIS

Where?

d'ANNUNZIO

England.

AÉLIS

Why? Why?

d'ANNUNZIO

To speak....The Communists wanted my tongue.

AÉLIS

You didn't help him?

d'ANNUNZIO

No.

AÉLIS

Tell me again!

d'ANNUNZIO

I gave him nothing. He risked so much and I gave him nothing.

AÉLIS

I'll have to go tell Finzi.

d'ANNUNZIO

Let Mario go.

AÉLIS

And lose everything. Finzi wants to have me deported. If he finds out about Mario, I'm finished.

d'ANNUNZIO

He's gone, Aélis. I failed him, I failed all my friends. What use am I? I couldn't even convince Tamara...the young talk differently —

AÉLIS

Then learn their language! It used to be yours. You think you led the people? No. It was the crowds' chant which drove you to become great. You were their Boccaccio, their Caesar, their da Vinci, their Garibaldi. Through you, they built Roma, crossed the Alps, conquered nations....

d'ANNUNZIO

Yes! Yes!

AÉLIS

You were strong and I will not let you be weak. Do you hear me? Mussolini would destroy you. I'm going to do for you what you did for Italia, I'm going to make you rise again. In the Roman way. To save us. To save our house. *(begins backing d'ANNUNZIO toward the bed)*

d'ANNUNZIO

Give me your tongue!

AÉLIS

(straddling d'ANNUNZIO on the bed) Remember Duse in your greatest play, *Francesca da Rimini?* In my dream, I see it —

d'ANNUNZIO

"In my dream, I see it as it was in very truth."

AÉLIS

"A naked woman running through the depth of the wood."

d'ANNUNZIO

"Torn by branches and thorns, weeping and crying for mercy —"

AÉLIS

(pulling him up to a sitting position) "....two mastiffs at her heels...behind her through the depth of the wood, mounted on a black charger —"

d'ANNUNZIO

"A dark knight, strong and angry in the face, sword in hand, threatening her with a swift death in terrifying words."

AÉLIS

"The dogs, taking hold of the woman's naked side, stop her."

d'ANNUNZIO

"And the knight, with sword in hand, runs at the woman."

AÉLIS

"Drives at her with full strength; so the sword goes through her breast, she falls. He draws forth a dagger, opens her by the hip bone...rips out her heart and throws the rest to the dogs."

d'ANNUNZIO tries to roll AÉLIS over on the bed.

Non! Non! Tamara! Tamara! Take her, like every great ruler who has conquered Poland. *(climbs off d'ANNUNZIO and shoves him toward the door)*

d'ANNUNZIO
What should I say?

AÉLIS
Nothing! Nothing! Just take her.

d'ANNUNZIO outside the Leda, takes a deep breath and bursts into TAMARA's room, PAGE 341. AÉLIS remains behind exhausted physically and emotionally, until she hears FINZI and MARIO arguing in the Atrium, PAGE 339.

SCENE S100

SERVANTS' HALL and MARIO'S ROOM

DANTE catches up with MARIO.

DANTE
Mario...is he leaving with you?

MARIO
No...I failed.

DANTE
It's his failure, not yours. Now, what are you going to do with Emilia; she thinks she's going with you, doesn't she?

MARIO
I had to lie...but it was one lie I wanted to be true.

DANTE

If you care for her, think of her safety. What kind of life would it be, crawling about the country—

MARIO

She should marry you, Dante.

DANTE

That's right. You have your cause, Mario; Emilia is mine.

MARIO

A cause, if only it was....You fight for Emilia, your love, your duty—

DANTE

They're the same thing.

MARIO

Not to the Visconti....Si, Dante...I am the Visconti, Marquess Mario Visconti.

DANTE

The son of the Duke of Milano, the Fascist?

MARIO and DANTE enter MARIO's room.

MARIO

Si. To my father my title is: coward. We were being overrun at Caporetto and I refused an order to hold the line....The choice was whether to sacrifice fifty men I loved or to save their lives and disobey an order.

DANTE

You retreated?

MARIO

Si...a court martial was ordered and I went underground. Father said I'd disgraced the family; the Visconti are military men...and now he has to make the same choice about me.

DANTE

What choice?

MARIO

Love or duty. *(begins to change into peasant clothes)*

DANTE
There is no choice.

MARIO
There is. And I don't know which one he'll choose....de Spiga just told me my father is dying.

DANTE
de Spiga?

MARIO
Surprised?

DANTE
The rich never surprise me.

MARIO
My father is in Nice and wants to see me...the government claims I'll have safe passage. Or is my father, as a Fascist, participating in a plan to trap me? Love or duty...an ironic dilemma for both of us.

DANTE
Don't go, Mario.

MARIO
I'm going....I'll be safe in Nice....I just won't take their ride to the border.

DANTE and MARIO begin to exit upstairs.

DANTE
Finzi has guards at all the doors....

MARIO
But you know a way out, don't you, Dante?

Pause. They arrive in the Atrium.

DANTE
The balcony on the second floor leads around to the cypress trees on the side of the house. From there you can make it to the east wall and Conte Leonni's property. Can you drive a boat?

MARIO
Si.

DANTE
His "Maz" is the fastest on Lago di Garda. From there you're on your own.

MARIO
Grazie, Dante.

DANTE
Hurry.

MARIO heads quickly up the stairs as FINZI calls out, PAGE 338.

SCENE S101

FINZI'S OFFICE

FINZI picks up the phone and dials the operator. He is from PAGE 313, out-side his office.

FINZI
Operator, get me 3-2-8-6...si...si...of course...Roma. I know the time! Yes, Ministry of State...Generale Foscarinni. Capitano Aldo Finzi! Good news! d'Annunzio's involved — with a young Communist named Mario....What? Il Duce! He wants to talk to....*(jumps to attention)* Capitano Finzi! Duce, it is an honour. Yes, Duce...Duce..I know what a jackass is. But....Who is he? The son of the Duke of Milano!...I understand his father is a friend...forgive me, Duce, I didn't mean to repeat what you...but you don't understand. He's involved in subversive activities. Si, I know Libya...very hot....No, Duce, I don't want to go there...but if....Hello? Hello? Duce? *(pause)*

FINZI hangs up the receiver. de SPIGA enters, PAGE 328.

SCENE S102

THE STAIRWAY TO LUISA'S ROOM

EMILIA helps TAMARA get LUISA up to her room.

EMILIA
You shouldn't drink, Signora.

LUISA
Emilia, don't stay, just get Dante and go away. Run as far away as you can. Go tonight. Leave.

EMILIA
I'll leave soon, Signora.

They start to ascend the stairs.

LUISA
Up. Up.
I step and stare.

TAMARA
(pointing to a step) Regardez

LUISA
Up. Up.
I almost touched but didn't dare. *(stops on the landing)*
Goodnight. I'll do it by myself.

EMILIA
I'll turn down the covers, Signora.

LUISA
No. Help Tamara. There's no helping me. *(to TAMARA)* Bonne nuit.

TAMARA
Nous avons peur toutes les deux, ma soeur — mais notre peur nous rend fortes. [We are both afraid, sister. But our trembling makes us strong.]

LUISA
Live...*(starts upstairs)* Go away, Emilia.

TAMARA
(to LUISA) Bonne nuit.

LUISA does not hear this.

LUISA
Up. Up.
He almost touched,
but couldn't care.

*LUISA enters her room, PAGE 333. As she disappears into her room,
TAMARA and EMILIA exit to the Leda, PAGE 334.*

SCENE S103

FINZI'S OFFICE

*FINZI has just hung up the telephone as de SPIGA enters. FINZI is from
PAGE 326, de SPIGA has come from PAGE 319, the Dining Room.*

FINZI
Do they think d'Annunzio is weak? One speech, just one, could spark a
revolution.

de SPIGA
For God's sake, Finzi, don't you understand who Mario's father is?

FINZI
Si, the Duke of Milano. Il Duce just told me. But I don't care if he's the king's
son, the man is still a Communist. Do they think Mario's on a school excur-
sion? He's dedicated; I'm sure he's killed before and he'll kill again.

de SPIGA
No, he won't. Tonight, he will drive Madame de Lempicka to Nice.

FINZI
Are you going to give him spending money as well?

de SPIGA
That does not concern you.

FINZI
(rises and goes to de SPIGA) First, you try to steal Luisa and now what is your
plan? To take all the credit for my operation?

de SPIGA
(rising) The word is "blame," Aldo, and I'll have no part in it. The boy goes free. Il Duce is just granting an old friend his dying wish to see his son again. Only that. Once the Duke dies, Mario will have an accident before he can assume the title.

FINZI
And d'Annunzio?

de SPIGA
(crossing to desk) Nothing changes. Containment. Observation. As before. Of course Emilia will have to be arrested in the morning.

FINZI
The aristocrat goes free and the poor peasant goes to jail. Go away. Get out! Just leave me Luisa.

de SPIGA
Luisa is not negotiable.

FINZI
You don't love her, leave her to me.

de SPIGA
She's had enough of politics.

FINZI
Francesco, leave me something!

de SPIGA
I'm taking her with me when I leave.

FINZI
I love her. Everything I've done, or try to do, to get back to Roma, has been for Luisa.

de SPIGA
Well, at least the old Duke will get his dying wish.

FINZI
A trip to the Riviera for the Communist!

de SPIGA
You will let him go! And that's an order.

FINZI

(sitting at his desk) This isn't life, Francesco, we're living in a waiting room. No wonder there's a resistance.

de SPIGA

I am going to sleep and I suggest you remain here. Do you understand? And as a precaution, I want your gun....

FINZI hands de SPIGA his holstered gun.

de SPIGA will exit to the Oratorio for his monologue, PAGE 330, below. After de SPIGA exits, FINZI quickly goes to his bed and pulls out a gun concealed under the pillow. He also takes the money he had found in MARIO's room. He goes to find MARIO and DANTE in the Atrium, PAGE 338.

SCENE S104

THE ORATORIO

de SPIGA enters the Oratorio, places the gun he has taken from FINZI on top of the piano, pours himself a drink, then sits down to play a few bars of LUISA's song.

de SPIGA

Luisa...what? What can I possibly say to her? The truth? It's not a question of how much I love, it's a matter of how much I hate. When you slapped me I saw your hatred and saw it again when you pulled the trigger. What did it accomplish? The hand will heal, and you will go on hating. But I — I, Luisa, have done something positive with my hatred — I've joined a...yes, I suppose our movement is a kind of club — where, the more you hate, the more likely you are to be admitted. And since I hate its members almost as much as I hate myself, I had no trouble getting in — *(laughs as he lights a cigar)* When they asked me to get invited here, I saw my chance. I knew Gabri would treat me like a long lost friend because he has no memory of the pain he caused me by stealing you away....For him, it wasn't stealing; it was as if he just borrowed an umbrella to go out into the rain. And then, one day, he forgot you, and found someone else. But I never forgot or forgave. Nor did you. In hatred, a good memory is essential. And what I remembered over the years was just how many women had become addicted to Gabri...yes, he is an addiction.

(takes out a vial of cocaine) That's when the thought occurred to me: cocaine. I wanted him to experience what it was like to have an addiction. So for the past two months I've been teasing him into it. I don't think he's even aware of it...but now he needs it. The way I need you. The way you need him. You said yesterday you wanted revenge...think of the despair he's caused you....Now, imagine what will happen when his supply runs out...come with me. We have a common hatred, Luisa. That's grounds enough for love. *(pause)* Why not tell her everything? If I can just get her away from him she'll soon be cured.

He exits to head for LUISA's room and comes across FINZI, MARIO and DANTE in the Atrium, PAGE 339.

SECTION T

THE FOLLOWING SCENES HAPPEN SIMULTANEOUSLY:

SCENE T105   LUISA, alone in her room.
PAGE 333

SCENE T106   TAMARA and EMILIA in the Leda.
PAGE 334

SCENE T107   FINZI encounters MARIO and DANTE in the Atrium.
PAGE 338

SCENE T108   d'ANNUNZIO enters the Leda, throws out EMILIA and at-
PAGE 341   tacks TAMARA.

SCENE T105

LUISA'S ROOM

LUISA enters her room from PAGE 328.

LUISA

Luisa was so frightened that in her trembling, her soul burst free. Now, she's laughing, right at me. *(putting on a white nightgown)* Luisa isn't putting on a shroud, she's climbing into a cloud. Shh. Gabri wants her to sleep. Luisa thought he'd taken her blood, but it's still in there....I'm so tired and I want to sleep. *(goes to bed and lies down)* Shh...Luisa go to bed. Luisa rest...shh....They pad her mind with silence...she eats it with a violence.

She sits up. On the table beside her there is a pitcher of water and beside it, a small bottle with a medicinal dropper top. She pours a small amount of water into the glass, then as she speaks, she begins to drop sleeping drops into the water.

Dottore Barzini said two drops, but I wake and we're still here. "Once we were other people, but we were people." Now, I've found my own way home, done it all, alone. And the woman I know best is the one I just met. It's not the loser, but the winner who pays the bet. Not stop by stop, but drop by drop. Up. Up. You must fill your cup. *(drinks her sleeping draught, then lies back on the bed)* I'm not sitting on a shroud. I'm floating on a cloud. Breathe. Deep. *(body begins twitching; pause)* Luisa was starting to shiver, she felt as if the frost which held her had begun to thaw; she could move her toes, she felt that if she wanted to stand or run or dance her legs would laughingly join her. She followed her feelings from toe to thigh. Even her womb, which had always panted to be filled began to blush and blow up. *(sits up)* I was sitting inside her when suddenly, even I felt happiness; fear is fun and what is crushing me is transforming me. I can move my fingers. Shhh. There is music. *(gets up and heads out the door to the top of the stairs. After a long silence, she speaks.)*

Clouds, clouds,
clouds and haze.
Thank god, *(stops walking and slowly sinks to the floor)*
The night
ends our daze.

As LUISA is lying on the floor, dying, FINZI shoots MARIO, PAGE 344.

SCENE T106

THE HALL and THE LEDA

TAMARA and EMILIA are in the hall. As TAMARA picks up her luggage, she mistakenly picks up EMILIA's suitcase.

EMILIA
No...no...Signora, allow me. This is my last night as a servant.

TAMARA
Ça ne me dérange pas de porter mes propres baggages. [I don't mind carrying my own luggage.]

EMILIA
What kind of woman carries her own luggage? When I leave I'll hire at least three maids.

TAMARA
(turning around) Comment? [What?]

EMILIA
(shakes her head) Nothing, Signora. *(to herself)* I could call her whatever I like and she wouldn't understand.

TAMARA and EMILIA arrive at the Leda.

TAMARA
Je m' inquiète pour Luisa. [I worry about Luisa.]

EMILIA
What? *(to herself)* I'll have to hire a translator to understand these foreigners.

TAMARA
(mimes slashing her wrists) Luisa. Peut être elle va essayer encore ce soir...de se suicider. [Perhaps she'll try again tonight...suicide.]

EMILIA
Luisa? No. Signora...Luisa wouldn't. I'll go to her....I'll go up....*(mimes going up stairs)*

TAMARA
Bien. Non....Non....Moi.

EMILIA

She'll sleep tonight. *(mimes sleeping with her hand clasped to one side of her face)* Sleep.

TAMARA

Ah! Dormir. Moi aussi. [Ah! Sleep. So will I.]

TAMARA opens one of her cases, looking for another blouse.

EMILIA is unconsciously folding some of TAMARA's clothes so she doesn't immediately notice that TAMARA has just opened her suitcase.

TAMARA

Ce ne sont pas les miens. [These aren't mine.]

EMILIA

That's mine...mine, my clothes. My clothes aren't as nice as yours but one day I'll go to finishing school and learn to be a lady.

TAMARA

Je ne comprends pas. Excusez-moi. [I don't understand. Excuse me.]

EMILIA

Your clothes...very beautiful. *(points to her blouse)* Very beautiful.

TAMARA

Ça...vous l'aimez? [This...you like it?]

EMILIA

Si.

TAMARA

(suddenly unbuttons her blouse and gives it to her) Pour vous. [For you.]

EMILIA

For me? I couldn't.

TAMARA

Non. Non. Pour vous. [No. No. For you.]

TAMARA gets the top and then returns to her suitcase where she proceeds to give EMILIA all the clothes in it including the gown d'ANNUNZIO gave her.

TAMARA

Tenez, prenez tout. [Here, take everything.]

EMILIA

Grazie. Grazie, Signora. *(takes the gown)* Can I put it on? *(mimes the question)* Put it on?

TAMARA

Bien sûr, il vous appartient. [Of course, it's yours.]

EMILIA

Dear Lord, forgive me for all the bad things I said about her.

TAMARA

(buttoning up her own top) Ils étaient tous des cadeaux de Monsieur d'Annunzio, mais maintenant je vous les faits cadeaux. Et contrairement à Monsieur d'Annunzio, je ne m'attends à rien en récompense. [They were all presents from Mr. d'Annunzio, but now they are my presents to you. And unlike Mr. d'Annunzio, I expect nothing in return.]

EMILIA

When we get to England I'll wear this to meet the King, and Mario will be so proud of me.

TAMARA

Mario, le nouveau chauffeur? [Mario, the new chauffeur?] *(mimes driving)*

EMILIA

Si.

TAMARA

Vous et Mario, vous êtes amoureux? [You and Mario are in love?]

EMILIA

I don't —

TAMARA

Vous et Mario. [You and Mario.] *(points to her ring)*

EMILIA

Si...but it's a secret. *(puts a finger to her lips)* Secret.

TAMARA

Je comprends. [I understand.]

EMILIA
Can you help me? *(mimes the question and turns around)*

TAMARA
Oui....C'est très belle. [Yes...it's very pretty.]

EMILIA
I'll have to alter it a bit....What am I saying; I'll have my own seamstress.
(pause)

d'ANNUNZIO's sudden entrance from PAGE 323, will determine where this scene ends. If he has not arrived by this point the scene will continue with the two of them attempting to discuss at EMILIA's instigation whether or not TAMARA is in love with d'ANNUNZIO.

Signora...*(remembering)* de Lempicka.

TAMARA
Non, non, appellez-moi Tamara. [No, no. Call me Tamara.]

EMILIA
Tamara...are you...you and Signor d'Annunzio in love?... *(points to TAMARA's ring)* You and d'Annunzio?

TAMARA
(laughing) Moi et d'Annunzio?...Amants? *(points to the bed)* Ici? [d'Annunzio and me...Love? Here?]

EMILIA
Si.

TAMARA
(still laughing) Impossible. Impossible.

EMILIA
No. *(shakes her head)*

TAMARA
Non.

EMILIA
And you still got all these presents. I don't understand it.

TAMARA
Comment? [What?]

EMILIA
Nothing...nothing.

The scene continues as d'ANNUNZIO enters, PAGE 341.

SCENE T107

THE ATRIUM

FINZI enters the Atrium from his office, PAGE 330. He intercepts MARIO and DANTE from PAGE 326. FINZI carries the money he discovered in MARIO's room.

FINZI
Mario, I know who you are!

MARIO turns around. As he does, he motions for DANTE to leave. DANTE stays.

MARIO
Fascists always know "who" — they're very good with names. It is the "why" which is important.

DANTE
Aldo, please —

FINZI
Stay out of this, Dante! Trusting servants, very foolish. An aristocrat like you should know how servants talk.

MARIO
I know why they talk! Force finds answers, but never the truth.

FINZI
And you have never used force, have you, Mario Visconti?

DANTE
Let him go!

FINZI
Two tellers shot dead at the Banco Ambrosiano to finance this little expedition. *(throws the money in the air)* Look at the money your hero robs from the savings of the working people. Look at it, Dante!

MARIO
The working people have no savings, they starve while the Fascists eat at the banquet!

FINZI
I hate your type. Rich people who pretend to understand the poor, who pretend to care. You care only when it's convenient, when you're not going to the opera.

MARIO
I don't pretend.

FINZI
Is it fun to play poor? To steal some peasant's clothes and then go rambling about the revolt of the masses? Who do you think you serve, you textbook Communists? I couldn't get a job until the Fascist party took me on. Who'd give a poor Jew a chance to prove himself? Not your kind. Even in the war they kept me in this accounting office because Jews are supposed to be good with figures. Every step I've taken has been covered in some aristocrat's shit.

At this point, de SPIGA has heard the argument from the Oratorio, PAGE 331. He decides to investigate. AÉLIS has also heard the two and comes out from d'ANNUNZIO's room, PAGE 323. She listens to the argument.

And now I won't get back to Roma because your father is a friend of Il Duce. How convenient it is for you to have a father in the party. He lets you play and then if things get tough, you just tug on the rope and he hauls you back in.

MARIO
My father has no cord around my neck. *(turns to exit)*

FINZI
(pulling out his gun) Wait.

DANTE stands clear. FINZI holds the gun to the back of MARIO's neck.

Empty your pockets.

MARIO pulls out a piece of paper and holds it up.

What's this?

MARIO
A note from d'Annunzio.

EMILIA enters from PAGE 341 after hiding behind a pillar; she now decides to sneak up behind FINZI and grab his gun.

AÉLIS
Non! Il Comandante didn't help him. He's lying.

FINZI
I'll judge that!

AÉLIS
(running toward the Leda) Gabri! Gabri! Quick, Finzi's caught Mario!

de SPIGA
Finzi, what are you doing?

FINZI turns the gun on de SPIGA.

FINZI
You see...*(holding up the piece of paper he has taken from MARIO)* evidence. Evidence! He isn't going to France. d'Annunzio and Mario were planning a revolution. And I found out! He's my prisoner. Mine! *(points gun at MARIO)* And I'm taking him to Roma.

At this point EMILIA has crept up behind FINZI and now starts to grab for the gun. They struggle.

DANTE
Emilia, no!

FINZI
Let go!

DANTE
Stop! *(runs to assist her but the gun is suddenly pointed at him and he backs off)*

EMILIA
Mario, help me!

MARIO pauses for a moment and then turns his back on EMILIA and heads out the front door to escape. Suddenly the gun goes off in the air. The scene continues, PAGE 344.

SCENE T108

THE LEDA

d'ANNUNZIO enters TAMARA's room from PAGE 323, his room. The room is dimly lit by a bedside light. TAMARA is talking to EMILIA, from PAGE 338.

TAMARA
(looking up) What do you want?

d'ANNUNZIO
Leave, Emilia! The hour of violence is here! Go.

EMILIA exits to PAGE 340.

d'ANNUNZIO
My tongue is stretched to the limits of my language, I can no longer plead with feeble words....

TAMARA
(standing) Get out!

d'ANNUNZIO tries to throw TAMARA to the floor. She continues to evade him. Finally he pins her up against the wall and begins kissing and fondling her. TAMARA knees d'ANNUNZIO in the groin. As he lies withering in pain she picks up his book.

Go on, get out, go fill your books with the names of all the women you have fucked...yes, fucked...because you've never loved anyone...and you'll never have me.

A shot rings out.

d'ANNUNZIO
Mario! *(runs out into the Atrium where MARIO lies dead, PAGE 344*

TAMARA
Luisa!

TAMARA hastens to LUISA's room via the interior staircase. Upon entering the room, TAMARA sees the glass of sleeping potion. She tastes it with her tongue and then spits it out and races from the room calling out LUISA's name. On the landing of the exterior staircase in the Atrium, TAMARA finds LUISA's body. She rocks LUISA in her arms, and tears run down her cheeks. She does not speak until PAGE 347.

SECTION U

SCENE U109   The final scene begins in the Atrium.
Page 344

SCENE U109

The final scene continues from PAGE 341. The gun goes off again.

LUISA
(on the top of stairs from PAGE 333) Listen, the sound of freedom. *(dies)*

MARIO turns around, there is blood coming from his abdomen. He's bleeding. He falls.

AÉLIS
(from PAGE 340, in disbelief) Mon Dieu! [My God!]

EMILIA
(from PAGE 341, quietly) Mario? *(goes to him and cradles him in her lap; he's dead)*

de SPIGA
(from PAGE 340) Finzi, why didn't you listen? I gave you orders. *(picks up the gun)*

d'ANNUNZIO enters from PAGE 342, the Leda. Upon seeing the dead MARIO he snaps.

FINZI
(dropping the gun) Emilia, why...why did you....I wasn't going to kill him.

d'ANNUNZIO
Orders? I give the orders.

AÉLIS
Stay out of this, Gabri.

d'ANNUNZIO
Is the Leda ready?

DANTE
He's dead.

EMILIA
(to DANTE) He's sleeping.

d'ANNUNZIO
Ah! I see Emilia has put down the carpet of roses.

FINZI
(to de SPIGA) It's in this note. They were plotting a revolution. And I found out. I told you the first day that he was a Communist. But you wouldn't listen. He's mine! Me...me...Aldo Finzi!

d'ANNUNZIO
Aélis, did you get all the presents?

AÉLIS
(understanding what's happened to d'ANNUNZIO) Oh!

de SPIGA
This note is about a gambling debt.

FINZI
No....No...I...I....It's in code. You aristocrats are all lying. Everyone here is lying! I've got to get to Roma. They'll see the truth. Luisa sees. Luisa! Luisa!

de SPIGA
Luisa cannot help you. She's mine. She always was. Now, get out. The party no longer needs you. Get out!

FINZI exits, running out the front door.

d'ANNUNZIO
Should I give her some earrings?

AÉLIS
Francesco, do something.

DANTE
Emilia, we're leaving.

EMILIA
(looking up to d'ANNUNZIO) Comandante, can I go?

AÉLIS
Francesco, help him.

de SPIGA puts the gun down and takes out a vial of cocaine and pours it on the floor and on MARIO's feet. d'ANNUNZIO, on his hands and knees, begins snorting it.

DANTE
Look at him. We don't have to ask permission for anything.

d'ANNUNZIO
(on his knees) I'll tell her that reading her letters is like watching a woman undress.

DANTE
(to EMILIA) Mario wanted us to go!

AÉLIS
He wanted to kill Il Comandante!

AÉLIS sees TAMARA on the stairs holding LUISA in her arms. TAMARA is shedding silent tears. She is from PAGE 342.

AÉLIS
Dante, take her to the station.

TAMARA gently puts LUISA down on the rail and heads downstairs.

DANTE
(to AÉLIS) There is no train.

AÉLIS
I don't care. Just get that woman out of my house!

DANTE
(to EMILIA) We'll get Caterina. Away from all this there is hope.

EMILIA
(crying) Take her with you. She's in the convent at Monte Cassino.

DANTE
Come with us.

EMILIA
I can't —

DANTE
I love you but I can't stay. *(runs out the front door)*

EMILIA
Dante —

de SPIGA
(seeing TAMARA following DANTE out the front door) Madame!

TAMARA turns and looks at him.

You're free to go. Eveything has changed. *(realizing she doesn't understand, he repeats it in French)* Pardon, Madame. Vous êtes libre. Tout a changé.

TAMARA
Oui...tout a changé! Luisa est morte. Morte. [Yes, everything has changed. Luisa is dead. Dead.]

TAMARA goes up to de SPIGA and points up to the dead LUISA.

de SPIGA
Luisa dead? *(seeing LUISA)* Luisa. *(runs up the stairs to LUISA)*

d'ANNUNZIO
But Aélis, since I've dreamt so much about her she may disappoint. Dreams kill reality.

TAMARA
(to d'ANNUNZIO) Fasciste! *(to everyone)* Fascistes! Fascistes! *(runs out the front door)*

d'ANNUNZIO
(rising) I am Gabriele d'Annunzio! Minister of divine mysteries...Prince... Prince...and...and....(keeps moving his lips but he's lost his voice)*

AÉLIS
(helping d'ANNUNZIO upstairs) Emilia, close the door.

EMILIA
Dante? *(running out the front door)* Dante!

AÉLIS
Emilia!

Pause, EMILIA slowly re-enters.

Close the door!

EMILIA slams the front doors shut.

Blackout

FINI

ABOUT THE AUTHOR

John Krizanc is a Canadian playwright with four plays to his credit. *Tamara* has been produced in Toronto, Mexico City, New York, and is the longest-running play in Los Angeles. It was the winner of the Los Angeles Drama Critics' Circle Award, as well as the Dora Mavor Moore Award in Canada. Krizanc's most recent play, *Prague*, won Canada's prestigious Governor-General's Award.

Krizanc, a native of Lethbridge, Alberta, resides in Toronto, where he is a founding member of the Necessary Angel Theatre Company.